Hiding in the Light
The Hunt: Book 1

Zachary,
May the love of the Lord always shine upon you. Continue to "walk in the light."

Blessings to you always,

Cy Emery 2017

Hiding in the Light
The Hunt: Book 1

CY EMERY

LIBRARY OF CONGRESS CONTROL NUMBER: 2017913716

ISBN: HARDCOVER   978-1-5434-4959-4

SOFTCOVER   978-1-5434-4960-0

EBOOK   978-1-5434-4961-7

Rev. date: 09/25/2017

To order additional copies of this book, contact:
Xlibris
1-888-795-4274
www.Xlibris.com
Orders@Xlibris.com
767246

CONTENTS

PROLOGUE

My mind raced at the speed of light. The Reaper's chill gave chase. Faster and faster went the drumming in my chest; its cadence pressed the back of my throat. Slipping into the world of shadows, I held onto hope...tied a knot at the end of its rope. A flurry of images passed in a blur; my family, friends, coach, my crew. When anxiety hit zenith, I pleaded with God, **"Don't let me go out like this."**

Oxygen depleting, pilot light faint, my life-force diminished. All struggling ceased. A peace, calm enveloped me. Only Mama mattered. Her love seized my final thoughts. The promise made to her cradled my heart. Fading deeper and deeper into the murk, I imagined her disappointment when they told her I was with a group of guys she warned against. Her reaction when she learned, I was found in a forbidden section of town. The tears when she got the news, "Her youngest son was dead." Our bond, our love, separated forever...the promise broken.

My efforts to fight back failed. Ritualized codes and rules peddled deceit and deception; a pretentious life. I wanted out, but the street had my number. An adrenalin junky with a lonely heart; a daily fix needed. So I answered the calls to scratch my itch.

A pawn in its' game of thuggery, dodging red and blue flashes, altered my family values. Out of place, out of step, out of time, a square peg found a fit. My ace and I, milk still on our breath, cruised the streets like a pair of Corvettes. It motivated my haters.

Finally, in a battle for respect, shots were fired. Clinging to my father's motto, "Keep your head up," I fired back. Bullets of anger, jealousy, rage, fueled the exchange. Using antiquated weaponry, I took hit after hit, an imminent retreat necessary... too late. My strong will, prideful spirit, and love for my crew wouldn't let me back down. My loyalty placed me back at the Reaper's front door once again. Now with one foot in death's abyss and the other with little fight to resist, I feel the need to explain *how I got here.*

This all started with name calling.

For years I was bullied by kids in my neighborhood. Smacked with mean, vicious names... harassed to shame. Their hateful rhetoric; society's prejudices, and the snubbing by the "well to do" in my community, wounded me deeply. Poverty and a dysfunctional home left their marks as well. I couldn't catch a break.

I searched to find myself...accept myself amidst the bullying, riots, marches. *Who was I, what was I and why was I the butt of the joke?* It was tough being me in the segregated south. I was different.

Lines were drawn. Pushed to the middle of the tracks, they snarled in disdain; "too light", "too dark", "too poor"... borders closed. Like tobacco juice spit into my eyes, an angry burn festered. Alone on the tracks, this striped lion prowled aimlessly until five kids from the west side took me in. A fun but dark path ensued.

I needed to find a way out, an escape from the hand I was dealt... but poverty offered few open doors. So I stood and fought the slings and arrows of my haters. I might have faired better if I gave in, accepted the bitter rhetoric spewed in my direction. They made me question my very existence. Every day I asked myself, will the world ever accept me? Could I learn to love myself enough to get past the hurtful verbiage? Will I get over my inferior feelings developed from a life of lack?

Mama said, *"In one's life some rain must fall. It makes you appreciate your sunny days."*

Mama, I need the rain in my life to stop! And I'm going to stop it.

CHAPTER 1

ODD BALL

My name is Joseph Graham. I was what you'd call an odd ball. Imagine all the kids in your neighborhood as solid colored balls. Well, I was the kid with the stripe, the odd one. For as long as I could remember I was made to feel different. My family told me I was special. My coach ran the game-winning plays to me. Even society labeled me as different. I couldn't get away from it. And through their bullying, some kids in my neighborhood never let me forget how different I was.

For starters, I looked different. I was this light skin, freckled face kid with reddish-brown hair living in the hood: or as I liked to call it, the jungle. I stuck out like a loose nail, and for that, they hammered me. Salt water, chlorine, and the summer haze added to my distinction; turning my mane a warm ginger. Locks not so tight, blacks called it, "Good Hair." I never understood that. Why was natural, kinky black hair, bad hair? Who told them it was bad? What was bad about it?

I also spoke different, had no choice. My mom and sister's rule… "No bad grammar." A whack to the head, a Herculean ear twist, or a Mr. Spock Vulcan neck pinch was punishment.

"Speak correctly," they warned. "Stop acting ignorant"

Being the youngest of four or as my dad called me, "The last shot in the gun," which was how he introduced me to his friends…they'd ask,"Hey Ike, is that your baby boy?"

He'd answer, "Yeah, he was the last shot in the gun."

I cringed, lips tightened every time he said that. What was I to him, just a shot of nature from his loins? I knew he loved me but he flipped-my-wig quite often pulling stunts like that.

As I was saying, being the youngest I inherited phone answering duties. My siblings would be seated right next to the phone when it rang and shout, "Joseph, come answer it."

I made them pay up for their collusion. After a while I took pride in the job. I'd secretly call the Operators and start a conversation so I could imitate them later when I answered the telephone.

"Good evening, Grahams' residence, Joseph speaking. Who's calling?"

By the time the greeting rolled off my tongue my siblings were over my shoulder.

"Hello, this is Mike, Debra, Carl calling," the voice on the other end would answer.

"Hello Mike," I'd say in a loud voice, turning to my family. "With whom would you like to speak?"

This gave them time to nod yes or shake their head no if they wanted to take the call. At which point I'd informed them, "I'm sorry, they're unavailable. Would you like to leave a message?"

My crew ripped me a new one about the way I spoke, especially if a big word slipped out. Once I explained I had no choice and I got paid for my phone duties, they eased up. In the jungle we didn't knock another man's hustle.

Smart skills under lock and key, kept on mute, street cred lost for sure if it got out... walked a thin line. The crew's code: "No nerds allowed." Disguised as a riddler, aloft inquisitions masked my brainpower. They found me amusing. The front grew tiresome.

Whiz Kid or not it seemed as if my brain moved at 45 RPM (Revolutions Per Minute) while the rest of the world moved at 33 RPM. Picture riding in a moving car at 45 Miles Per Hour and you pass a car moving at 33 Miles Per Hour. The car moving at 33 would seem to be in slow motion or going backwards as you pass it moving at 45. That's how I felt most of the time, like the rest of the world was moving in slow motion.

Unbridled curiosity put another stripe on this lion cub's back. Willfully, dangerously I pushed beyond my limits. Panting, prowling, wanting to see; know, touch, and feel beyond life... often before my canines were in. Diagnosed with an extreme case of Boyhood Wonderment, my strain had no cure. I lived for "the hunt," the exploits of my crew. They made me feel alive. They fed my passion for adventure, excitement, escapism; often taking me to the brink of no return.

The thrill of the hunts partnered with my fancy for girls, pushed me to the edge of manhood. They often substituted for each other. If not on a hunt with my crew, I was on another hunt, "Chippy Chasing." I only told my ace Benny Lee about my promiscuous acts. You didn't kiss and tell. That's where most guys made their mistake which left more "Bitties" for me. An exuberant joy I found testing the female resolve. My cheeks wore some disapproval but it was worth it. I learned early, "Sometimes the chase was better than the catch." The hunts and chasing skirts kept my mind off the bullying, at least for the time being.

A strained relationship with my father didn't help matters either. I hated him when he drank. He was an angry drunk: yelling, cussing, fussing, and tormenting the family until he fell asleep. I loved him when he was sober and spent time with me. He worked all the time. Exhausted when he came home, he had little or no time for me. He would retire to the sofa, a western on TV, and a bottle of Seagram's. Mama attended my school event. I went against my father's authority often without consequence. He and I had bumped heads from the time I could speak up for myself; like the time he accused me of taking his bottle of liquor.

I was coming from the kitchen into the living room, when he grabbed me by my throat and threw me into the hall. His fingers cupped my neck like a coffee mug.

"I know you took it...you wanna be a street punk," he said in disgust.

The odor emanating from him reeked of stale cigarettes and alcohol. They combined with onion to produce a sour stench. His eyes were glazed and dead, indicating my father had left. This was Mr. Hyde. He squeezed and demanded, "What did you do with it boy?"

Gathering a half-breathe of air, I whispered, "Do with what?"

"My bottle boy; my Seagram," he spouted, spraying me with his musty dragon's fire.

I didn't blink or flinch. I wouldn't give that weekend drunk the satisfaction of intimidating me. To hell with him! I looked him right in the eyes and told him, "I don't have your bottle, let go of me."

"I know you and your piss-ant friends are drinking. I smelled it on ya. If I catch ya I'm gonna send volts through your ass with that electric cord. You hear me boy?" He burped, hand still around my neck.

I became as steely eyed as he. Taking in another half-breath I told him, "If you're going to kill me, kill me, but I didn't take your bottle." I wanted that bastard to know I wasn't afraid of him. Whatever he was going to do, do it, and be done with it.

CHAPTER 2

NEEDED MORE TIME

I wanted to get him back but didn't know how. Then came the time I was stricken with an ear infection. My dad pitched a fit because I stayed home from school. He swore I wasn't sick. From the bedroom I heard him and Mama talking in the living room.

"Babe, we walked 5 miles to school with cardboard in our shoes, through all kinds of weather, with all types of sickness and ailments. Why can't he?" he asked her.

"That was then Ike, this is now. Kids today are different. They don't come up as hard as we did; they don't have to," she answered.

"See, that's what I mean. He needs to toughen his little ass up and go get something in his head so his kids don't have to come up so hard," he challenged.

Mama pulled her trump card to shut him up, "I thought you told me my job was to take care of the kids. Well, that's what I'm doing. He'll be back in school when he's able to sit, listen, and learn. You can't do that in pain?"

Mama had lowered the boom on him. Daddy had no come back. He went outside to have a smoke. I was lying in the bed seething after hearing the things he said about me, "I needed to toughen up," like I was some pussy. "I needed to get something in my head," like I was some dummy. I swear my dad knew how to yank my chain. I had thoughts of putting rat poisoning in his liquor bottle. Not enough to kill him, just enough to make him sick. Then I'd walk past him and say, "Aren't you going to work today? Man... you need to toughen up!"

We didn't have money for doctors so Mama treated my ear with an old home remedy: Sweet Oil and Prayer. She poured the oil in its bottle cap and warmed it with a match. Lying on her bed, on my right side, she poured two drops of the warm, soothing, pain reliever into my infected left ear. She quickly stuffed the ear with cotton, then took my hand and placed her other hand on the infected ear and prayed.

I had three of those treatments a day; morning, noon, and bedtime, until my ear was better. Before each dose she had me remove the cotton while she warmed the oil. The cotton had turned into a small greenish-yellow colored pellet. A foul, spoiled, repulsive odor drifted from the Cotton pellet...and I knew just the person who needed to take a whiff of that skunk musk. So I waited.

It was day four of my illness. Mama was outside taking the dried clothes off the line. I took my chance to get even. I had save three of the infected cotton balls from the previous day's treatment. I stored them in a plastic bag so the odor would keep. They had baked overnight and all day in our cedar block sauna of a house and were ready for my plan.

Daddy was lying on the sofa as usual watching a western on TV. I took the plastic bag from the closet in Lavelle's room where I had hid it. The time had come.

"Here Daddy, I want you to see how my ear is getting better. It's been draining, good," I said, with fake smile.

As he sat up I opened the bag, pulled out the putrid cotton ball pellets, and stuck them close to his face.

"See all the stuff...

Once he got a good whiff of my rotten cotton...

"What the hell is that? Get that away from me," he said as he pushed my hand away.

I intentionally dropped the cotton balls in his lap. He jumped up like his crotch was on fire. I backed away from him, biting my tongue to keep from laughing. It served him right for calling me a pussy and a dummy in the same breath. If a kid had said that about me, I would've smashed his grill into the back of his neck.

"Get that out of here," he yelled.

"I just wanted to show you my ear was getting better from the draining. That's all," I said in an innocent voice while laughing inside.

"I don't believe that came out of you. Throw it out. Throw it, now!" he yelled pointing to the door.

Mama heard all the shouting and came rushing inside. "Is everything alright?" she asked as she passed through the kitchen into the living room.

"Tell him Mama these are the cotton balls from my ear. He doesn't believe me. I just wanted to show him my ear was getting better because of the draining from the oil," I said turning on the charm as I picked up the rank cotton balls from the floor. I showed them to Mama from a distance. She recognized the color and a hint of the odor.

"Yes, those came from his ear and he's getting better. He finally ate some solid food today. He'll be back in school on Monday. Now put those in the trash outside and wash your hands for dinner," she ordered me. "Yes Mama," I answered. I gave my dad a slight smile as he sat down on the sofa. I wanted him to know he had been punked. He just glared at me as I went outside to the trash can.

My love-hate relationship with my father started around age seven or eight. My dad would always give me a dime to buy treats from the corner store. As I grew, so did prices. I began to ask him for a quarter; he continued to give me a dime. He didn't realize a dime had become chump change. One day as he lay on the sofa, I asked him for a quarter. He looked at me strange, then stood, ran his hand into his pants pocket, and gave me a nickel and five pennies. I asked if I could have 15 cents more.

"No! That's all you're getting," he barked as he lay back down on the sofa.

His refusal stung like boiling water. My veins bubbled. Glaring with rattlesnake eyes my body quivered. Tighter and tighter I clenched the coins. With my next breath, I threw the coins against the wall where he laid. CLING, CLANG, CLING-A-LING rang out as they ricocheted

7

off the wall. It startled him. I stood firm, arms stiff at my side, and shouted, "I can't buy anything with a dime,"

Mama's face turned pale as a ghost. Her eyes widened in shock at my protest.

"Go to the bedroom," she yelled.

Before I could move a muscle, Daddy ordered, "No! Sit right there."

I sat in the chair across from him. I knew I was going to get it this time but I didn't care. I was tired of him and his damn dimes. He rose from the sofa. I was sure he was going to get the electrical cord to whip me senseless. Well good for him, it was about time. With my behavior, I'd told him to go hang himself so many times. Now he was finally going to do something.

Remaining silent, he rose and gave me a hard look. Prepared for a reprimanding blow of some kind, I was surprised when he dropped to his knees and began to search for the coins. When the last one was found, he stood, put them back in his pocket, and walked over to me. I steeled myself, the anticipated slap to knock me into the middle of next week was about to be administered.

With his eyes slit, nostrils flared, my father leaned in toward me and said, "You once had 10 cents. Now you have nothing. Get out of here. Go to the bedroom. I don't want to see you!"

You ass! I thought as I walked to the bedroom. But he was right. I had given up what I had to make my point. I sat on the bed stewing.

"A bird in the hand is worth two in the bush." Meaning, you don't let go of what you have, to chase after something you don't have. That was something my father often said. Lesson learned. I also learned the importance of standing up for what you want. He never gave me a dime again…only quarters.

Although my father and I didn't see eye to eye most of the time, I still listened to what he had to say. I should've obeyed him more. His drinking clouded my perception of him. I cherished our time together when he was sober. I relished the fact that I had a father when many of my friends didn't, drunk or sober. Just wished he had more time for me. I don't ever remember my dad playing catch with me or shooting baskets with me or teaching me how to ride a bike or read to me or play board games with me. Yeah – more time would have been nice.

CHAPTER 3

CHOOSE YOUR WEAPON

Being an Odd Ball had many challenges. My haters made me overly critical of myself. I started to question everything about me. I'd noticed my thing was different from my two older brothers. I cornered my brother Lavelle alone in the bedroom. He was sitting on his bed doing homework. I sat across from him on Casey's, our older brother's bed.

"Lavelle?"

"What?"

"Why is my thing different from yours and Casey's?"

"Thing? What thing?" he asked still looking in the book.

"My thing, you know?" I repeated pointing to my pelvic area.

He looked over the top of the book at me.

"Your penis...why is your penis different?" he chuckled.

I nodded yes.

"Say penis."

"No."

"Say penis or I'm not going to answer your question."

"Okay, okay. Penis. Why is my penis different from yours and Casey's?"

"Now that wasn't so hard, was it? It's not like it's a bad word. And from what my friends tell me, you're not afraid to use bad words. They tell me about your dirty little mouth when you're out running the streets talking jive."

"Are you going to tell me or not?" I asked in frustration.

"Alright, alright, I'll tell you."

He set the book on the bed and turned to face me.

"Okay listen-up. You were born in the hospital. When boys are born in the hospital the doctor removes the skin from the head of their penis. You have a circumcised penis."

"A circum what?"

"You have a circumcised penis. That means you don't have any skin covering the head of your penis. Casey and I aren't circumcised," he explained.

"Why weren't you and Casey born in the hospital?"

"I don't know. You have to ask Mama,"

I went to find Mama.

I found her in the kitchen stirring a pot of beans. I called to her, "Mama!"

"Yes Joseph."

"Why was I born in the hospital and Lavelle and Casey weren't?"

"Well, by the time you came along the state had outlawed mid-wives."

"What's a mid-wife?"

She answered, "A mid-wife was a woman who came to the pregnant mother's home to help her deliver her baby. She was registered by the state to deliver babies. She would record the child's birth with the state. The state would send the child's birth certificate in the mail. The mother and child didn't have to go to the hospital. Lavelle and Casey were delivered at home by a mid-wife."

Mama paused for a moment, giggled, and continued.

"There's a funny story about the hospital and your birth. Well, it's funny now but it wasn't so funny back then."

"What happened, Mama?"

"As I checked out the hospital with you I noticed an error on the paperwork. They marked your race as Caucasian. I hit the roof! I wouldn't leave until all copies of the documents were corrected."

My face drooped. Waves of grief passed through me. Mama giggled remembering the incident while I couldn't breathe. As I turned and staggered back to the bedroom I thought, *my identity has been in question my whole life. The mislabeling, the name calling started in the cradle!*

Thanks Mama for being persistent back then. But how do I change the reality of today? *What could I use now to erase the image kids love to hurl names and insults at?*

Most of the kids in my grade liked me but my haters were relentless. They called me: Casper, Space Ghost, Kimba (the White Lion), High Yellow, Mutt, Mutter, House Nigger, the Massa's Child. They called me those names because of my appearance. My family said the name calling was nothing but jealousy. But why would they be jealous of me?

Mama said, "They wish they were as handsome as you."

I loved my family but they couldn't hear the grenades going off in my brain when I heard those names. Sometimes I wished I was invisible! I often cried myself to sleep, wishing things were different.

I couldn't physically beat the bullies, so I used my mouth as my weapon to fight back. I had a very foul mouth. You got a taste of it in my thoughts about my father. But I only cussed in the streets. I never swore at home or in school. So when kids started that name calling bullshit, I let them have it! I blistered their asses worse than a baby's bottom left in a wet diaper overnight. I busted their chops about their appearance, their clothes, and about their fat ass mama. Then I got in the wind.

One of those name calling dicks gave chase. He called me a "Lil House Nigga." After we exchanged obscenities I told him, "It's sad that your ass rides your back like a camel's hump. It's even sadder that your mama's fat ass looks like a double humped camel!"

That pissed him off. I went ghost, darting between parked cars, through the wash house, and back onto the street again. Dashing through traffic to the other side times two. All while calling for my brother, "Lavelle, Lavelle, help!"

Terry, the kid that gave chase, always called me names. I went extra hard at him. I totally embarrassed him in front of his two friends. They laughed aloud as he gave chase.

"Lavelle, Lavelle, help!" I continued to yell.

CHAPTER 4

JUNGLE JUSTICE

Zoom! Like a Ninja in the night, Lavelle appeared. He swooped Terry like a buzzard diving on a dead carcass. The fight was on. Terry was dead meat! His ass was grass and Lavelle was doing the mowing.

"Get him Lavelle! Beat his ass! That bastard's always dissing me!" I screamed.

I tried to kick Terry but the crowd held me back. If it wasn't for them I would have stomped his lights out. I hated that kid and all the others that called me names.

"Let me go! Get off me!" I groaned.

"Let it be a fair fight. Lavelle can take him by himself." One of the kids said as he put his arm in front of me.

He was right. I looked down and Lavelle was giving it to him!

Two men intervened; saved Terry's ass, pulled Lavelle off him. Lavelle walked over and stood in front of me. Terry tried to explain.

"He was telling mama jokes and–" Lavelle interrupted,

"Don't you ever fuck with my little brother again!"

"But–"

"Shut up! You're three years older than him."

Terry shut his pie hole as he wiped a gob of blood from his nose and mouth. Lavelle was built like a tank. Whenever he got pissed he didn't take no shit. He'd just open can of "Whoop Ass" and then gave it to you.

Lavelle turned, grabbed me by my collar, and literally dragged me home. Manic eyes, steam seeped from his ears, a thin red line trickled from the crease of his lips. The third fight I'd gotten him into that year. It was only February. We walked briskly.

"Joseph!" his voice rose. "You must leave the older guys alone. One of these days I may not be around to help you," he cautioned.

"Terry started it. He's always picking on me! I just gave it back to him and he couldn't take it!" I bragged.

Punching and kicking the air I continued, "But you showed him Lavelle. You showed that dick!"

Lavelle rolled his eyes at me, looked skyward, and shook his head in disbelief. When we arrived at our back door, he opened it, and shoved me inside. I stumbled through the kitchen into the living room.

"Mama," he called out in frustration wiping blood from his mouth.

Mama rushed into the living room.

"What's wrong?" she asked in fright.

"Please keep him home!" Lavelle begged.

"Why? "What did he do now?" she asked with sympathy.

"He got me into another fight," squealed Lavelle.

I dropped my head, gave Mama my sad puppy dog eyes, and mumbled,

"The other kid started it."

A low growl came from Lavelle. He gave me a pit-bull glare that punched me in the gut.

"What did he do?" she inquired.

"He called me a name."

Mama shook her head in anger as she peered into my soul.

"Joseph, how many times must I tell you? Don't let the devil steal your joy! Don't let anyone touch you that deep. Sticks and stones can break your bones but don't let words hurt you." She instructed.

I wanted to scream, *Those names hurt! Words do hurt, Mama!* But I couldn't.

I looked over at Lavelle standing in the doorway listening. I began to feel bad. I'd gotten him into another fight. It wasn't his fault I looked the way I did. It wasn't his fault I'd chosen to defend myself with words I couldn't physically back up. My eyes welled up a little. I loved Lavelle. He was always there for me.

Seeing the fullness in my eyes, he warned, "Don't do it! Don't you dare! You were tough enough to speak your mind on the streets. So don't get all watery-eyed now."

I walked over to him, buried my head in his chest, and wrapped my arms around his waist.

"I'm sorry," I whispered fighting back tears.

He slowly put his arms around me and hugged back.

"Just leave the older guys alone," he said

"Okay." I sniffled.

My family didn't get it. Neither of my brothers had light skin, freckles, and reddish-brown hair. They weren't odd ball. It was tough for me on the streets. I probably should've stayed at home, but the streets called to me. It was exciting out there, and if I were going to wander the terrain, I had to get my respect. I lived in the jungle and *in the jungle you're either the predator or the prey. That's the rule of the jungle and the rules don't change!*

I struggled to survive out there but if I was going to make it, I had to fight. There were several ways to fight. It started with choosing your weapons. Some chose non-violence, other used brute force, their fist; while others used more lethal means. Words were my weapon of choice, against the bullies.

I was in the jungle by chance, others by choice. It didn't matter how you got there. What mattered was your survival! You couldn't show weakness in the jungle. If you did, the wolves came after you every day. They'd pick and eat at you until nothing of yourself remained. The weak survived only when protected by a pack.

CHAPTER 5

FAMILY SECRETS

Whenever I was on punishment or confined inside, I would walk through the house yowling like the Wolf Man. No lie. It drove my family crazy.

"Yooooowl!" "Yoooowl!"

Over and over, again and again I'd yowl with only a breath in between. My soul, my spirit yearned to run free. The primitive utterance also served as a pressure release from the hate I was getting on the streets. I kept it up intermittently until my dad came home. Then it became a stare down session.

He sat on the sofa, I in the chair. My jaw tightened, my fangs grew, saliva seeped. I glared at him as he watched TV. When my X-ray vision finally pierced his consciousness, he spoke.

"What's wrong with you?"

"Nothing."

"Well, don't you have somewhere to be? Go."

"I can't. I'm on punishment. Don't you remember? You gave it to me."

"Oh – yes, I did. Well you shouldn't have been up there cussing and fussing with those street punks on Franklin. I was very embarrassed when my friends told me they saw and heard you. Now get out of here. Go to the bedroom."

He was clueless to how I was getting verbally trashed by those kids and I wasn't about to tell him either. I stalked him as I got up to leave. Fangs exposed, foam at the corners of my mouth, salvia dripped down my chin. I stopped in front of the TV and in one deep breath I let out a ferocious yowl. I must have held it for a minute or more.

"Yooooooooooooooooooooooooooooooooowl!"

My siblings rushed to the doorway to take a peek. Daddy's chin dropped. His eyes swelled, pushing his brows to the ceiling. When I was done with the longest Wolf Man yowl on record he jumped up and shouted,

"That's it!"

He came toward me. I braced myself for a clocking in the kisser. Instead, he blocked my path and called for Mama.

"Babe, Babe!" That was his pet name for her.

My siblings stood in the walkway between the bedrooms cracking up.

"Yes Daddy." She called him by her pet name for him as she pressed past the crowd.

"Go up to that school and have this boy checked by that counselor lady.

My brothers and sister chuckled. So did Mama.

"I'm serious!"

"Aw Daddy, he's just a growing boy with a lot of energy. That's all"

"How are his grades? Has his grades dropped?

My siblings and Mama laughed.

"Come here Joseph."

I walked under his arms to get to her outstretched hand. She wrapped her arm around my shoulder. She looked at me as she spoke. I eyeballed him.

"His grades are good and no discipline reports. All his teachers like him. Go to the room Joseph," she nodded.

I turned and walked away. They continued.

He said, "Babe, that boy—"

Mama interrupted, "That boy is special and you know it. Leave him alone. Now go and wash up for dinner. I'll make you a plate" she chuckled.

"You keep saying that but I wonder sometimes," he said slow stepping toward the bathroom.

"You know it's true. Stop wondering," she shouted from the kitchen.

Wait, what did they mean by special? Was I some reject or something? I knew I had issues but come on. My own parents were raking me over the hotcoals. I sat on the floor at the end of the bed. My siblings were posted up. Jeanie sat at the dresser writing a letter. Casey and Lavelle were sitting up in their bed looking through car magazines.

"When are you going to learn to stop pissing off the old man? You only get yourself in more trouble." Casey chuckled.

"No, when is that little half breed going to stop pissing off the older kids? He's gotten me into three fights in two months! Lavelle barked.

Already frying over Mama and Daddy calling me some special bobbing head doll, I rose to my feet and lashed out.

"Bite it Lavelle! If I'm a half breed then all of us in this room are half breeds, including you." I fired back.

Casey slowly lowered his magazine, gave me a bewildered look. He called to me,

"Joseph."

"What!"

"Didn't you read the memo?"

"What memo? What are you talking about?"

"It was from Mama and Daddy."

"No. Did I get a phone call or something?"

"No, you didn't"

"Was it something from school?

"Nope."

"Then stop jiving me. What are you talking about?"

"The memo was to all of us. It read; "To our children, yes, you all are half breeds. Casey and Lavelle you are half black and half Indian. Jeanie and Joseph you are half black and half white."

They all laughed. I wasn't humored.

"Watch it Casey." A half-hearted threat from Jeanie broke through the laughter.

"Piss on you Casey," I said as I turned to leave the room. I stood between the two bedrooms, arms folded, back against the wall.

"See what you've done," Jeanie mildly reprimanded.

She joined me in the walkway.

"You know they were just joking," she whispered.

"Yeah I know. I just wasn't in the mood for it especially after hearing Mama and Daddy call me some special nut job." I whispered back.

"They didn't say that."

"Yes they did. They called me special."

"That means you're smart, gifted, anointed. It's a good thing."

"Gifted? Anointed?"

"Quiet. You worry too much. Come, I have something for you."

She grabbed me by my arm and led me into our parent's bedroom.

"Sit down," she said pointing to her bed.

I sat quietly.

She reached into the dresser drawer and pulled out her purse. She sat on the bed beside me.

"I forgot I had this for you... your payment for taking my phone messages."

She reached into her purse and pulled out a $1.50 and gave it to me.

"Thanks for the messages."

"Wow, no Jeanie, thank you."

"Well, you know we light skin, half breeds have to stick together," she said with a smile, nod, and a wink.

I smiled, nodded, and winked back.

CHAPTER 6

A LOOK BEYOND THE VEIL

Growing up in my home there were two rules you didn't break. 1) Going to school. 2) Going to church.

Going to school was my father's anthem. A headache or a stomach ache wasn't a good enough excuse to miss school. You had to be sick… like a 103 temperature with diarrhea, and snot running out your nose sick – to miss school. His song titles: "Go to school." "Make good grades." "To get ahead, get a good education." Lyrics tattooed on my gray matter.

Church was my mom's thing. She didn't care how late you stayed out Saturday night, you had to get up and go to church on Sunday morning. No excuses. Her daily sermons: "Say your prayers," "Bless your food," "Be kind to others." A picture of Jesus hung on the wall sporting blond hair and blue eyes. I'd never seen a Jew with blonde hair and blue eyes. Anyway, he was the God we prayed to. I doubted if he was listening! The God hanging on my wall looked a lot like the men spraying black people with high pressure fire hoses. He looked a lot like the men accused in the bombing of a black church that killed 4 little black girls inside. I had doubts about the God that hung on our wall.

My home was a happy place until Friday night. Most weekends my father drank too much. He became mean, verbally abusive… aiming his fury mainly at my mother. Cussing like a sailor, he made false accusations; accusing her of infidelity, squandering his money, giving his money to other men. The only child at home, Mama and I bore the weight of his verbal assaults. My older siblings were usually out enjoying their weekend. By the time they returned Daddy would be asleep, his drunken rant over. These episodes infuriated me! Mama was numb to it. She rarely said a word in her defense. She just watched and prayed. Let him get it off his chest.

One night I couldn't take it any longer. Mama and I were watching TV in the living room. I lay on the floor in front of the set, while Mama sat at the dining room table. Daddy came in, sat on the sofa, and started his drunken routine. I tried to ignore him. As he continued to rant and rave, the top of my head blew off. I rose to my feet in front of the TV and turned to him. My hands felt like they held two large stones. I could have beaten him to death with them.

"Move out of the way," he shouted.

I stood firm. Tears started streaming down. I couldn't control them as I shook in anger. Finally, in a fit of rage, I began screaming, "Stop it! Stop it! I'm tired of your lies. Stop it!"

I repeated it over and over until I couldn't hear myself anymore. Mama tried to get through to me. She was like a faint voice from another zip code, "Calm down, stop screaming."

I couldn't respond. I had drifted into blank space, a dark void, an eerie place. Life, death, nothing mattered. Lost inside of nothingness, my circuit board shot sparks, flames. I had blown a fuse. Sparks continued to fly until a soft, tender voice brought me back. It called to me.

"Joseph. Joseph. Calm down." It was Mama standing in front of me.

My eyes cleared, darkness faded. The room came back into view. My body went limp. Mama caught me and sat me in the chair. We cried…I trembled…She hugged my angst away. Both were jolted by my rage. Concern smeared their faces. I couldn't remember if I hit him. I would never do that, even in a fit of anger. He finally sat up. He was pissed. Of course he blamed Mama for my blackout.

"You got that boy acting like some crazy fool. It's your fault he acts that way," he grumbled.

I wiped my face and stood.

"I'm leaving. I want you to come with me," I said to Mama.

"Where are we going?" she asked.

"I don't know but we're leaving here!" I said glaring at my dad.

Mama could sense the anger rising in me again.

"Sure! Sure! Let me get my purse," she answered in a huff.

She rushed to gather her things. Together we left. Daddy didn't say a word. He just mumbled under his breath and laid back down on the sofa. We walked across the field to cousin Mae's house. Her dad was my second cousin on my mom's side. There we stayed until my dad was asleep.

CHAPTER 7

BLOOD IS THICKER THAN MUD

We were a proud but poor family. The menu- mayonnaise sandwiches, onion sandwiches, syrup and water for Kool-Aid. For dinner it was always Pork but not the good pork: ham, pork roast or pork chops. No! We ate: pig ears, pig tails, pig feet, ham hocks, hog maws, pig intestines. Every meal was served with white rice and beans. Pinto beans, Lima beans, Navy beans, Kidney beans, or Black Eye peas. I ate beans and the worst parts of a pig every week day. It gave new meaning to the phrase, "Pork and Beans!" I shouldn't complain. Several of my friends didn't have anything for dinner a couple of nights a week. We ate our best meal on Sunday, chicken.

When the electricity was turned off, one of my brothers would hot wire the electric box by placing a penny behind the fuse and screwing it back into the slot. This kept the lights on until the bill was paid. Sometimes we had to borrow the penny from a neighbor! The lights and the telephone were never off at the same time. I asked Mama why?

"Some months I have to decide which one to pay," she said.

When the telephone was off we made calls from the phone booth at Ray's Groceries. Once, I went with my parents to call my Uncle Tony, my Dad's younger brother. He lived in New York. He was one of my mental escapes from Reservoir City. I loved bright lights, and New York

City had lots of them according to Eloquent Magazine. Whenever my spirits were down I imagined running away to live with my Uncle Tony, a kind, soft spoken man who didn't drink, smoke, or swear, who often came to visit for the winter. I slept with Lavelle during his stay. He was the opposite of my Uncle Mack, my Dad's older brother.

Uncle Mack was from another planet! No, really. He was definitely from another world! Known as one of the Town Drunks, his antics were off the hook! I had my own problems to deal with. I didn't need Uncle Mack's chaos in my life. He was a loose nail sticking out which gave my haters another reason to hammer me. But I was taught, "Blood is thicker than mud," but Uncle Mack's zaniness made me question that phrase several times.

Whenever he was drunk he came to my block to direct traffic. You heard right, "Drunk directing traffic!" I kid you not. It was total bedlam, madness personified! It was the funniest, craziest, scariest thing ever. He stood on the center line as cars and trucks raced past him. He spun around like a dog chasing his tail blowing that damn whistle…. yes, he had a whistle! He blew it at the motorists. They beeped their horns back. He fussed and swore at the drivers. They swore back at him. He yelled obscenities. They yelled them back. It was a live comedy show in the middle of Franklin Street.

And in a supreme act of buffoonery he bellowed a tune. "Stop, in the name of love, before you break my heart."

That was over the top, a total spectacle. A crowd had gathered to enjoy the entertainment. After the song he began to run after the cars; right, left, forward, back. After a few chases, he stopped again. This time he broke into a jig. He did his "Happy Dance" on the center line. Unbelievable! Several cars and trucks came dangerously close to hitting him. The crowd was hysterical with laughter. His last antic was to call for his brother, my dad.

"Ike. Oh Ike! You and I have some things to discuss. You John Brown right!" He belted.

He ended each sentence with, "You John Brown right." I never knew why. He would continue yelling for his brother until someone from my family came to get him out of the street. It was a routine my family knew all too well.

Although it was entertaining for most, his life was still in danger. Yes, his behavior was quite embarrassing but he was still family and "Blood is thicker than mud." When I became of age, it was my job to go get him. All my siblings had their turn as Uncle Mack's retriever. They refuse to do it anymore. I was up! It was never easy convincing him to get out the street. I stood at the edge of the road. I begged, pleaded with him.

"Uncle Mack, please get out the street. I'm scared for you," I cried out.

No response. He continued with his antics.

"Uncle Mack, come down to the house to get something to eat."

"Where's ya paw boy? Get him up here," he demanded.

"Daddy wants you to visit. Come get something cool to drink," I begged.

Hearing my desperate attempts, the crowd began to encourage him to get out the street. In a light bulb moment, I got an Uncle Mack idea. We were definitely related. In a leap of faith or desperation, I ran out to him.

"Joseph, what are you doing? Go back," he slurred.

"No! I want to direct traffic with you. Let me blow your whistle." I playfully requested.

The crowd's faces went from jovial to terror. Now there were two nuts on the center line.

"Joseph, you go back now! It's dangerous out here," he demanded.

"Nope! I'm not going anywhere. The only way I'll leave is with you," I insisted.

Pause.

Quiet.

"Okay! Okay! I'll go. I'll go with you," he finally agreed. My heart sang.

I extended my hand. He covered it in his softball mitt of a hand. I led him out the street to the roar of the crowd. When we were clear of the traffic, I took a bow. They cheered louder. Although Uncle Mack was inebriated, he considered my health and safety above his own. I guess blood was thicker than, well, alcohol.

CHAPTER 8

BRAIDED STRANDS

My mother, Ruth Ann "Babe" Graham was my heart, my protector, defender; my blanket of love and affection. I once said to her, "If you die, I'm going to climb in the casket and go with you!"

She smiled and replied, "Oh baby, you don't have to worry about Mama dying. I'm going to be around for a long time."

A beautiful, quiet spirit, I never heard her speak an unkind word. "Treat others the way you want to be treated," she taught.

Mama was a praying woman. During my tender years, she held my hand several times a day, placed her free hand on my forehead, and prayed. She gave me a sense of God and faith. What little moral and ethical character I have came from her. She reminded me daily, "Joseph, don't steal! If you're hungry, ask the store owner if you can sweep the floor or take out the trash for something to eat. But don't steal!"

She branded my heart with it. When I was older I found the nerve to ask her, "Mama, why do you always remind me not to steal?"

In an instant she replied, "Being labeled a thief is one of the worst things to be branded as. Once you're labeled a thief, no one will trust you again. Trust is very important. You want people to trust you!"

My father, Isaac "Ike" Graham was a hard-working man, a good provider. I can only remember him missing one day of work. I got my strong work ethic, self-motivation, and determination from my father. His motto: "Once you start a job, you stay on that job until it's done!"

He wouldn't let me quit anything! "If you start it, you finish it!" he'd say.

For years he worked for minimum wage. It haunted him. He wanted more for himself and his family. This drove him to drink heavily on the weekends. By all accounts, he was a weekend alcoholic. A Dr. Jekyll, Mr. Hyde clone…alcohol, the activating potion.

He was small in stature but stood tall on principles. He often said to me, in his sober state, "Joseph, you are a Graham. Always walk with your head up! The world would love to see you walking around with a broken spirit. They'd love to see you with your head hung low. Don't do it! You keep your head up!"

My father was a hotel maintenance man for most of his adult life. When I was younger he would take me to work with him about once a month on a Saturday morning.

"Bring your swimming trunks today," he said.

"Great, we're going to the beach," I answered with glee.

He didn't reply. He just smiled and continued to put on his shoes. After tying them we headed for the door.

"Do you have them?" He asked.

"Yes, they're under my shorts," I answered.

When we arrived at his job, we walked toward the front office. He had to check-in with management. Without warning he said, "Go get in the pool."

Wait. What? He wanted me, his black son, to go swim in the white folks' pool? I didn't hesitate. Peeling off my shorts and shirt, I jumped right in as he entered the office. He knew I wasn't welcomed in the water by management. He blocked the window and distracted the owner with small talk while I swam. He came out later and pretended to clean leaves from the pool. He continued to block the owner's view of me in the water. He wanted to show them the water wouldn't change colors and no one would get sick because I swam in the pool. It was also his way of exposing me to the things white kids were privileged to.

Finally the owner spotted me. She stormed out, snarled, and yelled, "Ike!"

He turned to acknowledge her.

"Oh Mrs. Caroline, he's not hurting anything. It's just water."

He knew how to play the subservient role when he had to. That's how he made his living. But he was no one's dummy! He wanted to prove his point.

She gave him the evil eye and marched back inside. Her jaw dropped when two white kids joined me in the water. We played for hours. Their parents looked on from the 4rd floor balcony. Maybe from that distance they couldn't tell I was black. Did my amber tone and curly ginger locks fool them or maybe they just didn't care? They were Northerners from New Jersey.

My father took me once a month to swim there. Those experiences taught me not to be afraid of white people. They were kids just like me. The only difference was the color of our skin. And with me there wasn't much difference in that department either. He also took my siblings to work when they were younger, but none swam in the pool. He had grown weary of the racial remarks thrown at him. Having me swim in the pool was his personal protest.

My three siblings were much older than me. My sister Jeanie was 15 years my senior. She worked at the beauty shop on Franklin Street. Her dream was to own her own beauty shop someday. She was smart, outgoing, and unassuming. Her heart danced for fast cars and miniskirts. Mama didn't agree with her wearing miniskirts. Not to dis Mama, Jeanie carried the skirts in her purse. She changed into them after she left the house. She was a fox and she knew it! She was light skinned like me and Mama. Girls teased her when she was growing up. Mostly whispers though, nothing like my haters. The guys liked light skin girls, called them "Red bones."

Whenever she caught up with me she took me places with her. Said I was good company. Because of our resemblance, and the big age difference, some assumed she was my mom. When asked if I was her son, to most she told the truth. But if there was some sucka trying to hit on her in a store and she disapproved, she'd call to me in this manner, "Joseph, Joseph, come on son!"

I'd come around the corner from the next isle over to join her. The guys would take one look at me and move on. I'm glad they didn't persist with their advances. The situation could have gotten ugly. Jeanie carried a switch blade in her purse and wasn't afraid to use it! She had several academic scholarships to college. She lost all of them when she got into a fight at school. She pulled her knife on a girl.

"Come on hoe! You want a piece of me. I'll cut you too short to shit bitch!" she told her. Well, at least that's what the suspension notice read according to Lavelle.

The girl didn't press charges but Jeanie got a 10 day suspension. The colleges got wind of the fight and the suspension. They withdrew their scholarship offers. That was years ago.

When we were out together Jeanie often corrected me. She groomed me on how to speak and act in public. If I followed her instructions, a burger or ice cream awaited as my reward. Butter Pecan was our favorite flavor. Other than my parents, Jeanie was the most influential person in my life. She listened to me with compassion. She never dismissed any of my questions, thoughts or concerns. On one of our outings we passed a cemetery. I said to her, "I don't like graveyards." Without taking her eyes off the road, she said, "You don't have to be afraid of the dead. They can't harm you. They're dead! The ones to keep your eyes on are the people walking, talking, and breathing. Those are the ones that can hurt you."

My fear of graveyards was cured.

Casey, my oldest brother, was 10 years older. He worked as a night janitor at the all black high school he once attended. He and Jeanie were close. Every day they discussed plans to leave the neighborhood. Casey was a real charmer with the girls. His pecan tan complexion, like my dad and Lavelle was adored. Combine that with his high cheek bones, a bushy mustache and you had a Billy D. Williams look alike. He loved to dress like Billy D. with clothes from the second hand store.

Casey preferred Otis Redding's music over James Brown. He fancied whopper burgers, horror movies, and luxury cars. A Cadillac was his dream car. I told him, "Good luck with that brother! No one in this house can afford a Cadillac."

He drove a Volkswagen Beetle. It was the first car I learned to drive. I was ten. He sat me on his lap while he operated the gas, breaks, and clutch. I would steer and work the gears. I was only allowed to drive on the rocky road leading to our house. By the time I was 12 we switched seats and I drove, operating all systems by myself.

Casey took me places as well, mostly to the carwash. I was cheap labor. My pay was always food, a welcomed break from pig ears and pig tails. One day on the drive back home, we got the surprise of our lives. As Casey made the left turn onto the rocky road from Franklin Street, the car door swung open. I was catapulted into oncoming traffic.

A human bowling ball, I rolled toward the gutter. Careening cars, screeching tires sounded the alarm. Tailpipe fumes, burnt rubber, singed my sniffer. Angelville prepared my wings. Inches away from being a pancake, I reached the curb…a much appreciated gutter ball thrown. Casey ran to me as did one of my near executioners. Disoriented I tried to stand.

"Sit down. Are you alright?" Casey's voice shook.

'I'm okay," I answered with a slight moan.

"Are you sure?" The motorist asked.

"Yeah, I think so," I groaned.

"Let me see," Casey requested.

He searched my body for injuries. A few scrapes on my arms and one on my knee. They weren't serious. My hip was sore from the landing. I was more frightened than injured. He looked into my eyes.

"Are you alright?' he repeated as the motorist looked on.

"Yes, yes. I'm good," I answered with a slight groan as I stood to my feet.

We started walking back to Casey's car.

"You're one lucky kid. I barely missed you," the motorist said.

"I got him from here. He's my little brother," Casey said to the driver.

"Man, your little brother has an angel on his shoulder. Glad you're okay li'l buddy," he said in departing.

"Thank you Sir." I replied.

Casey and I opened the car doors and got in. He turned to me and said,"Please don't tell Mama"

I gave him a bewildered look and sarcastically asked, "Don't tell Mama what?

We smiled. He started the engine and continued home. I was lucky that day. I cheated death by inches, a foreshadowing of things to come.

My brother Lavelle was my hero. I openly bragged about him. He was five years older and had mega street cred. In sports, he was the man. Recognized as one of the best athletes in the county; football, basketball, and track. No one was better. He had granite for muscles, and I worshipped the ground he walked upon. Moments with him and his friends were golden. When I couldn't find my crew I searched the streets for Lavelle. Once I found him, he and his crew treated me like royalty! Lavelle never allowed anyone to dis me. After chilling for a few minutes, I was sent on my way.

Lavelle was a great brother but at times he behaved like a certified nut. He was definitely related to Uncle Mack, nuttier than a fruit cake. There were times he couldn't sit or stand still. His legs twitched. His arms shook. His fingers tapped nonstop. When he was younger our parents had to tie a rope around his waist or his wrist. A strong, heavy object supported the other end. This kept him from running away. If left unattended for any length of time, he was ghost.

Once, he was gone all day. Eluding Casey and Jeanie's search party, he returned to find Daddy waiting with the electric cord in hand. His amps up to max, the electrical storm began. A barrage of lightning strikes rained upon Lavelle. Bolt after bolt, so intense, I began to cry. When the thrashing was over I went to Lavelle. He sat on the floor at the end of the bed in the bedroom he and Casey shared. I sat beside him. With us hugging each other he whispered, "Stop crying. I mean it. Stop! You must be tough Joseph. Don't let nothing or no one stop you from doing what you want to do!"

"I won't." I sobbed quietly.

CHAPTER 9

THE GREAT PRETENDERS

In the months, years that followed, Lavelle's creed encouraged me to just do it! Don't fart around. If you're going to do it, do it…and don't let anything stand in your way. Sure, there were consequences but, the rewards for doing what I wanted to do was worth it. He helped release the lion within me. To boldly go and do what most kids my age only dreamed of!

Lavelle was my real life hero. However, my Silver Screen hero was Bond. Through him, I imagined the life I hope to have someday. He became my alter ego. After seeing my first Bond flick, I knew I was destined to live my life as a Double-O. I'd never connected with a movie or TV character as much as I did with James Bond.

All the males in my house had an action hero. Daddy's hero was John Wayne. He'd watch John Wayne movies all night if Mama let him. Lavelle's was Bruce Lee. Casey's hero was some guy with girls dress-up like bunnies. Whatever! And my hero was James Bond. I would've preferred a black action hero but there were no positive black images to imitate or emulate in the movies or on TV. The blacks were casted as maids, butlers, chauffeurs, or slaves. The closest to black was Tonto, the Indian side kick to The Long Ranger. Everyone in the hood cheered for Tonto. The biggest joke on the Silver Screen was Tarzan, a white man yelling through the jungles of Africa wearing only a loin cloth. He wrestled and tamed and killed lions with his bare hands! They called him the "king of the jungle." Get the fuck out of here! No one on the west side of the tracks believed in Tarzan…a white man the hero of Africa. Far out man! That was too much to stomach.

I didn't care that Bond was white. Besides, your hero should match your personality, not necessarily your race. He should have traits you identify with other than race. He's someone you looked up to. A person you aspired to emulate. He has qualities that make you root for him. For me, that was James Bond.

I loved everything about him: The accent, the clothes, the adventures. Don't forget the cool gadgets, the travel, and of course the girls. Can you image having a girlfriend named, Pussy Galore? That was Bond. He was hood with an accent. As bond, I imagined going to exotic places with a pretty girl for an exciting adventure. On the streets and on the phone with a girl, I was Bond, a Double-O.

I know I rambled on about my family but in the end they're all we have. They wanted the best for me. I should've listened more. Bear with me. This last story puts a bow on me and my family.

We had an old record player that hadn't played in years. It sat in a corner of the bedroom my brothers shared. One day while they were out, I decided to tinker with it. A mound of cluttered blocked my entry. The heap found a new home at the base of the mahogany frame. Rising to survey the inner workings a squeaky hedge, dust, cobwebs gave a salute.

After a half hour of cleaning and sneezing, I plugged it in. Nothing! A quick inspection revealed the power supply knob was in the off position. When I moved the knob to the on position, the turntable got its groove back. Each revolution cranked my smile wider.

Sifting through the mound, a record album emerged; The Platters. On the turntable it went. The melodic cords grabbed Mama's attention. She entered.

"Oh my, I haven't heard that song in years. What did you do to get it to play?"

"I cleaned tons of dirt and dust from the turntable and adjusted the needle."

"You used water? Joseph, you know better! Never water on electrical devices."

"The power was turned off Mama."

"You know the rule. Next time, please ask for permission."

"I'm sorry. Next time I will. I promise."

Leaving the room she turned around, smiled, and said, "It does sound good though, puts a little joy in the air."

As the album played I became fond of one song in particular, "The Great Pretender." I played it two or three times.

It was a sad song about a guy who broke up with his girl. On the outside he pretended to be happy. While inside, his heart ached for her. I identified most with these lyrics,

"Oh yes, I'm the great pretender," and "My need is such I pretend too much."

Weeks passed. I played the song religiously. In fact, it was the only song I played. And then out of the blue, the record player stopped working. I would wager a bet Mama sabotaged it. Too late, the lyrics to the "Great Pretender" were etched in my brain. The song mirrored the story of my life, my family's life. We were all Pretenders.

My father pretended to be happy working for minimum wage. My mom pretended to ignore my father's drinking. Lavelle posed as Jim Thorpe, the world's greatest athlete. Casey pretended to be, "God's gift to women." Jeanie faked being happy stuck at home helping with the bills, which denied her the opportunity to get her own beauty shop. And me, I was a Double-0 agent. Oh yes, we were the great pretenders. It was how we dealt with our dysfunction. It offered a temporary escape from our reality. Pretending bought us time to work through the many challenges of living on the rocks in the jungle.

CHAPTER 10

BRUISES FROM
THE ROCKS

My hometown Reservoir City, a beach resort, was named for its many waterways. Sunny days, tropical nights, made it a year round tourist trap. Population: 42,000. Sea Garden, eight miles north and Rising Tide, ten miles south, were our tourist trap neighbors. Monopa, the largest tropical magnet, set 30 miles farther south… population, 300,000.

Segregation and southern towns went together like grits and eggs. The railroad tracks the divider. Blacks lived on the west side, Whites on the east or beach side.

Before tourism set in, farming was the bread winner in Reservoir City…beans, tomatoes, corn. All fields on the west side. White farm owners recruited black laborers, paid by the day, named them, "Day Workers." My mom was once a Day Worker.

Picked up at the crack of dawn, yawning, wiping sleep from their eyes, they crawled into the cab. Side rails completed the cattle like enclosure. They sat swaying in the morning mist. Four miles later, the cab door opened to the bliss of the owners. With aching backs they waded through muck and fertilizer picking crops to earn their pay.

In the scorching heat, shot gun carrying overseers, supervised the slave labor. Their disclaimer; "The guns were needed for snakes." The workers knew who the snakes were!

Acres of farmland as far as the eye could see separated the workers from town. Trapped in the middle of nowhere, black women became delectable for the supervisors. Scratching, kicking and clawing, they were wrestled to the barn. Brute force tamed their protest, their prized possession taken. Muffled whimpers emanated from the rafters. Agonizing screams permeated the air. Black men rendered helpless. Attempts to assist could result in loss of life. So everyone kept quiet about the on goings in the fields. Bullies strike from a position of power.

Prior to my and Lavelle's birth, every year during high harvest season, January through May, the School Boards of Reservoir City officially closed all black schools. Black students were only allowed to go to school six months out of the year; June through November... and two weeks in December. They were encouraged to pick crops for "The Man" the other half of the year. Even worst, while white kids and their teachers were home enjoying their summer vacations, black kids attended school if they wanted an education. Black teachers had to teach twice as much material to their students if they were to pass to the next grade. They never got a break: school and pick The Man's crops... modern day slavery.

My two oldest siblings participated in that atrocity. Depriving black children of their education to help anyone gain their riches during school hours was criminal, bullying at its best. Thank God laws changed by the time Lavelle and I came along. I would've told them all where to go if they thought I was going to help them become rich while they called me; nigger, coon, monkey, jungle bunny, jigaboo.

Worst yet, this hell hole had a bottom; my neighborhood, Jefferson Quarters...the only section in Black Town without paved roads. Rocks cut the paths between the eighteen mustard colored, flat roof, 25 foot by 22 foot cinder block boxes...the eye sore of the community. Another nail sticking out for my haters to hammer me for. I despised the place! It irked me to hear or say the name, Jefferson Quarters. Built by Bill Jefferson for his farm laborers, I never referred to it by name when asked where I lived. I'd say, "I live off Franklin Street behind Ray's Groceries."

Some jokers would continue as if they didn't know where I meant. "You mean Jefferson Quarters?"

Forced to answer, I'd nod yes in shame. Butt-holes!

Endless clouds of dust and white sand generated Visine eyes. Chalk colored clothes, a cough. Each lair room for 4, we packed 6…tighter than sardines in a can. No inside doors, bed sheets hung instead. Roaches and mice were co-tenants. The Reservoir Canal provided a view… some water front property. Four dimly lit street lamps shadowed the crime infested dump. The mailman refused to deliver. The kicker, my home address: #1 Northwest 8th Place was bogus. There was no street named, 8th Place. According to the US Mail, my home, the Quarters didn't exist. Mail pickup, Ray's Groceries, Box 27.

Wooden shacks once the skyline of the Quarters. Taken by hurricanes, only one survived. A blessing or a curse, the Quarters were in the heart of the Black Business District, Franklin Street. Muscle Cars and Hot Rods cruised 30 yards from my backdoor. If you were looking for a good time, Franklin Street was the place to be; bars, night clubs, pool halls, diners, the movie theatre, clothing stores, grocery stores, corner stores, and more.

The energy on Franklin was uncontainable! From uptown to downtown, excitement rode shotgun with danger on Franklin Street; fights, stabbings, shootings, muggings were common. Drugs, alcohol, prostitution, gambling- parts of the landscape.

I prayed to leave Jefferson Quarters. The rocks depressed. When I stood on them; the hurt, pain, sorrow of lost dreams and broken promises penetrated my senses. Hopelessness, disappointment, and the poverty of generations past hovered above. Their ghosts haunted me, urging me to participate in their life of despair. No way! I rejected their invitation. I left those rocks every chance I got. I prowled Franklin Street like a young lion, searching to find what was out there for me. I wanted a life far greater than the one I was living. I refused to participate with "The Skeletons" of Jefferson Quarters.

CHAPTER 11

THE FIRST CUTS WERE THE DEEPEST

My first friends were the Davis girls next door: Gracie, Ola, and June. Gracie and I were the same age. Ola, a year younger and June was two years my junior. The older two made a fuss over me all the time. I was too young to understand. Growing up with the girls I learned a lot of girly stuff like braiding hair, playing jacks, jumping rope. They also taught me how to kiss.

When we were younger their father built them a playhouse. Its' pint size ceiling hid us from the burning rays. Wide cutouts for windows welcomed the sweet-lemony-scent of Magnolia blossoms riding the breeze. Miniature doorways offered safe passage to and from. Their favorite game, Playhouse, was enjoyed in the afternoons.

The object of the game was to pretend to be a family. Since I was the only boy I was always the father. Gracie and Ola argued constantly over who would be the mother. Whoever lost the argument was the older daughter. No complaints from June. She was always the baby. As time passed I figured out that this was their made up version of a kissing game. If you were the mother you got to kiss me on the lips. If you were the older daughter you could only kiss me on the cheek.

Here is how it worked; when father left for work the older daughter kissed me on the cheek and mother kissed me on the lips. The same was true when father came home from work and when we pretended to go to church, the grocery store, and when we lay down to go to sleep. Gracie and Ola orchestrated everything. I followed their lead. Gracie was the aggressor, bossy, always pulled me to her before planting a firm wet one on me. Ola was softer. Her kisses were gentle, almost apologetic.

I could never fully appreciate going to the movies and seeing some 14 year old sapsucker on the screen having a problem asking a girl for a kiss. Man, I'd been kissing girls on the lips since I was 6 or 7. That early start gave me "Beaver Fever!" Good or bad, the fever was real. My temperature rose, as well as parts of my body, as I got older.

Years passed, kissing grew into fondling when three girls from the Heights Apartments joined the mix; Tracie; Bonnie, Amber. The Heights was 75 yards across the weeds and bush. A dirt path gave access. These girls, especially Amber, were like octopuses. Their tentacles had no bounds. They taught me how to find my mark. Our games of "Hide and Seek," played at dusk in the dust, weren't innocent anymore.

After playing Hop-Scotch, Jump Rope, and braiding hair for years with the girls; I leaped with joy when Adam Evans moved into the Quarters. Although it was creepy at first, it was awesome just the same. Looking at him was like looking into a mirror; light skin, freckles, and fire engine red hair. An odd ball to the max! It was too good to be true and he lived only a house away. Finally I had someone I could do guy stuff with. The same age, in the same grade, my first male best friend. Best of all, he was an odd ball. Mama babysat his little sister while we were at school. After school, we walked to my house where he and his sister were picked up by his older brother or older sister.

Crazy how much we had in common besides our looks; yoyos, marbles, spinning top, football, basketball. Jamming to our favorite music was another afternoon favorite. Milk money saved, a dash to Betty's corner store, the jukebox blared. James Brown, "I feel Good" for my dime. Jackie Wilson, "Higher and Higher" selected with his coin. Our dance contests were epic. With Mrs. Betty as the judge, I was James Brown while Adam did his best Jackie Wilson impersonation. Mrs. Betty usually called the contest a tie. So amused by our effort she put another coin in the jukebox to break the tie. Dripping with sweat, Mrs. Betty, once again, declared another tie. She gave us each a candy bar for the show.

Laughing and joking who was better, we waited at the crosswalk. On the other side three older boys stood pointing and whispering. The light changed, we walked toward them. They snickered as we passed them. I glared out the corner of my eye. I wanted to jab my pencil in their butt or something…anything to stop them from snickering. We picked up the pace.

"You see those fart faces pointing; what's their problem?" Adam asked.

"Welcome to the neighborhood. I get that all the time," I said.

"Yeah, I do too. It's so stupid. My mom says to just ignore older kids. They're nothing but trouble," he said.

"My mom said the same thing but it's hard to ignore them when they do that kind of stuff right in your face."

"True but what can we do? We can't beat'em."

"I know, but I still wanna poke'em in the eyes or something."

Adam chuckled. "Yeah, like Moe on the Stooges. But then what, we take a massive beat-down and get dumped into the trash? Not me! Let's just keep walking."

"You're right but someday…"

"Yeah, but your someday is not today," he said as I opened my backdoor.

It was good to have someone who shared my frustration, felt my pain…someone to discuss it with. He talked me into my first adventure.

School was out for the day. Kids raced past playing tag, chasing each other, goosing and giving wedgies. The last day of the week, the celebration was on. You would've thought it was summer vacation, not just the weekend. The sun was warm but not blistering. The haze was purple, blue, and yellow, not its customary fireball red and orange. Preadolescent sweat and cheap dime store perfume took their individual paths toward home. I caught up with Adam at our usual meeting spot, the gym equipment room.

"You want to stop by Mrs. Betty's to play some tunes?" I asked.

40

"Nah, I spent my milk money today," he said.

"Well, I have a dime. We can at least play one song," I offered.

"Nah, I'm not into it today. I want some mulberries," he said.

"Mulberries?" I questioned as we neared the outside basketball court.

"Yes… mulberries. That stupid Eddie Reed, all he talked about today in school was how he was going to his aunt's house this weekend and pick mulberries. How he and his sister will pick and eat them and his mom and aunt would bake mulberry pies. Man, he made me hungry for mulberries all day. Let's go pick some."

"We'll have to find a tree first," I said.

"There must be one around here somewhere," he said.

We veered off our beaten path to pound the pavement next to the school for a mulberry tree.

After several minutes, we came up empty. Then I remembered April telling me her grandma had a tree. April was my best girl. She wasn't a typical Bond girl, a little pudgy in the middle but had headlights. The best kisser in school, she was fond of pressing her stubby fingers underneath the elastic below my belly button. I returned the favor. Her grandma lived only a block away.

"Adam!"

"What?"

"Let's go to April's grandma's house?"

"Why? So you can play suck face with her."

"No! Her Grandma has a mulberry tree. She told me."

"Really?" he asked.

"Yep."

"Point the way."

"Her Grandma's house is on the next street over, but we can't stay long," I said.

As we walked toward the house, I joked, "Man it would be nice if April was there."

"Joseph, you're such a horny toad!"

"I know. Don't tell anyone," I admitted with a smile.

We arrived to find no one at home, several knocks proved it; we journeyed around back to the tree. A big sucker it was! We turned to each other, a devilish smile, and attacked it. A third of the way up, we parked, and dug in. We ate until our faces were covered in purple juice. Throwing the green berries at each other, we laughed and talked about everything; from my teacher Mrs. Cramer's fish tank, to wanting a ride in his teacher, Mrs. Parker's Mustang.

"Mrs. Cramer is such a witch."

"Why you say that?"

"She thinks she's doing me a favor by letting me clean her fish tank," I complained.

"I thought you didn't have to do any class work when you're cleaning it?" he mumbled with a mouth full of berries.

"I don't, but I'm tired of sucking up that fish shit through the hose to get the water out the tank," I grumbled.

"Joseph, I knew some day you'd make a good shit eater," he joked.

"Shut up you turd!" That's why I spit that fish shit on her shoes one day. She was standing near the bucket. I was like, take this! Splat! Fish shit all over her new shoe. She hopped around like she was being bit by red ants. Oh, I'm so sorry Mrs. Cramer, I said. The class fell apart laughing."

Adam and I laughed for a minute straight, spraying purple slime everywhere. We continued to chat until a faint sound broke through our chatter,

"Adam! Joseph!"

Silence

We paused, looked at each other. The voice came closer.

"Adam! Joseph!"

"Oh Man! That's my mom," Adam announced.

We only meant to stay a little while. It was evident, our time had run out. The fat was in the fire. We hit the ground running.

"Adam! Joseph!"

"Over here. Here we are," we answered.

As we approached, anguish left her face...a scowl replaced it. A belt was at her side. We didn't stand a chance. She whipped us all the way home with a scolding between the lashes.

"Where have you been?" Lash! Lash! "You both should've been home an hour ago." Lash! Lash! "Y'all had Mrs. Graham and I worried to death." Lash! Lash! "This better not happen again." Lash! Lash! Lash! Lash!

Mama picked up where Mrs. Evans left off. It was a fact of life. If an adult caught you doing something wrong and they knew your family, they'd beat you on the spot. Then took you home, explained what you did, and your parents gave you another whippin. Mama explained it this way: "It's embarrassing that you did something wrong. It's worst that a friend of the family had to correct you. And its triple embarrassing they brought you home to tell me what you did."

Although I got it twice for our escapade it was the best time ever! I couldn't wait to do it again. My first cut down the path to adventure went deep, exhilarating. Exploring without permission intrigued me to no end.

We were both grounded for a week. We could only see each other at school. When we got to my house from school Adam's older brother or sister was there waiting for him to take he and his little sister home.

Our friendship was never the same after our adventure. Whenever I went to visit him I wasn't allowed inside. He was only allowed to talk a few minutes though the screened door, agonizing! I guess his mom blamed me for the escapade but it was her son's idea. I just knew where a tree was. But I wouldn't rat him out.

A few months later, he and his family moved across town. I walked down one Saturday to find an empty house. They moved during the night. He said nothing about it at school on Friday. I never got a chance to say good-bye. I guess they didn't want any of us dust buckets following them, can't blame them for that. Just hurt, real bad.

Without Adam it felt as if someone was sitting on my chest squeezing the life out of me. My first male friend, my twin was gone for good. But that's how it was in the hood. Important people in your life came and went without warning.

CHAPTER 12

BLOOD BROTHERS

Three months after Adam's exit, Life had mercy. As we finished the pledge to the flag and the morning-prayer, Mrs. Cramer announced,

"We have a new student, Robert Mason. Will you stand Robert?"

He was seated behind me, two rows to my right. As I turned to look back, my smile grew wider than the clowns' in the circus. Robert Mason was an odd ball! If the desk top wasn't affixed, I would have leaped out of my seat.

He had the whole package too; light skin, freckles, dark brown hair in a bulky body. I thought I'd never meet another odd ball. Now I had one in class with me all day every day...too good to be true. Mrs. Cramer continued, "Class say hello to Robert?"

"Hello Robert!" The class chanted.

"Hello!" He echoed and waved.

I wanted to know this kid. A thousand questions I had. Where did he come from? Were there other odd balls at his old school? Did he have brothers and sisters? Were they odd balls too? Where did he live? I was beside myself with glee but I didn't want to scare him away. Getting to know him meant a lot to me. I needed to move slowly

It took two weeks to get the skinny on Robert. We exchanged phone numbers, talked regularly. Thank God my phone was on! He moved here from Pittsburgh, Pennsylvania. He told me all about the snow, deer, and bears in that neck of the woods. He had two older Brothers. They live with their mom on 12th Avenue, four blocks from me behind the Heart Beat Theater. We both liked many of the same things; Football, basketball, marvel comics, peach cobbler, and Gayle Page; one of the hottest girls at school.

Robert had an unfair advantage with Gayle. They lived on the same street! He got to walk her home from school every day. That was hard to compete against. I could have used my Bond skills to win her over but I had enough action. Besides, I wasn't going to let some girl come between me and another odd ball. His friendship was too important to me. Unfortunately, we lived four blocks apart, not much hang time together after school...only an occasional visit by me on Saturday. Bell-Tel built our bond. I still longed for a friend to handout with though.

Saturday morning; wiping sleep from my eyes, I waddled to the toilet. Pulling back the sheet hanging across the doorway, I opened the flood gate. Between the rapids crashing below and my sleep induced coma, I heard Mama talking to Jeanie in the bedroom.

"He was talking in his sleep last night. I think it's starting," Mama said

"Are you going to tell him?" Jeanie inquired.

"Not yet."

"When? He deserves to know."

"In time I will but not now. I want you to promise me that if anything happens to me you'll look after him.

"Mama, don't talk like that."

"Promise me Jeanie."

"Okay, I promise."

"Good. Thank you."

Who and what were they talking about? Who deserves to know what? I tried to put my Double-O skills to work but the fog from my sleep hadn't lifted. I left it alone, grown folks business.

Still struggling to welcome morning, I stumbled into Casey and Lavelle's room to get dressed. Lavelle stood to tuck in his shirt.

"Joseph"

"What?" I growled.

"Were you dreaming about Army War Games again?" he chuckled.

"No. Why would you ask that?" I questioned thinking he might have intel about Mama and Jeanie's conversation.

"Well, your private is still standing at attention." He smirked. "Or should I say your thing is still at attention," he chuckled more.

"Shut up you goof! I said pulling my shorts and shirt out the drawer. "Why are you all spruced up?"

"I'm going to Rising Tide at noon to give a radio interview at WRBZ. When I get back, Lacy and I are going to the movies."

"Ah, and who's private will be standing at attention then? I joked. We laughed.

Still laughing, he ordered, "Get out of here you little perv. I have some phone calls to make before I go."

I finished tying my sneakers and went into the living room to start my chores; cleared the sofa of my bedding, folded it and put it away, swept the living room, and took out the trash. With the Sun's smile begging me to come outside, I grabbed my basketball from behind the storm door in the living room and tracked outside. Looking up to take my first shot...

"For crying out loud, they took it again!" I yelled.

Someone had stolen my basketball hoop. I was fit to be tied. I'd have to wait until Christmas to get another one. The hoop was one of the few things I asked for and got for the holiday. I voiced my disgust walking back inside.

"They stole my hoop again!" I ranted as I smacked my basketball in disgust.

"Again, how many times is that?" Lavelle questioned sitting on the sofa watching TV.

"That's the third hoop they've stolen it," I growled. Mama, can I go to McKenzie to shoot some hoops?"

McKenzie School was two blocks away. It had an outside basketball court.

"Are all your chores done?" she shouted from the bedroom where she and Jeanie were folding the wash.

"Yes," I shouted back.

"You took out the trash?"

"Yes"

"Okay, make sure you're home by dinner."

"I will."

"Come here before you go."

I pulled the sheet back and entered.

"Yes Mama."

Like so many times before, she took my hand, put her other hand on my forehead, and prayed. Jeanie stilled herself and bowed her head.

Taking my usual route, I tucked my ball under my arm, and hopped on the dirt path near my backdoor. Within minutes I was at the red light between Ray's Groceries and Betty's Corner Store. The aroma of Don's BBQ ribs sailed on a faint breeze from the west. Hickory smoke meat, his award winning sauce turned my head to the left. Nose skyward to catch a whiff, my mouth watered for a bite size morsel. The light changed, saving me from drowning in my taste buds' demand. Crossing Franklin, I hit the dirt path behind Betty's, a straight shot to McKenzie School. This path ran along the creek. The creek weaved its way behind the Franklin Court Apartments. The McKenzie Bridge connected the apartments with the school's enormous Recess Fields.

Along the trail I spotted three kids from my gym class leaving the fields. One held a football. *I liked football too*, I thought. We waved to each other as they crossed the bridge. I wanted to meet them but they kept walking. I continued down the path, across the fields to the basketball court. The three kids watched me for awhile from the back of the apartments. I shot baskets until dinner time. On my way home I took the McKenzie Bridge to the apartments. A brief search for the kids proved fruitless. I dribbled my way up to Franklin Street.

All I could do was shake my head in pity and shame when I arrived. There, in the middle of the street going through his drunken antics, was Uncle Mack. Running back and forth, cussing, screaming at the motorists, and singing for the crowed. The small gathering was hyped and cheered him on. I put my head down and turned away so he wouldn't see me. He was down near Betty's Corner Store. I crossed the street in front of the apartment and hit the rocky road for home. I loved

Uncle Mack but I was tired and hungry. I wanted to eat first before I did my retrieving duties. Of course I went and got him after dinner.

Monday in gym, I approached two of the three kids I saw crossing the bridge on Saturday.

"Hey, you're the guys I saw on the bridge Saturday. I'm Joseph."

"Hi, I'm Booker and this is Benjamin. Everyone calls him Benny Lee," the smaller one said.

"What's up," I nodded to Benny Lee.

"What's up," he nodded back.

"Aren't you Lavelle Graham's brother? Benny Lee asked.

"Yes, I am. Do you know Lavelle?" I questioned.

"Who don't know your brother? He's only the best football and basketball player in the county," Booker raved.

"We saw him run for 132 yards in the game Friday," added Benny Lee.

"You were at the football game? So was I! Where were you guys sitting? I asked

We flapped our gums so much we barely made it out for roll call. Instant friends we were. We hooked up at lunch time, sat at the same table. My friends Robert and Matt joined us. Matt was a friend I met last year. His brother was good friends with my sister. He lived uptown. No odd ball but he and Robert had football bodies. They came in handy if either was on your pick up football team. After school Bennie Lee, Booker, and I walked home together. They knew everything about me but I knew nothing about them.

"Why are you always by yourself?" Bennie Lee asked.

I hadn't thought about it but since Adam moved I'd been riding solo.

"Most of my friends in the Quarters have to stay inside until their parents come home from work. They're not allowed to come up to Franklin Street. So I do what I do by myself," I explained.

"That's not a smart thing to do in this neighborhood," Booker warned.

"I know. It's cool. I'm not scared," I said shrugging my shoulders.

They looked at each other with raised brows. Taking the McKenzie

Bridge to Franklin Court, we stopped by the apartment of the third kid I saw on the bridge. He wasn't at school. Benny Lee wanted me to meet him. He also wanted to see if he was ok. Benny knocked on his door. The kid answered.

"What happened to you today?" Bennie Lee asked

"I was sick, stomach ache. Grandma gave me some meds that made me crap all day. I never knew using the toilet could make your stomach feel better," he laughed wildly.

Okay. My first thought was, *this kid's elevator doesn't go all the way to the top.*

"Oh, this is Joseph. Joseph… Otis," Bennie Lee introduced.

"What's up," I nodded.

"What's up? I know you. You live in the Quarters. We have gym together," he recalled.

"Yes we do. You think you'll be back in school tomorrow? We're starting football in gym," I asked.

"Yeah, I should be back tomorrow," he answered.

"Cool! See you then," I said.

After saying good-bye to the others, I crossed Franklin Street for only the second time without the cross-walk between Betty's Corner Store and Ray's Groceries. I liked it, daring. I crossed this time in front of the "New Do for You" beauty shop where Jeanie worked. Over the next month, Bennie Lee and I became best friends. We had much in common; pinball, youngest in our families, born in the same month, and Marvel over DC Comics. Both enjoyed sports; his favorite, football. Mine was basketball. But the main attraction was we both were men for adventure! If you said, "Let's do…" before you could finish the sentence one of us was doing it. We roamed around town searching for adventure. We were as close as brothers. He was the brother close in age I didn't have. A brother I could talk to, confide in. The person I could tell all my secrets to. I became the brother he didn't have. He had two older sisters. I was the brother he could talk guy stuff with and do guy things with.

Benny Lee wasn't an odd ball. We looked nothing alike. He had brown skin, no freckles, and black kinky hair. In fact, I looked nothing like any of my new friends in Franklin Court. We accepted each other for who we were, not how we looked. Man, did I need that!

On one visit to Benny's, he introduced me to Elijah, another kid in our grade from Franklin Court. He lived in the end apartment next door to Otis. Elijah had a body like Robert and Matt. He weighed a good twenty pounds more than the rest of the kids in the apartment. He was a quiet kid. Not a lot of rough around his edges. He struck me as a little different from the others. Elijah brought the total to four new friends I had in Franklin Court.

Benny and I were always together on weekends and holidays from school. No one could say anything bad about the other in our presence. We were best friends in every sense of the word. We shared everything 50/50, Benny insisted. We often broke away from the group to go on our own hunts.

One of our earliest hunts was the bottle hunt; penniless most of the time, our adventures centered on getting money to buy food. One bottle earned one cent at Ray's or Betty's. On our first bottle hunt I spotted a 24 count bottle container under a carport. Benny snuck up to the house and took it. On a good day we filled the container to overflowing. When we were done, we stashed it in the bush behind Betty's near the creek.

Our most challenging bottle hunt came on the bank of the Reservoir Canal. It was always wicked down there; snakes, Water Moccasins, river rats loomed near. No fear though. If there were discarded bottles there, they were ours! One day our courage got the best of us.

Standing at the Franklin Street overpass, two bottles winked at us from below. Securing our container we looked for an entry point to the embankment. Twelve yards down we descended to the edge of the canal. Walking toward our treasure, we spotted what appeared to be a body lying between us and the bottles. A hat and a large green coat camouflaged the figure. Face turned away, no life or sex could be determined.

"Is he dead?" Benny whispered

"I don't know…Let's go get some help.

"Let's get the bottles first."

"But what if he's dead?"

'Well, if he is, he won't mind us having those bottles, will he?"

"Yeah, I guess you're right."

Benny Lee looked around.

"What are you looking for? I asked

"This! He picked up a long, thin tree branch, and moved closer to the body. Standing shoulder to shoulder, he jabbed the body with the stick. No response. He pokes him again…nothing.

"He's dead. Let's go get help."

Benny Lee turns to me, smirked and said,

"Well, if he's dead go get the bottles!"

Silence!

Benny Lee turned back to the body. We leaned in until our ears touched. We shared the same breath as he jabbed the lifeless body for a third time.

"Hey, what the hell's going on?"

What the …! He's alive! We jetted. Benny Lee slightly ahead lost footing. A snake saw the mishap. Their eyes met. Feet still pumping, a handful of shirt pulled him upright.

"Get up! Come on!" I implored.

Our no named sneakers dug us to safety. Camouflaged coat didn't pursue. The serpent slithered past, dinner denied. Hands resting on our knees, vitals stabilized, we glance up at each other and smiled.

"He's dead. Let's get help." Benny joked.

"Dead my ass! When he popped up like Frankenstein, I was in the wind!"

"Me too! Then I fell, looked over, and a damn snake was staring me in the face."

"That was crazy. Let's get the crate."

We moseyed back toward our container of bottles.

"You didn't know it was a garter snake did you," I said laughing

"Hell no," he squeaked.

"Man, that bum can keep those bottles."

"You damn right! He scared the shit out of me."

"What did you expect? You were jabbing the man in his back with a damn stick!"

Arriving at our container we took inventory…3 bottles short of full. We lugged the container to Ray's for the exchange. Twenty-one cents was the payout; ten cents each and a divided piece of bubble gum…50/50.

Another favorite hunt was the hunt for money! Open season declared on all vending machines, in stores and on the streets. I took one side of Franklin Street. Benny took the other. We checked the change return slot on all; pay phones, candy, soda, gum, cigarette, and Pinball machines. If there was nothing in the coin return slot, we'd press the coin return button. Still nothing, we struck the machine near the coin entrance and pressed the return button again. Sometimes up to 50 cents fell into the return slot. We often got free sodas, candy and gum when we struck the machine in the right spot. We also hunted money at the Laundry Mat and the State Farmer's Market.

At the Laundry Mat it was all about the coins that had rolled beneath and behind the machines. We brought along sticks for this hunt. Using the stick we'd rake the coins to us. We also took bubble gum, chewed it until soft, and placed it on the end of the stick. This allows us to pick up the coins that had rolled behind the machines.

For the Farmer's Market money hunt we each took a fork from home. There were food venders on the platform at the market. The costumers dropped coins all the time. Some fell through the cracks in the boards. The platform sat 4 feet from the ground. This allowed the drivers to back their trucks into the dock to load/unload their cargo. It also sat high enough for us to crawl underneath to reach the area of the food booths. We'd start in the shadow of the food booth. Some coins fell directly though the cracks. Other coins hit the platform and rolled. Armed with fork in hand, we moved the soil to uncover the lost treasure. It was dark but not pitched black. Some days we spent hours in the soil. We had to be careful not to get bit by the rats that lived under the platform. They dined on the food swept through the cracks from above. We saw 2 or 3 on the regular. Big, shiny suckers, teeth exposed; they didn't scare easy! Armed with our metal fork we were prepared to do whatever necessary to keep from getting bit! We were determined to get our meal money!

During one money hunt at the market we found enough money to buy milk shakes. As always, Benny Lee and I divided our find 50/50. We took our milk shakes to the steps leading to the platform. There we sat enjoying the payoff from the hunt.

"Benny, we're two poor scavengers that love to hunt money for food." I joked.

"Scavenger, what's that?" he asked.

"A scavenger is a poor person who looks for lost objects."

Benny Lee turned to me, lowered head, horizontal eyes, and said, "Joseph, you're not poor!"

"Not poor! What do you mean, not poor?"

"You live in a house. Your family has a car and you have a telephone. That's not poor."

"Benny, I live on rocks! There's dust everywhere! I have dust with every meal. I breathe dust when I sleep. Our phone is off more than it is on. And the car – hasn't run in 4 months," I whined.

"But at least you have them! You can always get them fixed or turned back on. Plus you have a family that loves you. Those are things…"

He paused, a deep swallow, voice cracked, he continued, "Those are a lot of things we all wished we had."

I had no come back. In that moment it became apparent there were different levels to being poor. I was poor but Benny was po! So needy he couldn't afford the last two letters in the word poor. By his estimate, I was a step or two above po. There seemed to be more he wanted to share but stopped. He was hiding something.

"You think I have it Good?" I asked. "You have no idea. Man I wish I could come live with you on the weekends. My dad is such an ass when he drinks. He comes home drunk most Friday and Saturday nights. He cusses and fusses half the night; such a pain."

"So is that where you learned to do all that crazy cussing?" Benny mused.

"Come on man, I'm serious."

"I would never have thought your dad was like that. He seems to be a nice man."

"He is most of the time, except on weekends when he turns into Mr. Hyde! He argues, cusses, and complains until he falls asleep. It's not good man! Sometimes I want to run away ... let's run away Benny?

"Where would we go?" he asked taking a sip from his milk shake.

"We'll go to New York City. My Uncle Tony lives there. We can stay with him," I said with glee.

He raised his head, turned to me, and said,

"And how in the heck are we going to get to New York City?"

I starred in the distance daydreaming. I took a sip of my milk shake and answered,

"I don't know. Maybe hop a train like in the movies."

He chuckled to himself, shook his head slightly and said, "Okay Box Car Willie, we have no money, how will we eat along the way?"

He sipped from his shake and raised his brow.

Still looking afar, imagining the bright lights in New York City, I was brought back to reality by his question.

"I don't know...I guess running away isn't such a good idea. Then maybe I can stay with you on the weekends?" I asked as I turned to him excited.

His tone changed as he looked down and stirred his drink with the straw.

"Coming to live with me is an even worse idea. My two sisters are pure evil! If they could ride a broom they would! Plus they don't like light skin boys. You'll also have to deal with my mom. She's the queen of the broom riders. A bunch of evil witches they are," he answered.

"Well, come stay with me on the weekends. That way we'll have each other to talk to, watch TV with. We can help each other drown out the noise in our lives," I suggested.

"If I came to stay with you on the weekends, where would I sleep? You're always complaining about sleeping on the sofa. That sofa ain't big enough for the both of us. At least at my house I have my own sofa to sleep on, " he replied.

Quiet.

We both took sips from our drinks.

"I guess you're right. I'm just irritated by all the bullshit in my life. It's not fair. What did I do to deserve this? I must be a bad person. It's God's way of getting back at me. He's probably pissed because of my anger, or the girls, or my disobedience to my father?" I confessed.

"Man...God has nothing to do with it! You're the best friend I ever had... someone I can count on. You always come through for me. You're nothing like the other people in my life. You complain about your differences. So what? Yeah, you're light skin with freckles. Big deal! There ain't shit you can do about that now! You use big words that the guys and I don't understand. Who gives a shit?! And... you're the biggest perv I know with the girls," he smirked and playfully shoved my shoulder.

I looked at him and smiled. His voice grew stronger as he continued, "But those are the things I like about you, you're different! Everyone around here is liars and cheats. You can't trust any of them. I never have to worry about that with you. We all pretend. I pretend to be good when I'm really not. You pretend to be bad when you're really not. We hide who we are. We don't want people to know who we really are," he concluded.

Once again, I had no comeback. I was speechless. Benny Lee just read my mail. He told me my Christmas and birthday gifts without opening the packages. That's why I loved him. At times, he knew me better than I knew myself. But I couldn't let him get away with calling himself a bad person.

"You're not a bad person. You're my best friend too! You're the bravest kid I know and you always look out for me. I know you stick up for me with the guys when I'm not around. I know they bust on the way I look, my big words, and how I talk. But you don't let them get away with it. A bad person wouldn't do that."

"How'd you know about that?" He asked in awe.

"I didn't. You just told me," I said with a smirk.

"What! You really didn't know?"

"No, I really didn't. But it's what I'd do if anyone tried to bust on you. I knew you'd do the same for me. That's what good friends do. They look out for each other."

I didn't want to use my Bond skills on my best friend to get intel. But he needed to know he wasn't a bad person. Bennie Lee was a realist. I was an idealist. He had accepted our social and economic situation. I hadn't. He knew the deck was stacked against us, so did I. But I continued to hope, dream of a better day, no longer harassed, free from the rocks.

"Yeah, I guess you're right," he said.

We sat quietly for a moment, taking sips of our creamy delights.

"Benny!" I whispered.

"What – now?" He moaned.

"Let's become Blood Brothers.

"What's that?"

"It's when you cut a body part and mix together the blood of each person."

"I won't get freckles or anything, will I?" he joked.

"No you dick, you won't get freckles. But you might become a perv," I teased.

We laughed as we walked down the steps to search the area for something sharp to make the cut.

Benny Lee found a sharp piece of glass.

"Will this do?" He asked as he gave it to me.

"Yes! It's perfect," I said as I ran my finger along the edge.

The middle finger, left hand, won the nomination. Edge pressed to flesh, a quick jerk, and blood dripped. The ceremonial edge passed to Benny. When his cut was complete we pressed the fingers together combining our plasma. Blood trickled down between our fingers into our palms. We locked our remaining fingers, bringing our palms together. We raised our intertwined, left hands to the sky.

"Okay, blood brothers on three." I suggested.

He nodded. We counted off; "One, two, three... " Blood Brothers!" we shouted.

I'd never felt more accepted by any friend than in that moment. There I stood, blood streaming down my arm declaring blood brothers with a friend that was closer than a brother. A kid who didn't have much but shared whatever he had 50/50 with me. He was a friend who defended my honor no matter what. That was more than friendship, it was love. He had no idea how much that moment meant to me, or maybe he did. He was much smarter than kids gave him credit for. We did the blood brother ritual but in my heart, Benny Lee and I had been brothers since the first day we met.

CHAPTER 13

THERE'S POWER IN THE NAME

Bright lights fascinated me; Christmas, my favorite time of year. Blinking, twinkling stars and silver bells, my heart swelled. Carols played as I sat in the shadow of our Christmas tree. Reflections danced on my skin like no one's watching, lifted me to stardom; I'm on stage, or in a Bond Movie, or making the game winning shot. Suddenly I'm inside their interworking. I shined, sparkled, made people happy. No more bad names, no more weird looks. Just happy faces enjoying my glow.

Carnival Lights did the same thing. Every year the Carnival came to the Recess Fields at McKenzie School. I could see the Ferris wheel from my back door. When I wasn't participating in the Carnival festivities, I admired the bright, flashing lights. I'd walk back to the entrance to watch from afar. I asked myself, how many cities had they been to spreading their joy? You rarely see anyone sad at a carnival! Kids run, laugh, eat, and have a good time. I wished I could be a bright, flashing light; to bring joy and happiness to people. I wanted kids to run around, smile, laugh, and play in my glow. But that seemed impossible in Reservoir City. Instead of shining like a star, I was made to feel like I didn't belong. I was pushed to the corner of the room to live my life as a fictional character to drown out my hurt, sorrow.

For years, I had a recurring dream that I could fly! I had no cape, no wings, or a rocket belt. I didn't save or rescue anyone nor act like a superhero. I was just this regular guy with the ability to go airborne at will. My friends greeted me as usual when I flew up to roof tops to meet them or landed on the playground to join them in a game of football. Although they did tell me I couldn't fly during the games. They weren't in awe or afraid. I soared over rivers, canyons, mountains. The best was gliding over the city at night. A spectacular light show; street lights, car lights, traffic lights, shop lights, neon everywhere. A rainbow of fireworks exploding in my eyes provoked an effervescent smile.

I told Mama about the dream. I asked her, what did it mean? She didn't say much the first couple times I asked her. By the third time, she called me to her and said, "Someday you'll be very successful. People will look up to you. Don't let those people down, especially the people who put their trust in you."

She paused, grabbed my hand, and continued, "You have something special."

"What do I have?"

"It'll become clear to you later. Just know you are meant to do great things. Promise me you'll finish high school and go to college," she pleaded.

"I promise. I promise I'll finish high school and go to college," I assured.

My promise was important to her. She made me swear it two or three more times over the years. With empty pockets, it seemed impossible but I needed to keep her hopes alive. This was her dream for me. So I obliged whenever asked.

What did she mean, "I have something special?" Was it some super power? Was that why I could fly in my dream? I had more questions than answers. I needed help to process Mama's interpretation of the dream. I tried to apply my Bond skills but I didn't have enough intel to process. I needed to know, what would be made clear to me later? Bond was many things but a mind reader he wasn't. Whatever it is, it had something to do with me finishing my education.

I came home from school to find a huge tent in the field across from my house. I could see the inside from my front door. The weeds and bush were cleared away for the business of the tent. I thought, *how great, the circus had come to my neighborhood! But where were the animals?* I rushed into the house,

"Mama, Mama!" I yelled.

"Yes Joseph," she answered surprised.

"Can I go to the circus?"

"What circus?"

"The circus in the big tent outside"

"There's no circus."

"What? No circus…. Then what's the big tent doing out there?"

"There's going to be a Tent Meeting tonight."

"A Tent Meeting – what's that?"

"A Tent Meeting is similar to having church with a few exceptions. The speaker is called a prophet. He lays hands on the people to pray for their healing and deliverance. He may also give a prophecy," she explained.

"What's a prophecy?"

"A prophecy is when you look into the spirit world and make a prediction about a person's future. A strong prophet can tell you many things about your past as well as your future."

"Was that a prophecy, when you told me I would be successful someday? That people will look up to me? Was that a prophecy when you told me I will do great things?"

Mama smiled, pulled me to her, and gave me a kiss on the forehead… but didn't answer.

I felt a strong need to see this prophet. He must be a big, powerful man, like a super hero or something. He must have some great power to be able to heal people and look into their future. My curiosity meter reached its apex. I begged Mama to let me go.

"Please, can I go to the Tent Meeting?"

"Why are you so excited? You're more excited about going to this Tent Meeting than going to church on Sunday."

"I need to see how he does it. I've never seen anyone do those things before."

Mama finally agreed but only for an hour. It was a Thursday night. I had school the next day. I dressed in my best school clothes with my Sunday shoes. Mama said the meeting started at 7:00. She gave me a quarter to put in the offering.

"Put it in the basket! Don't cheat God," she ordered.

"I'll put it in," I answered opening the front door.

I heard music coming from the huge structure. I closed the door and walked toward it. Each note gave the tent a pulse. It exhaled on each beat. Stepping through the arched opening, a world of mystery revealed. A radiant glow, five flood lights equaled the sun. Red, yellow, and blue speckled the platform stage. I froze to take it all in. A small ensemble to the right provided the pulse. Motor oil, gasoline fumes, freshly cut grass circled on the wind from the large fans at each end of the stage. A man in all black stood in the back behind a huge box with a gazillion knobs. He continuously played with each, turning his ear toward the band.

It was tight up in there, only a few open seats. I spotted one near the back along the outside aisle to my left. The crowd sang along with the band. I knew the song, "Just a Closer Walk with Thee." I joined in. The Prophet rose from his seat to lead the final song before he preached. He wasn't a big man at all. He did have on a cool suit with a cape. That was hot! Did his powers come from the cape? Hmm...The title of his sermon; "There's power in the name."

When he finished his sermon they passed the basket for an offering. No, I didn't cheat God. I put the quarter in the basket. Then he asked all those who needed prayer for healing to come up to the front. A line formed that stretched to the outside of the tent. When they left their seat I moved toward the front for a better look. When the people approached the prophet, they whispered to him what their needs were. Two males and a female stood next to the Prophet to assist. As he listened to the needs of the first person, one of the male assistants moved behind the man. The prophet placed his right hand on the forehead of the man and prayed.

Ah heck, Mama does that to me all the time, I thought to myself.

At the end of the prayer the prophet stomped his foot on the wooden planks and simultaneously shouted in a loud roar, "In the name of Yeshua!"

Plop! The man fell back into the arms of the male assistant standing behind him. The assistant laid him down on the planks. He was out like the bedroom light. What happened? How did he do that? Did he punch the man? A woman was next in line. I told myself to watch closer this time. He placed his hand on her forehead. Once again he prayed, stomped his foot and shouted simultaneously,

"In the name of Yeshua,"

Flop! Out she went. As the second male assistant laid her down the female assistant covered her with a small blanket from the waist down. It was crazy! How was he doing it? People dropped like flies being sprayed with Raid.

Next, a woman brought her 15 year old daughter forward. I heard her whisper to the prophet something about bad spirits. The Prophet told the people near him to move back. He told his assistants to get behind him. He placed his hand on the forehand of the girl and spoke into her ear,

"Come out! You have no place in her. She's a child of the righteous one. Come out!" He commanded.

She let out a deafening shrill.

"Come out! Come out in the name of Yeshua!" The Prophet shouted over her.

When he stomped his foot the girl crumbled to her knees. Screaming she began to shake her head. The Prophet kneeled beside her, puts his hand back on her forehead,

"Come out! Come out in the name of Yeshua," he commanded once more.

The girl went limp, melted like butter to the planks. Her screaming stopped. The Prophet turned her head to the side. Thick, white, foamy goo oozed out.

The crowd sighed, "Oooh!"

What the...? Oh my.... That was the wildest yet! I looked at the man's watch seated next to me. I had to go. It was 8:15. I should've been home 15 minutes ago. I ran home to tell Mama what I saw. I opened the front door.

"Mama, Mama!" I called.

"What! Are you alright?" she asked.

"Mama, people were falling out! They passed out like they were at a funeral. They were foaming at the mouth!" I rambled.

"Slow down! Slow down Joseph so I can understand you," she insisted.

My mouth was moving faster than my thoughts. I told her about the girl. How there was thick gooey stuff flowing from her mouth as the Prophet shouted, "Come out! Come out!" Mama's face went from interested to concern. She grabbed me by the arm.

"Did you touch her?" She asked with a firm grip.

"No!" I answered.

"Joseph, did you touch her?!" She repeated.

"No Mama! I didn't touch her," I assured.

She pulled me to her and gave me a hug.

"Why did you ask if I touched her?" I questioned.

"Well, it's late and time for bed. You have school in the morning," she said.

I changed and got in bed. Well, on the sofa. My Double-O senses were fired up! Why didn't she answer my question? I played back everything I saw and heard in the tent. The Prophet was the only person to touch the girl. What or who was he talking to when he said, "Come out?" I didn't stay long enough to find out.

I told Benny Lee and the gang at lunch about the tent meeting. I told them everything; the prophet's cape, people screaming, shouting, falling out; foaming at the mouth. Their eyes stretched to the size of half dollar, mouths fell open; bodies went stiff as a board.

"You got to come with me tonight!" I urged Benny Lee. "It's the craziest thing ever!"

He just stared at me with squinted eyes.

Silence!

"Are you coming with me or not?" I asked.

Shaking his head he said, "Nah man, you got that! That's the craziest shit I've ever heard! I want no parts of it. It sounds like Voodoo to me!

"Nah man, no way; you got that man." The rest of the table replied.

It was Friday night. I wanted to go back to the tent meeting. I needed to find out where the Prophet got his powers. Men who were drunks yesterday were sober today. They carried bibles. They were telling everyone how much God loved them. My Dad and Uncle Mack could use a touch from the Prophet. Maybe I could learn how he does it and use the powers on them.

"Mama, can I go to the meeting?"

Mama squinted at my request. Her lips tighten. She didn't want me to go alone. She checked with my sibling, all had plans for the night. And of course, Daddy would be at Jake's Bar. She didn't want me to go by myself after I told her about the girl last night.

"I think I'll go with you tonight. I haven't been to a tent meeting in several years."

"Mama, you won't believe the things this guy can do."

"Well, let's get dressed. We don't want to miss the singing."

We arrived to find the tent near capacity. The scent of Jasmine and magnolia sailed on a breeze floating through the aisles, replaced the funk of cut grass and motor oil. Lights flashed, tambourines jingled, hands clapped to the beat; Mama was not impressed. She had seen this "Dog and Pony Show" before. We spotted two open seats four rows from the back on the left side, close to where I sat the night before. The same early routine: music, sermon, offering. Money collected, baskets placed on the stage, the Prophet made an announcement.

"Because of the long line last night, I ask those who only need prayer for blessings to stand at your seat".

About 20 people stood up. The Prophet continued.

"When I point to you I want you to raise your hands."

He stood in front of the podium. He pointed his index and middle fingers at the first person to his right with their hands raised. When he prayed his fingers shook like an earth quake. He stomped and shouted, "In the name of Yeshua!" And down goes Frazier! Right back into his seat like a bolt of lightning struck him! The same was true with the next person, and the next. I turned to Mama, who was seated to my right. She raised her index finger to her chest. She spoke loudly without saying a word.

His second announcement was to have all those who needed a special healing to come up front. A lady with two small kids came up to the Prophet. She told the Prophet she didn't need a special healing. She wants him to touch and pray a special prayer for her children; for their protection, to have a good life, a good future. As she gave the microphone back to the Prophet, I slid to the back of my seat. Man, what a light bulb moment! The epiphany blew me away.

It all became clear. That's what Mama had done all those years. She prayed for my protection and for me to have a good life, a good future. I lay my head on Mama's shoulder. As I sat there it occurred to me there was something about the name Yeshua. Every time he said it something happened. Hey, that was the title of the sermon last night, "There's power in the name". Is that where he gets his power, Yeshua?

Mama and I walked home in silence after the meeting. When we reached the front door, I asked, "Who is Yeshua?"

As we entered Mama pointed to the picture on the wall.

"That's Yeshua."

"The blond haired, blue eyed, Jesus! Is that where he gets his powers?

"Yes!"

She tossed my brain into the blender, turned it on high, and walked away. I was not ready. I needed time to rethink my position on Jesus, Yeshua or whatever his name. I wanted his powers. I could use them to help people. Well, let's be honest, to help my dad and Uncle Mack. What if he has some powers for me? How would I get them? Is that what Mama meant by, "It will be made clear to me later?" Mama knew something but wasn't saying.

CHAPTER 14

CROSSING BRIDGES TOO SOON

Being the telephone operator in my home, I knew everyone's business. Jeanie had a new boyfriend.

"Who is this guy Arthur?" I asked her. "He sounds like a school Teacher, real proper."

"He's just some guy," she answered.

"So where did you meet him?"

"I meet him at church; stop being nosey."

"At church," I said. "So you went to the cross to find this one huh?"

She laughed and blushed at the same time. We laughed together. I called out to Mama.

"Hey Mama, I think he's the one!"

"Shut up boy! You're so crazy." Jeanie chuckled.

My fee for my phone services were any spare change or the promise of spare coins later. There were times when my siblings demanded their messages without making any payment arrangement. I gave them up but they were sorry later.

The next day they inquired about their calls.

"Did I have any phone calls?" They asked.

"Yes, you did," I answered.

"Well, who was it?" They asked in anticipation.

"I don't know. I didn't ask," I told them.

"Why didn't you ask? The call could've been important!" They argued.

"Well, you didn't pay for your last messages. So I assumed your messages weren't important to you anymore," I informed them.

They got my message! No pay or promise of pay equaled no messages. I'm no dummy. I knew the only reason I got away with it was my age. There were advantages to being the youngest in the family! My second reward was listening in on my brother's conversations when they returned calls to their girlfriend.

I'd snake under the sheet into the bedroom, lie on the floor out of sight at the foot of the bed, and listened. Sometimes I walked into the room pretending to look for a lost item. I'd start at the dresser moving objects around; used a few choice words under my breath, to express my disgust. Sink to the floor I'd check under the beds. Then creep over to the tiny closet and rummage through the mess. Ten minutes or more of romance lessons before I'm kicked out. I put my Bond skills to work deciphering the intel.

Girls and basketball took up a lot of my time when I wasn't with my friends. I was improving at both. In the library at my school there was only one book about basketball. My name was the only name on the checkout card. I checked it out once or twice every month. It had great illustrations explaining the skills and how the game was played. Ms. Gilbert, the librarian often teased me about checking out the same book.

"We do have other books in here, if you haven't noticed," she would joke.

"I know but this is my favorite," I'd answer every time.

One day I went to check out the basketball book and it wasn't on the shelf. Someone had checked it out. I morphed into a fire breathing dragon. I glided on the winds of pissedtivity to the circulation desk.

"Who has my book?" I asked Ms. Gilbert in not such a pleasant voice.

She began laughing, but I wasn't in a laughing mood. As I stood there, five cuss words popped into my head. Each one would wipe that damn grin right off her face, inch by inch.

"You're really attached to that book," she said.

She had no idea. That book was my basketball bible. I had read it so often I knew the words on each page. For the past two years, I studied the book to help me with my basketball knowledge and skills. Now someone else has it, my greatest fear. What if they lost it? What if they damaged it? What if pages were missing when it was returned? I broke into a cold sweat!

"When is it due back?" I asked.

"In 10 days," she answered.

"10 days! What am I supposed to do for ten days?" I groaned.

"Ah... read another book!" She said with a smirk.

I squinted. She was really grinding my gears. To keep from exploding, I gave her the middle finger behind the desk where she couldn't see it. I left in a huff.

It was Saturday morning and time to practice. With my ball tucked under my arm, I was off to the courts at McKenzie. I took my usual route. I crossed Franklin Street at the cross walk between Ray's Groceries and Betty's Corner Store and hopped on the path behind Betty's. In the distance I saw Sheila coming toward me. She lived in the house across from the church I attended. I waved to her sometimes. She was pretty but two grades ahead of me. As we approached each other, she stopped in front of me.

"Don't I know you? What's your name?" she asked.

"I'm Joseph. And yes, you do know me. I see you on your porch when I'm going into church," I answered.

"Yeah, that's where I know you from," she beamed.

I smiled as she scanned me from top to bottom. She continued,

"You're cute. Come give me a kiss," she ordered.

"Okay, sure!" I answered.

I didn't know what she expected me to say or do but kissing was my game, well; along with hoops. As I stepped toward her she grabbed my upper arms and pulled me into her. She put her lip lock on, ecstasy began. Without warning she slipped part of her gum into my mouth.

Before I could back away I find myself tugging at it. It wasn't her gum! The intensity grew as I tugged on her tongue. Sheila pulled back for air. I slowly opened my eyes, took a stepped back to take it all in.

"You're cute - and a good kisser too," she exhaled.

"Thank you." I said.

Panting, she made her demand.

"Now you do it to me!"

Wow! I'd never been kissed liked that before. She took me to school but I was a quick learner. I closed my eyes and leaned in for round two.

Accepting her request, I eased my taster between her lips. Gently she tugged, over and over again, shooting fire through my wand. The stiffness tried to break through the skin. My ball dropped. Ah... my basketball; freeing my hand to join the other around her waist. I pressed my heart against hers. Each tug from her kisser, the inferno grew. Hips gyrating; stomach muscle pulsated to the rhythm. The fire was too hot. I didn't want to be rescued but I couldn't control the blaze. I slowly pulled away keeping my eyes closed, trying to hold onto the last flame.

"You're my little boyfriend now," she ordained.

I was so aroused I couldn't speak, I could barely breathe. Only after clearing my throat was I able to converse.

"Sure... I... I'd love to be your little boyfriend!"

"Okay then Joseph – my little boyfriend."

"Okay then Sheila – my big girlfriend."

"Well, good-bye for now," she smiled and waved as she turned and walked away.

"Bye Sheila," I smiled waving back.

Retrieving my basketball, I strolled down the path toward McKenzie School like my shit didn't sink! No one could tell me I wasn't the man that day. To Hell with all my haters... cause not one of them could get a kiss like that from Sheila; even if they paid her a $1000 bucks. She was one of the hottest girls around. I was beginning to think my family was right, my haters were jealous. Unfortunate for me, their jealousy caused them to hate me even more.

I shot hoops for hours with a smile on my face, couldn't get serious. The five minutes of bliss over powered my senses. Back on the path heading for home, smelling Shelia, thinking I was grown; it occurred to me, I didn't get her phone number. How was I going to get in contact with her? I was too young to go calling on her. I had to play my role, out of sight, her little secret.

So I sat and waited at the back of Betty's for Shelia to come down the dirt path. Three times a week, an hour a clip, I waited. An old paint can my seat, I longed for her, my first crush. Sparks in my heart; the thought of her started my ignition. I wanted to burn again.

After three weeks my heart hung low, thoughts of giving up surfaced. On Friday, in the cool of the evening as the sun set across the fields, a silhouette appeared on the path. I wasn't sure. I had been wrong so many times before. As the likeness came closer, my heart cried, my eyes watered too. It was Sheila. She couldn't see me crouched in my hideout. I wiggled around the corner to pretend I was just getting on the path. I wiped my face, put on a Bond face, and slowly walked toward her. Twelve strides down the path I hear,

"Is that my little boyfriend?" she called.

"Yes it is!" I answered.

"Then come and give me a kiss."

"I'm on my way."

There we were once again kissing on the path between Betty's Corner Store and McKenzie School. I didn't wait for an invitation. I slip my tongue in her mouth, and waited for the fire truck. I burned again. It hurt so good! I know that sounds weird, but it did. After our second meeting I never saw Sheila again. Rumor had it she went up state to live with her aunt. That's how it was in the hood. Important people in your life came and went without warning. But she had left her mark on me. She improved my Double-O status too. I introduced every girl I could to my new skills. A few slaps across the cheeks but most approved.

My curiosity about the female anatomy was heightened. I wanted to see it! I wanted to see a real one. Not a drawing on the bathroom stall or a picture in a magazine. I wanted to see a real live one in the flesh. After weeks of trying, I finally convinced Amber, one of my old Hide and Seek partners to participate. Her deal was, you show me yours and I'll show you mine. Even though I hadn't done this before, the arrangement was fine with me. Lavelle told me, "If I really wanted to do something, don't let anything or anyone stop me."

I walked over to Amber's. She lived across the field in The Heights Apartments; the same field where the Tent Meetings were held. Her apartment was on the second floor.

I quickly, quietly climbed the steps, two at a time. I struck twice at her door. The curtain moved. I coiled my neck to see. It closed, the door opened…it was Amber.

"Hi! Come in," she invited.

"Hi," I answered slithering inside.

"What took you so long? After a while I thought you weren't coming."

"I had a few chores to do before I was allowed to leave."

No other words were spoken. She took my hand and led me toward the back. We stopped in the hallway just before the bathroom. She smiled as she released my hand. I nervously smiled back. She leaned back against the wall. Staring me in the eyes, she slowly put her hands under her skirt. Softly she worked her underwear past her knees. Maintaining eye to eye contact she flipped up her skirt and there it was! She giggled. My mouth swung opened like the front door. If there were flies in the room, they circled through twice before I closed it. The muscles in my stomach began to do that pulsating thing again, caused an involuntary twitch in my right leg. The flesh beneath my shorts expanded.

"Now show me yours," she said.

While still staring at hers, I grabbed a handful of shorts and underwear and yanked them to my knees.

"Ooouch!" I moaned.

I should've unbuttoned my shorts! Man, did that hurt! She giggled again. I managed a fake smile but quickly shifted my attention back to her private part. I was hypnotized. I couldn't look away. I felt my hand starting to reach for it when my brain slapped that nerve. I had my hands down her pants a dozen times but there I stood hypnotized. Now all of a sudden it seemed sacred, off limit; do not touch. Amber broke the ice.

"Yours looks different," she said.

"Uh…" I mumbled coming out of my trance.

"Your thing…it's different."

"Oh! I was born in the hospital."

"What does that have to do with your thing?"

"When you're born in the hospital the doctor cuts the extra skin away," I answered.

"They cut on your dick!"

"No just the extra skin at the top. Some boys still have the extra skin."

"Oh! That explains a lot."

It became obvious she had played this, "Show me yours" game before.

Silence.

"What do we do now?" she asked.

"Uh," I uttered pretending I didn't hear her.

"What do we do now?" She repeated.

Oh boy! I hadn't thought passed seeing it. She was moving too fast! There I was, caught physically and mentally with my pants down without an answer. I couldn't let her know I hadn't thought this through. All I wanted to do was see it but she wanted to do it too. My Bond skills kicked in to save me.

"What if your parents came home?" I asked.

She didn't respond. I pulled up my pants, paying close attention not to injure myself again. She pulled up her clothes as well.

"I'm Sorry! I'm sorry!" I frantically apologized.

"No, no! It's okay. Calm down, she implored.

Too late, I was spooked! My heart bounced like a basketball. What was I thinking? What was I doing? I headed for the door. I turned to her as she was on my heels.

"Thanks Amber. I'll see you later." I said.

"You don't have to leave. You can stay if you like," she pleaded.

"But what if your parents caught me here? I better go, I don't want to get you in trouble," I said closing the door.

I hurried down the steps and scampered home. I was in a full sweat when I reached my front door. I had travelled only 75 yards! My heart beat like the marching band! I should've been with my friends shooting baskets, or playing football, or pinball. But no! Instead, I was standing in front of Amber with my pants down staring at hers. This was the first time my curiosity had gotten the best of me. My mind and body was not prepared for what came next. Mama always said,

"There are some bridges you don't cross unless you're prepared to go the rest of the way."

Meaning, there are some things we shouldn't say or do unless we are prepared to back it up. Because once you've done it or said it, you can't undo it! I had just crossed a bridge I wasn't prepared to cross. I couldn't undo it but I decided to stop travelling down that road for a while. At least until I knew what I was doing and where I was going. For the next few days I dreamed about the event at Amber's. I continued with the heavy petting with the girls but I kept my pants up!

I could only tell Benny Lee about the girls. I caught up with him coming out of Ray's.

"Hey Benny, wait up!"

"Joseph, where you been? I haven't seen you for a couple days."

"I've been around. Where are you off to?"

"I swiped some cigs from my mom's purse. Wanna go to the creek?"

"Sure. Let's go."

As we sat shirtless, smoking cigs in the heat, I told Benny Lee about my episode with Amber. We finished our cigs and flicked the butts in the water.

"Where do you get these thoughts from?"

"I don't know. I wanted to see a real one so bad. She was the only taker."

"Well, at least you picked a pretty one. She's hot!" He drooled as we threw rocks in the creek.

"That she is."

"Did you do it yet?"

Oh man, Truth or Dare. I couldn't tell him Amber wanted to do it and I backed out. I would be the biggest pussy in the neighborhood.

I could lie and tell him I had done it but he would never lie to me so I told him the truth.

"No – not yet, but I've gotten close," I bragged.

He looked over at me, "You lucky dog."

We laughed.

He tossed his t-shirt in my face and proceeded to playfully tackle me in the sand. As we rolled around he shouted," You're sick Joseph, really sick!"

Still laughing we sat up. He looked over at me and asked,"You actually stood in front of her with your pants down?"

"Yep, my sword was sticking out a mile long."

"Man, you're the craziest cat I know."

"I know…I'm a perv. I need to go to church and pray." I said with a devilish grin.

"No, we need to go hunt for money. Then you can buy a cold soda, drink it too fast, and get a damn brain freeze or something. That'll stop them crazy thoughts of yours. Come on, let's go!" he ordered.

Brushing the sand from our shorts, away we went. Still covered in sand he removed the grains from my back with his shirt. I did likewise when he was done. Aces!

CHAPTER 15

THE FRANKLIN COURT CREW

The crew had grown to six. Duke, the latest member, was Benny Lee's cousin. Duke was two years older. We tried to make him our leader. He didn't want any parts of it. He announced,

"You are your own leaders! You make your own decisions. Don't wait for me to tell you what to do!"

Although he made his little speech, we still followed his lead. He was our unofficial official leader. We called ourselves the Franklin Court Crew, "FCC" was our tag. The apartments were our home base. It and the Quarters were in the heart of Black Town. The extension of the creek behind the apartments was our meeting spot.

Living on the "Strip in the jungle," we rambled its' ten blocks from the Farmers Market downtown to Jakes Bar uptown. Whatever you wanted you could find it on the strip: bootleg tapes, jewelry, knock-off jeans, sex, drugs, Rock 'N Roll, gambling: dice, cards, and a game of Pool at the Pool Hall. Four bars, four restaurants, three grocery stores, and a movie theatre on the main drag. Burnouts, wheelies, cruisers were on display. You could juke and jive on Franklin 24/7! Well, for us, at least until the street lights came on.

We were a bunch of dare devils. That might be why they accepted me. I was as uninhibited as they were, maybe more! The exhilaration from our hunts was my high. I was a Double-O. They didn't come anymore fierce. We weren't bad, thug kids…just mischievous. We were more likely to hurt ourselves than someone else. But we did steal. Well, the other crew members stole. Smoked our parent's cigs, looked through nudies, and sipped wine down at the creek. It was easy to get wine, "Pay a bum a dollar and he'd buy you a bottle." Duke got most of our stash. The nudie mags we found in an abandon house. We never looked for trouble but if you wanted to start something, we didn't mind finishing it.

Our rival, the Hula Poolas were a bunch of panty wearing assholes! Smoked weed, drank cough syrup with beer, and showed little respect for adults. Their tag, "HP", sprayed everywhere. They bullied kids and fought girls! I wanted to mash their faces in. The crew felt the same way, but Duke disagreed.

"Since they haven't crossed our path, they're not our enemy," he said.

The Hula Poolas pretended to be tough. But they knew if they crossed us, they were asking for a beat down. We also knew a rumble was coming, just a matter of time. So we waited.

The FCC Crew Members:

Daniel "Duke" Rivers: the oldest, wisest, strongest with the most street smarts. But he was never demanding. If he said something we didn't agree with he never got upset. We just moved to the next thing. He only got angry when one of us did something dumb which brought negative attention to the group. He really did look out for us. Someone had to.

Booker Wells: the smallest of the bunch was quick witted. He loved to crack jokes or bust on you with a rhyme. He was a step ahead of all of us when we planned the hunts. He had a plan B and C ready if plan A didn't work. He analyzed the end at the beginning! I learned that from him. But he didn't apply himself much in school. He also liked to make dumb bets.

Otis Beacom: The Iron Man of the crew, 2nd strongest behind Duke. An only child, he lived alone with his grandmother. He was a street kid that loved to fight. Suspended was his middle name, at least twice a school year. An insane laugh he had. Spooky! But he was 100% FCC. Glad he was on our side.

I called Elijah "Lijah" Walters our part-time crew member. He didn't roll with us much. He had three younger siblings he watched while his mom was at work or running errands. He usually hung out with us at the apartments and the creek. Lijah was a big one, more round than tall. Football was his favorite sport. He didn't speak much but was always encouraging.

Benjamin "Benny Lee" Rivers: was soft spoken but firm when necessary. He was the leader of the pack in Duke's absence. Benny Lee was funny, tough, and sensitive all at the same time. He struggled to hide his sensitivity. Only I knew his softer side. He would fight if provoked. There was something bugging him. Something he wanted to say. Whenever he tried to talk about it he'd clam up.

We all had poverty issues. No one said it but we'd love to live like the Parkers. When I was 6 or 7 years old I invited a few friends to my birthday party. The gas was turned off the morning of the party. We couldn't boil the hotdogs. Mama and Jeanie used pots of hot water to try to cook them but the center wasn't cooked. A few kids complained. Thank goodness Mama baked the birthday cake the day before. It saved the party. I was so embarrassed by the hotdog incident I never asked for a birthday party again. I went through childhood with only one birthday party! Same was true for the other crew members. If we got a homemade cake and a gift or two, we made out good on out birthday.

We all had parental issues. **Elijah** was angry at his dad for running out on his family. He use to come around when he was younger but he hadn't heard from him in years. He was also angry at his mom for making him babysit his siblings all the time. He felt trapped by them. He couldn't wait until they could look after themselves.

Otis had issues with both his parents. They left him to live with his elderly grandmother when he was four years old. . They moved to Texas. Promised they'd send for him when they were setup with jobs and a place to stay. They never did. Grandma, too old to properly care for him, he'd basically raised himself. His mom use to call him on holidays but not anymore. He swore never to speak to her again. He hasn't spoken to his dad in 7 years. He assumed they weren't together anymore.

Booker lived with his aunt and uncle. His mom died in a car accident when he was 5. His aunt was his mom's sister. He had guilt and anger issues with his aunt and uncle. He rebelled often, especially when they tried to discipline him. He threatened to run away if his uncle tried to discipline him again. He also threatened to call the cops and report them for child abuse. Although he never met his father, he still hated him for not taking him when his mom died.

Benny Lee had issues with his mom. She was cheating on his dad and he knew it. She once sent him to the man's house with a note! He figured out what the message meant. She made him give her half the money he earned from our hunts. He often lied to her about having money. Whenever he lied his sisters would rat him out. They loved to get him in trouble with their mom. Whenever he spoke of his family, he went to a point and stopped. My Bond skills suspected a secret of sorts. I didn't press him on it.

Duke, our elder statesman, had issues with both parents. He overheard them say they couldn't wait until he was old enough to drop out. They wanted him to get a job to help pay the bills. Duke played on the football team. His dream was to become the starting running back for the varsity like my brother Lavelle. But he had no support from his parents. They never attended his games. They criticized him for playing sports, often asking him to quit and get a job.

We did all our venting at the creek. If we weren't on a hunt or playing sports, we shot the breeze at the creek. Once there, we dug up our stash of cigs, girly magazines, and a fifth of Bali Hi wine; only a swig allowed. All were wrapped in plastic and buried in a large cookie can on the upper bank. The creek also served as our meeting place for birthdays and when one of us was in the dumps. Those were our "Crew Therapy Sessions."

In one session I griped about the name calling. The day before, a kid in the barber shop busted on me with his friend saying,

"Doesn't he look like Howdy Doody?"

The two kids laughed! A couple adults in the shop snickered. The comparison said loud enough for me and others to hear it; a cruel, dirty trick. Their laughter took turns punching me in the heart. My insides ached from the beating, my eyes welled a little. I wanted to go at them so bad. I would've cussed and busted on their mama for a half hour straight. Then we'd see who was laughing at whom when I was done. But out of respect for Mr. O'Dell I pretended not to hear the insult.

Mr. O'Dell gave them a tongue lashing. The kid tried to clean it up with a weak apology. I gave them a fake nod in response, but the damage was done. They had crossed the bridge. I left shortly afterwards. Duke interrupted,

"Yeah, I know. I hear the guys at school talking about you. How you flip out on them cussing and busting when they call you names. They call you those names because they're jealous of you!"

Bewildered I asked, "Why are they jealous of me?"

"Well, some are just haters. But others have little sisters that like you. They hear them on the phone talking about what they did with you. They push your buttons to get back at you for fooling around with their sister. It's a game to them until you embarrass them."

"Well, fuck them and their game!"

Everyone chuckled but me.

In earnest Duke asked, "Did you really call David Brown's mom a fat, watermelon head pig with holes in her underwear?"

We all laughed. Otis mocked,

"A big watermelon head pig."

We laughed more. Duke continued between the laughter,

"That was a good one! We laughed at David for a week over that one."

Still laughing, he said,"Just remember, it's a game to them. Don't let them push your buttons so easy."

"Man, I'll try not to. Thanks for the heads up."

Duke was the man! He always saw the big picture. He really tried to keep us hellions under control. I must admit, he did have some Bond skills. But he wasn't a Bond disciple. He, like Lavelle, was a Bruce Lee man.

Duke had given me good intel but my first impressions were;

a. He had no idea how those names made me see red. Easy for him to say ignore them.
b. If this was a game, I refused to let them score without scoring back.
c. Since name calling was their way of scoring points then I'll do the same and throw in some fat mama jokes to take the win.

I refused to be their prey. One rule of the jungle; "If you get hit, you better hit back." I would get my respect one way or another, or so I thought.

CHAPTER 16

THE HUNT

The crew had seven rules. Duke came up with them.

1. Respect each other.
2. Protect each other.
3. Care for each other.
4. Share with each other.
5. Stick together. No matter what!
6. If chased by the cops, don't hide together
7. If caught by the cops, don't give up your crew members

These rules bonded our crew. A copy was buried with our stash out at the creek. Each crew meeting started with the reading of this list. If caught in violation of a rule you could get voted out of the group.

By 11 am the growling of our stomachs declared a food hunt; guava, mulberry, and mangos our favorite, avocados and kiwi on occasion. Dangers, hazards lurked: dogs, wasp, bees, weak branches and stomach aches. Too many mulberries; the toilet was your friend for two days as Adam and I found out. Too many guavas, you couldn't go to the toilet for two days.

Bellies full the fun began..." Food fight!" Hanging 25 feet up, one hand for safety, the other fired away. Dipping, dodging, the green fruit projectiles, we shrilled of joy and pain. Welts and bruises remained.

Rotten guavas exploded on impact. Smelly slime, seeds, worms ooze down the victim's face. Funniest thing ever!

Mango hunts more serious, a pretty penny they brought. A mango was a large, sweet fruit grown in tropical climates. A tree could grow up to 35 feet depending on the type of the fruit. The Haden was most popular in Reservoir City. It brought the most money on the street. When ripe the fruit fell from the branch; many preferred them picked, no bruises. Either way it was easy money.

When Benny Lee and I were younger we hunted mango on the west side of town. Back then, we ate our takes. Most of the black tree owners sold their fruit. So we didn't collect much, just enough for lunch. After a few summers passed, the crew often walked into White Town on mango hunts; several large trees just across the tracks. Our parents forbid us from going over there. But the rewards of having lunch and making money outweighed their consequences.

Some tree owners on the east side allowed us to use their long pole with a hook at the end to pull the fruit from the branch. Others allow us to climb the tree but warned, "Don't climb to the top," but that was where the best looking fruit was. We took large grocery bags with us. No bag, we took off our T-Shirt, tied a knot at the bottom, and filled from the neck, sleeves.

We always knocked to get permission to have some fruit. The crew always chose me to knock and ask. They stood about 10 feet behind me. It wasn't until years later I learned why they always chose me to ask. Most of the owners said yes. I guess they felt sorry for a pack of orphan-looking black kids and a half breed begging for fruit. Some owners said no. We were polite when they refused and moved on, but remembered the house. If our bags were low on the way home, we'd go back by that house. If the owner's car was gone, we'd hit their tree; raked clean in 5 minutes or less. If no one was home when I knocked the first time, we'd hit their tree and gone.

We faced several frightening situations on mango hunts in White Town. Like the time the owner came home while we were in his tree. We were up near the top laughing, talking, and picking fruit. No one heard the car drive up. He went into the house, got his shotgun, and demanded we get out the tree. Once on the ground he cocked the trigger.

"Get out my yard you little coons," he warned.

We ran like our lives depended on it! Dashing to out run each other, we left our bags behind. We stopped running after a block or so. Out of breath with our hands on our knees, we looked to see if everyone was okay. After a minute, nervous laughter took over.

Wheezing for air, Duke mumbled, "Can you believe that cracker drew a gun on us?"

Otis, between his insane laughs, mocks the owner, "You little coons better get out my yard."

We let out a gut busting laugh which broke the tension. We gathered our composure and continued the hunt.

Then there was the time when we were given permission. We entered the fenced in back yard and prepared ourselves to climb the tree. The back door swung open.

The woman yelled, "Get 'em!"

Two Dobermans came charging out the house! Holy guacamole! An all-out sprint to the 6 foot fence ensued. I had never leaped over a fence in one bounce before. But I was never chased by Dobermans either! None of our feet touched the top of the fence as we went over it. Having built up momentum from the life or death sprint, I leaped, grabbed the top of the fence, and vaulted over. Once my body cleared the fence, I quickly removed my hands as the dogs snapped at them. We ran across the street.

"That'll teach you little niggers about begging me for my mangoes," she barked!

A wimpy group would've given up and went home, not us. We completed the hunt! Many things delayed us but few stopped us. Those shots of adrenalin were the best! We retold the stories as we toked cigs at the creek.

But the worst mango hunt was when Benny Lee died. It still hurts to talk about this.

It was a clear, bright day, not a cloud anywhere. On days like such the crew would go swimming in the Intracoastal. But Benny Lee's and my pockets were registering past empty. We decided to go on a mango hunt for some quick cash. We tried to get the crew together for the hunt. Everyone was on assignment. Otis had to run errands for his grandma. Booker took his little cousins to the playground. Duke went to work with his dad. Elijah, as usual, had to babysit the youngins. That left only Bennie Lee and I. Just like the old days!

We head out on the eight-block hike to the tracks. We talked about everything along the way; Spinning Tops, Sling Shots, Yoyos, and of course, girls.

"What if you get caught?" Benny Lee asked.

"Well, the objective is not to get caught," I answered.

"But what if you do? I'm telling you, they're going to put you in Juvie.

"For what?"

"If you get caught the girl will lie. She'll say you made her do it. Or it was all your idea."

"Why would she say that if she's doing those same things to me?"

"She'll lie because she's daddy's little girl! They aren't supposed to do things like that. You must remember I have two sisters. My dad barks at them all the time about how they better not do this and they better not do that."

"I hear you man. Juvie's the last place I want to go!"

Benny Lee was concerned. He was warning me to dial it back a notch. Juvie was short for Juvenile Detention Center. In other words it's jail for kids. My Bond skills sensed he was telling the truth. He'd given me good intel to consider.

As we approached the train tracks the conversation changed.

"Be alert, move quickly but don't run. Don't bring attention to yourself. Smile, be polite, and say please and thank you. Don't look them in the eyes." We said to each other.

They don't like when you look them in the eyes. To us, it was one big con. We give them what they wanted so we could get what we wanted. About a month earlier we spotted one of the largest mango trees on the east side. We saw it on the way back from swimming in the Intracoastal. It's near the big church on Northeast 10th Avenue. The tree stood about 35 feet high. It took up the owner's entire back yard and part of the neighbor's. When we were younger we dreamed of hitting a tree that big. As we drew near, the tree got larger and larger. Like a huge mountain. Upon arrival at the house I knocked on the front door. Benny stayed on the sidewalk. A beautiful woman answered. In her southern drawl she asked,

"Can I help you?"

"I was wondering Ma'am if my friend and I could have some mangoes from your tree out back?"

She looked at me, then Benny, we both were dripping with sweat, and said.

"You boys look hot. Meet me around back."

We walk to the back of the house where she met us with two bottles of soda.

"Here you go," she said.

"Thank you Ma'am," we replied.

"You boys can have some mangoes but don't climb to the top. That's a pretty big tree!"

"Thank you, Ma'am."

As we drank our sodas the lady went back inside. Benny and I looked at each other as we sat on the back steps. We didn't say a word, gestures indicated, "I don't know why she's so nice but this soda hit the spot!"

We finished the sodas, left the bottles by the door, and walked toward Mt. Everest. Out of respect for the nice lady, we didn't climb to the top. We went two-thirds of the way up. We were about 30 feet in the air. We decided to leave our bags on the ground and go with our shake method. It's a lot of fun. We would shake the branches which caused the fruit to fall to the ground. This would make up the time we lost enjoying the soda. Curfew was the street lights on.

We stood on separate branches. Now it was time to make it rain! We shook the branches with great force. "Thump, thump, thump!" The mangoes dropped to the ground. We may lose a little profit due to bruises but we'd make it up on the number of fruit sold from the huge take. We laughed and yelled as we shook. Okay, on to the next branch.

We can't lose any more time. We still had to collect from the ground and load them in our bags. We counted down,

"Three… Two… One… Make it rain!"

"Thump, thump, thump."

"Oh Joseph…"

Benny's foot slipped, he lost his grip, and disappeared from sight!

"No! Benny!" I screamed.

I was helpless as he hit branch after branch on his descent.

"No! No!" I screamed, "Benny".

I got to him as fast as I could. I called out as I shook him repeatedly.

"Benny! Benny Lee!"

No response!

He laid flat on his back motionless. His eyes were staring into space. I listen to see if he was breathing. I heard and felt nothing!

"Help…. Help…!" I yelled.

He still wasn't breathing or moving.

"Benny, please don't die," I begged kneeling beside him.

In that moment I remembered the Prophet. I remembered Mama. For the first time in my life I prayed to white Jesus for help. I placed my hand on Benny's forehead.

"Benny, be healed in the name of Yeshua." I whispered with puddles in my eyes.

"What happened?" The lady asked as she stood at the backdoor.

I turned to her as she's running down the step.

"He fell out the tree," I answered.

"No!" She gasped putting her hands to her mouth.

I turned back to Benny to find him blinking his eyes and moving his head.

"I'm alright," he said as he sat up.

I went numb! Now I couldn't speak. One minute Benny was dead. I prayed and now … I was spooked! I kneeled next to him with my mouth gaped. He looked at me.

"Are you okay? You look like you've seen a ghost," he said.

Still silent I gave him a hug.

"I thought you were dead. That's all," I said as tears fell on his shirt.

"Are you alright?" The lady asked.

"I'm okay,"

"But you're bleeding, I'll call for help."

"No!" We both shouted in unison.

Benny got up to show the lady he was okay.

"It's just scrapes from the branches. I'll clean them when I get home."

"Okay boys. Come up to the porch when you're done collecting your mangoes."

"Yes Ma'am," we answered.

"Benny, are you alright?" I asked.

"Yeah, I'm ok. Just my back's sore. That's all"

"Let's get these mangoes and get out of here."

"Okay."

The lady watched from the backdoor. She looked to see if Benny was alright. When we were done we went to the steps. The lady came out with a wet and dry cloth. She cleaned and bandaged Benny's wounds. When she was done, we thanked her and went on our way. I had never met a white person with that much compassion. She offered us another soda but we politely refused saying, "We had to be home soon." We both knew we only had a couple hours before the street lights came on and we still had to sell our take.

As we walked backed across the tracks into Black Town, I confessed to Benny again, I thought he was dead.

"Man, don't scare me like that again. No jive – I thought you were dead. Were you?

"I don't know. I could see the sky but I couldn't move or breathe," he shared. "I guess I was half dead."

"Were you scared?"

"A little, I could hear everyone. By the way, who's Yeshua?"

"That's the God we pray to."

"I thought his name was Jesus?"

"Jesus is his English name. Yeshua is his name in another language,"

"That makes sense."

"So could you hear me when I was next to you?"

"Yeah, I heard you. 'Oh Benny Lee, please don't die,'" he joked.

"Don't goose me man! I was so scared you were dead."

"I know…I'm sorry. I wanted to tell you I wasn't dead. But I couldn't talk. That's why I think I was half dead. Thanks for praying for me."

"It's cool. You would have done the same for me."

"Yeah, I would've but you'll have to give me some lessons first."

I turned to him. "Later," I smiled.

He smiled back. "Cool."

We continued side by side carrying our take. I had never felt closer to God than in that moment. I didn't know if Benny was dead, half dead, or what. I didn't care! What I did know was when I needed God, he showed up for me and my ace. He saved my best friend from dying. We had our biggest pay day ever from a mango hunt. Benny made $3.50. I collected $2.50. He tried to give me .50 cents to even out our cash.

"No Benny, you've had a rough day. You keep it."

He insisted, "No way baby, 50/50! That's how we roll. Blood Brothers, right?"

"Yes, Blood Brothers forever."

I took the 50 cents.

"Thanks. See you tomorrow," I said as I turned toward home.

"Yep, see you tomorrow," he waved.

For the first time, I really appreciated hearing him say, "See you tomorrow."

Chapter 17

THE STORMS KEPT BLOWING IN

A storms a comin'.

The town was in a frenzy! Hurricane "Lucille" approached. Reservoir City was in the middle of the hurricane zone. We got three or four a year. I'm sent to the store to get the usual staples to ride out the storm; bread, spam, peanut butter, and jelly. My brothers helped Daddy secure the windows and doors with plywood. Outside, they tied down all loose property of value. Jeanie helped Mama collect water in gallon jugs. The weather man said this could be the worst hurricane to ever hit the region. He predicted wind speeds up to 160 miles per hour, a mega storm, scheduled to hit around 9:00 pm. Rain started early that afternoon. It was a little pass 5pm when we all were finally gathered inside. We awaited Lucille's arrival.

Coal black inside, no power since 4pm. Our voices danced in the dark, trading partners to find each other. Mama and Jeanne lit candles. Gathered in the living room, Casey brought in the radio from the bedroom. We huddled for the latest report. The broadcaster announced,

"Lucille has hit Manopa and is moving north toward Rising Tide and Reservoir City with winds between 140-160 miles per hour. It has destroyed hundreds of homes and buildings in its wake. The strong winds have eroded the coast line. This will be one of the worst storms to hit Reservoir City!

Daddy added, "If wind's gets to 160 miles per hour, this will be the worst ever!"

Oh no, Matt and Robert lived in wooden houses. I frantically fumbled my way through the dark. Items crashed as I bumper car my way to the phone. I fumbled in pitch black to deal. Robert's line gave a disconnected signal. The same was true for Matt's. I tried again. My line died in the middle of the call. I began to unravel, my glue was melting. I hid my angst in the darkness.

One of the few bright spots about my home: it was "Hurricane Proof!" Made of cinder blocks it blinked at hurricanes. My parents always said,

"Don't complain. There's always someone worse off than you!"

In other words, there are others who wish they were in your shoes. I think that's what Benny Lee was trying to tell me. Now I knew what he meant. I complain about my home for various reasons but two of my friends are riding out the worst storm in history in a wooden house. I was coming apart at the thought. I battled my way back to the living room.

Lucille arrived an hour early. Cross currents swirled. A loud freight train circled the house blowing its whistles. Debris slammed into the structure from all directions. Rattling plywood fought back, keeping the windows and screen doors intact.

"Bang, bang, bang."

"Quiet! Did you hear that?" I asked.

"Hear what?" Daddy said.

"You probably heard the junk hitting the house," Casey suggested.

"Bang, bang, bang" went the sound again.

"I heard it that time. It's coming from the back door," Jeanie said.

Daddy got up from the sofa and went to the backdoor.

"Don't go out there Daddy," Lavelle warned.

He opened the thick wooded storm door and listened.

Not only was our house storm proof because of the cinder blocks, it also had thick wooden storm doors and shutters on the windows. The plywood was added for extra protection. I thought about how William Jefferson made sure his black slave laborers stayed alive to pick his crops! I knew I was being a dick for thinking such a thing at a time like that. There we were trapped in a deadly storm and I was angry about what happened 30, 40 years earlier. Mama's always said, "Some things you must let go of or they'll eat you up inside."

"Bang, bang, bang" went the sound for a third time.

"Someone's banging on the plywood," Jeanie announced.

"My God, Ike, someone's out there!" Mama cried.

"Come help me Casey." Daddy asked.

Casey and Daddy kicked and pushed until the plywood fell. There, standing in the Hurricane was the Dawson Family. They live in the wooden house behind us, the last wooden structure in the Quarters.

"Come in, Come in!" Daddy invited.

In stepped Mr. and Mrs. Dawson and their two sons, Ralph and Anton; both in their early 20's. The family was soaked!

"Thank you," they said in unison.

Mrs. Dawson started explaining how the hurricane ripped through their home. She sobbed. Her family tried to console her. She continued,

"The wind blew open the back door. We went to close it but it was gone! After the front door flew off, we gathered in the living room to ride it out. When half the roof blew off, that's when we knew it was time to go," she explained.

My anguish, anxiety just turned to panic! I grabbed Lavelle by the arm and pulled him into the bedroom.

"What's wrong?"

"Robert and Matt"

"What about them?"

"They live in wooden homes. When I tried to call them earlier, their phones were dead," I explained.

Lavelle heard the concern in my voice. He pulled me to him. He wrapped his arms around me and held me tight.

"They're ok. They live in the newer, stronger built wooden homes," he encouraged.

Mama entered the bedroom.

"Is he ok?" She asked Lavelle.

"Yeah, he's alright. He's worried about his friends that live in wooden homes," he answered.

"Joseph, you pray for your friends and their families. Give it to God," she suggested.

For the second time in my life I prayed to God for my friends. Casey and Lavelle went to find some dry clothes for the Dawson brothers. Mama and Jeanie got dry clothes and blankets for Mr. and Mrs. Dawson. Casey talked with the brothers about cars. Mama, Daddy, and Jeanne talked with Mr. and Mrs. Dawson about their plans after the storm. I didn't say much to anyone the rest of the night. I gave up my sofa so the Dawson's could sleep together in the living room. Jeanie retired to her bed in my parent's room. I slept in the bed with Lavelle. He continued to try and ease my concerns.

"Are you going out for the team this year?" he asked.

"I don't know. I might. I still have to work on my shot," I answered

"Well, like I told you before, you let me know if you need help."

"Thanks, but they keep stealing my hoop!"

"Yeah, I know, but they don't keep it long though. These hurricanes come through and blow that hoop into someone else's yard. Some little kid walks out after the storm and says, "Hey look what I found," he joked.

We laughed.

"Yeah, you're right. After every hurricane I have to go looking in the field to find the pole I nailed it to. I'm glad the storms blow my hoop away from the loser that took it," I cheered.

He talked until I fell asleep. We were trapped for the night.

By morning, Lucille had passed. It was time to inspect the damage. Daddy and my brothers removed the plywood, letting the light in. Shut in for nearly 15 hours, it was blinding. Water, mud, trash, clothes all over the Quarters. Huge palm trees uprooted. Tree branches on every roof top. I ask if I could visit Robert and Matt; not allowed, too dangerous. Electrical lines on the ground everywhere. Phones were still off. I couldn't find out if my friends had survived. The suspense tormented me! Mama told me to, "Give it to God." I had no other choice. There was nothing I could do. God came through for Benny Lee. I hoped, prayed he did the same for Robert and Matt.

The Dawson's home was destroyed. There was no front or back door. The roof was gone. All window frames and panes, blown out. The family salvaged what they could and moved on. They told my parents they were going to live with relatives in Rising Tide. I didn't worry about the crew. The apartments were concrete solid.

It took a full day to restore phone service. I called Robert and Matt. Both were fine. Yes! I clicked my heels the rest of the day. Most of the electrical lines had been repaired. I went to visit Benny Lee and the crew. They didn't have telephones. All were fine. They were gathered in front of the apartments checking out the damage from Lucille. They're talking and laughing when I walk up.

"What's up," I greeted.

"What's up" Benny answered first. The others followed.

"So which one of you girls pissed your pants when the wind began to howl like a pack of wolves outside your window?" I joked.

All heads turned to Booker.

"Why are you pussies looking at me? I wasn't scared," he barked.

"Sure you weren't," Otis said.

"I wasn't," Booker insisted.

"Man, whatever! Just cool it. You jitter bugs are always clowning." Duke groaned.

I proceeded to tell them about the Dawson family banging on our back door during the storm. Their eyes stretched in amazement.

"Let's go check it out." Elijah suggested.

We walked across the street from the beauty shop to take a look.

"Well, there it is or what's left of it," I said.

"Wow! I've never seen that much damage to a house before," Booker confessed.

"Me neither," Otis agreed.

Duke's assessment, "They'll have to tear it down, way too much damage."

"Yep, that's a goner," Benny agreed.

"Let's check out the creek," Elijah shouted.

"Well, look who's on the go today," Duke smirked.

We chuckled.

"Damn straight, I'm so glad I don't have to look after the rug rats today. My mom got a day off because of the storm. So let's get out of here before she starts looking for me," he answered.

We walked around to the creek to check the height. When we got 8 feet from the back of the apartments, the creek met us. We marveled how we'd never seen that much over flow before. We wondered about our stash. On days when the creek and canal overflowed, we usually went car surfing. Not today, too much debris around. We walked uptown to check Lucille's destruction and to get Elijah away from his mom and the rug rats.

After four days off, school was back in session. The buzz was Lucille's devastation. Final count; 26 dead and 76 injured. Smart move doing my homework before the storm, grumpy teachers gave no mercy. Then another storm blew in!

CHAPTER 18

ROOSTERS IN THE HEN HOUSE

Assignments rushed, mid-day approached. Provisions waited. Feet pattered, eyes hurried the clock. Finally, a muffled bell released the hungry herd. The hallway exploded with clamor. Panes rattled as we rambled, cafeteria bound. Crinkled bags of deli meats, assorted cheeses accompanied the crowd. Then, without warning, turbulence hit! A breeze so cool it filled the hallway hush. His gale pressed backs to the wall, allowing passage. With a proud peacock strut, his swag rippled a gasp.

"Hello," he greeted with a Colgate smile.

The girls' legs went noodle. Both hands rose to their blush. Star spangled oculars. The guys glared. I asked myself is he real? His eyes danced with his smile. Silky golden brown skin set the corridor a glow. His store like mannequin clothes and curly black hair filled the picture frame! He was real alright. He was Lindsey Gomez, the new kid!

Within a week, all the girls in school were riding his jock. His name was scrolled all over their folders. There was a new rooster in the hen house! For the first time, I saw green! The other boys did too, but theirs' was nasty, mean spirited. They called him gay, queer behind his back. They pronounced his name, "Lindsey", in a high pitch, girly voice. They passed their cup of "Haterade" but I wouldn't drink. I did not participate. I knew the pain of name calling. Their jealousy stemmed from Lindsay's looks and good behavior, and the teachers' adored him. I didn't care about any of that. No, really. I didn't.

My concern was, he was stealing my thunder with the girls. If I was James Bond, he was Napoleon Solo or Tony Stark. Before he arrived, my gum and candy take from the girls was a pocket full every other day! I had dropped to only 5 or 6 pieces a week! The girls said they still liked me. But that was probably because I didn't make fun of Lindsey. I wanted to know him. I needed to find out what made him remain cool, calm while kids made fun of him. I would have wigged out, cleaned their clocks. But he strolled above it. I knew I could never be like him but I needed to know where his swag and peacock strut came from. Having that intel would improve my Double-O status. I gave Lindsey odd ball props on his looks and behavior, defiantly a different breed of cat.

His body was smaller than most, but not by much. But a feisty competitor when it came to sports. When he first arrived he was always chosen last in gym class. I changed that when I was team captain, I picked him second or third. It pissed off my friends. But Lindsey was an odd ball in a new school. He needed friends and respect. I also invited him to eat lunch at the table with me and my friends. The guys began to accept him. *We all wanted to feel accepted!*

Over the next month Lindsey and I became good friends. A talker he was! Our best conversations were at the end of Chorus class. Hey, don't judge! The choices were Art or Chorus. And I couldn't draw! I encouraged Lindsey to take the Chorus Elective. We sat next to each other in Chorus. He was easy to talk to, polite, never interrupted. Born in Mexico, he came to America when he was three. He lived with his mother and little brother. They moved here from upstate, after his father kicked them out. *Another damn bully! I hated bullies!* Lindsey's passions were reading mystery books and playing baseball. His favorite team was the New York Yankees. He knew the names of each Yankee team member! I told him I had an uncle who lived in New York. Lindsey took his turn to ask questions at the end of class.

"Joseph, why don't you want the other kids to know you're smart?"

"It's a long story."

"That's not fair! I gave you my life story and you clam up on my first question."

"You're right. You've been honest with me."

"I watch you finish your class work before the rest of us but you turn it in after us. You help me with my math when I need it. So why don't you want the kids to know you're smart?"

"Shush, keep it down! I can't let that get out. I have a group of friends I hang out with. We do a lot of cool and crazy things together. We call them "Hunts". They're great adventures, the best! We're also a tight bunch, get along real well. If they found out I'm a nerd they'll kick me out of the group."

"Not all smart kids are nerds you know!" he said with a smirk.

"You're right; I'm sorry, but to them – we are."

"Man, that's great you guys do some neat stuff. And your crew seems to be a together bunch. But *it can't be too great if you can't be your true self around them,*" he said.

Pause.

Quiet.

"I guess you have a point," I answered.

I wanted to tell him, "I don't know my true self." I've been pretending so long, but he probably knew that too. We went to the door and waited to be dismissed back to class. We stood at the back of the line so no one could hear us.

He continued, "Why do you cuss and fuss with the older boys?"

"How did you find out about that?"

"I asked around. I wanted to know about my new friend, Mr. Bond," he teased.

Before I could answer we were dismissed back to class. Chorus was held in the music room outside of the main building. We took the walkway back. Away from the other kids, I was free to answer.

"Well, I cuss and bust on them when they call me bad names. I could be walking down the street minding my business; when one of them will start with the name calling."

"What kind of names?"

"Mean names, very mean! I've been called Casper, Half Breed, Mutt, and House Nigga just to name a few.

"Man, join the club. I get it too. I've been called Spic, Frito Bandito, Little Taco, Burrito, Speedy Gonzales," he complained.

"I hear you man. That's why I cuss them from tip to toe! I do my best to humiliate them. Well, that's what they're trying to do to me! I've gotten my older brother into so many fights because I won't back down from them."

We dipped into the restroom to take a whiz. Lindsey was on a roll with his inquisition. I told you he liked to talk, "But if you cuss, bust, and call them names doesn't that make you like them?"

"No way, I'm nothing like them!" I protested. "Most of them are at least two years older than me. I don't say anything to them until they start with me. I give everyone their respect until they disrespect me. My Daddy said, "Let a sleeping dog lie. Wake him and you might get bit." Well, I try to bite their head off when they start the name calling."

"But still, you both are calling each other mean names! It doesn't matter who started it. You're allowing them to pull you down to their level. They're making you act like a jerk with them! If you don't like hearing the names, just stay home more."

"Lindsey, I would shrivel up and die if I had to stay at home. I love the happenings in the street. And I've learned if I'm going to be out there I must get my respect. If not, they'll continue to harass me. They'll start to take my money, my lunch, my basketball. I won't be their prey, ever!"

We washed our hands and went upstairs toward our classrooms.

"I hear you. But I just ignore them. I've found when people call me names, they're just jealous."

"My mom said the same thing. So did my older friend Duke. He's the leader of our crew. He said they're jealous because their little sisters like me. Well, they did like me until you came along," I chuckled.

"What do you mean by that?" he asked with concern.

"I'm just kidding," I smiled. "Duke said the name calling is their way of getting back at me for making out with their little sister. He said they call me names to watch me flip out. It's a game to them and I shouldn't let them push my buttons so easily."

"Well, why don't you listen to him? Don't let them push your buttons. It would save you a lot of trouble."

"I'll try. Next time I'm called a name, I'll ignore them. Will that make you happy? " I asked sarcastically.

"Don't do it for me. Do it for yourself," he urged.

We split off to our classrooms.

"See you at lunch," I said.

"See you then." He yelled back.

That's why I liked him. He didn't sugar coat things! He was honest, sincere, and in control. Lindsey was a good kid. I wished I was more like him. *He was free inside!* Not bound by the social pressures of the jungle. He just went home, hid in his lair, and came out the next day. But unfortunate for him, he was still in the jungle. *And Rule #1 was, "You can run but you can't hide!"* Meaning, you've got to face your haters sooner or later. Lindsey was prey and I knew it. In order to survive he needed protection. *There was safety in numbers.*

The day came for the "Big Question." I fought against it as best I could. It was something the guys were dying to know. Since I was closest to him, I was chosen to ask. I didn't want to. I could lose his trust. His friendship meant a lot. But I gave in. I promised the guys I would ask at lunch. As usual, the cafeteria was packed.

Squeaky sneaks and ponytails scurried about. Squirrely voices caromed off the ceiling. Plastic trays clashed. Hair netted ladies on the line, Beefaroni filled the air. Teachers spied our every doing. Warnings issued, few punishments given.

Table 3's Finger Football game chanted, "Dolphins, Eagles, Jets, Redskins." Quarreled, who's the best? Players named, scores repeated, no champion declared. No love loss, a daily routine.

Table 4's Rock, Paper, Scissors turned heads. Napkins tossed, patience tested, brows dripped. Sweaters removed, sleeves pulled back, sweaty pits reigned supreme. Too intense, teacher interrupted, settled for a draw.

Table 5 was glam, girl power ruled! Flirt Flare flew. Finger painting, lip gloss, whispers all around. Finger pointing, heads on a swivel, placed boys in lost and found. Dollar perfume shared, the touching of hair, where was the sense in that?

Table 6's Spit Ball battles, epic! Balls of goo propelled through straws. Pellets found their mark. Glasses, hair, nothing was sacred. Girls squirmed on misfires. The fury felines of table 5 readied their claws but alerted the spies instead. Straws down, food consume, they waited to resume. No luck, the spies convened, Table 6 was where they settled.

Meanwhile at Table 7 I stalled as long as I could. I tried to interest the guys in a round of Finger Fighting. No Takers. Kicks and nudges beneath the table forced my hand. The time had come. Lindsey sat in his usual spot, right in front of me. Matt sat on his left, Otis to his right. Booker was to the right of Otis. Robert was seated to my left and Benny on my right. Elijah was to the right of Benny. The lunch bunch was in full force. It was show time.

"Lindsey!" I called.

"What?" he replied between bites.

"You know I'm your friend right?"

"Sure Joseph."

"So don't get angry at me for asking this."

"Ask me what?"

With six sets of eyes staring down my throat, I froze! My throat swelled like a Bull Frog! Air flowed in, grunts came out. Paralysis strangled my vocal cords. My eyes fixed on his. He returned the stare with a slight squint. After a series of welt forming pinches to both thighs from Benny and Robert, I finally snap out of it. I leaned over the table.

"The guys want to know – do you like girls?" I asked in shame.

Their head and eyes snapped to Lindsey.

I sat down. The room became distorted, everyone bending horizontal. My lunch jabbed my belly button. Salt filled my mouth. I chewed a carrot not to blow chunks. I wanted to take it back but before I could speak, he laughed!

"Sure I like girls! And yes, I have a girlfriend too," he answered.

"Who?" Seven squeaky voices asked in unison.

"Her name is Maria. She goes to my old school," he confirmed.

"Aw Man!" We all sighed.

"What about all the girls here"? Benny asked. "They love you."

"I know. They're nice to me, but I have a girlfriend," he answered.

"What about Tanya? She beats up every girl that mentions your name," Robert asked.

"Pee Yew, I hate her! She's always grabbing me from behind with those big hands of hers and kisses me. Yuck! She's too big and rough for me," Lindsey answered.

We burst into laughter! So did Lindsey. The commotion caused the monitors, the spies, to come over. This was the best lunch ever! As we threw away our trash, all I could think about was… the girls were all mine to chase again. Lindsey had a girlfriend!

That was one of the hardest things to do, ask someone something so personal. Our friends push us to do a lot of things we would rather not do! We do or say it to win or keep their friendship. I was glad Lindsey was a good sport about it. He was an odd ball like me. His friendship meant a lot to me.

It was mid-October and the World Series was underway. In honor of the sport Mr. Daniels, our gym teacher had us play softball in gym class. Lindsey brought his glove to show me. It was a Rawlings, the best! I tried it on. Soft leather, good webbing, snug fit. It was a gift from his dad for little league. He looked down and away after he told me. I gave it back as we went out to class.

The sun beamed down on tender blades of grass. No place to hide its' face. Not a cloud to be found. The White Sand Field made ready for our youthful vigor. A fresh raked infield rose to greet us. Bases marked its' diamond face. Grass, weeds, sand spurs, made his brother outfield. Shoes stayed in place!

Red flags marked foul territory. One yellow sat in center field, a home run. A slight breeze paraded their colors. Home plate sat 150 yards from the creek. Every kid's goal, hit it in the creek! No fence to stop it. Orange cones marked the dugouts.

Behind home plate; spectators on chin up bars, girls jumping rope, car horns beeped. Motorists passed nearby. A delivery truck left in a rush. Tires burned, caused a fuss. Church bell rang mid-day prayer over. They waved to the kids, a daily routine.

"Hey batter, batter swing!" My team chanted.

"Strike three, change it up!" Mr. Daniels yelled.

We dropped our gloves and ran to the dugout. The score was tied in the bottom of the 2nd inning. Lindsey was up to bat. He was good! And fast! Pitch #1 was thrown,

"Ball one!" Mr. Daniels shouted from 2nd base.

Lindsey told me to never swing at the first pitch. He said, hopefully it's a ball and you'll be ahead of the count.

"Hey batter, batter swing!" The other team screamed.

Pitch #2, crack! "Wow, he got all of that," Robert declared.

It sailed beyond the yellow flag!

"Homerun," Mr. Daniels yelled.

Our dugout went wild, cheered out of control. Even the girls jumping rope on the blacktop noticed. Lindsey put our team up, 4-3. We mobbed him at Home plate. Finally, his hair was messed up. But a snake lurked in the sand. He raised his head to strike, injecting his haterade. As we walked back to the dugout he took his opportunity.

"You got lucky faggot!" said Rosco, the catcher for the opposing team.

Lindsey stopped dead in his tracks and turned to Rosco.

"What did you say?" he asked as he started toward him.

Lindsey's face matched the sun's blaze, sweat rolled. Veins the size of string beans raised from his neck. His knuckles lost color as he stormed forward. He was fed up. It took four of us to hold him back!

"You heard me!" Rosco taunted.

"Say it again! You *Hijo de puta*!" Lindsey yelled.

"He's too big. Let me take him. I don't like him anyway," I whispered to Lindsey.

Rosco ran with the Hula Poolas, a bunch of punks who thought they were tough. They always made trouble. The crew and I wanted to rumble with them so bad but Duke always said no. It pissed us off to no end.

"Let me go! I can take care of myself." Lindsey demanded.

As Robert and Matt continued to hold him, I walked over to Rosco, stood face to face with him, looked him in the eyes and said, "If you say that to him again I swear I'm going to beat you to sleep!"

"Why won't you let him fight his own fight?"

Benny had joined me on my right. Otis stepped up to my left. Two of his crew joined his flank; Jamal and Leon.

"You heard him Rosco! Say that to Lindsey again you dick and you're gonna get it," Otis warned.

My scowled face, mashed teeth continued to sneer him down. An inflated chest rose to greet him. Under the sizzle of the sun my brow dripped drops of fire. White hot knuckles ready to pummel him into submission.

Sneakers crunched sifting the sand as dugouts cleared. Jeers from the crowd added sparks. Fuel for my balloon sized heart. Who would cast the first blow?

In a distance a hawk's cry, a death dive, a field mice's last rite. A boy's delight on a regular day, it drew no cheers as booming bellows from 2nd base rushed near. Mr. Daniels arrived on a cloud of dust. Tiny grains peppered our eyes.

"Hey, what's going on?" He demanded.

Neither crew flinched! Threats were made, you didn't back down. Teacher's presence didn't matter. A rule of the jungle, "Show no weakness!" Jeering ceased, stilled bodies peered, a reverent fear emerged. An ass kicking awaited any snitch! Another rule: "Snitches got stitches!" Mr. Daniel tried again.

"You heard me, what's going on?"

Again, complete silence!

"Well, if nothing's going on let's play ball," he ordered.

Both teams slowly withdrew. No backs turned. The game resumed without incident.

That punk Rosco tried to steal my friend's moment. Not on my watch! My friends and I wouldn't allow it! Lindsey was one of us now. Well, at least at school. He didn't have any more problems out of Rosco or anyone else after that day. *He finally stood up to the bullying!* They all saw he had friends who had his back. He wasn't alone in the jungle.

Sometime later in Chorus class he asked, "Why'd you do it? Why were you willing to fight Rosco for me?"

"Ah, what happened to, "If they call me names I just ignore them" crap?" I teased.

While we both laughed, I continued,

"I did it because you're my friend. And friends look out for each other. If I was at your old school you would've done the same for me. What did you say to him in Spanish?"

"I called him a Son of a Bitch," he laughed.

I laughed with him.

Even the best of us had buttons, bruises, sore spots no one should press too often.

During Thanksgiving Break Lindsey moved back upstate. His mom and dad got back together. I knew that made him happy but I missed him. He was a good kid, good heart. Serious most of the time but liked to laugh too. His swag didn't come from his looks, his clothes, or his smarts, it came from within. He knew who he was and he let it show on the outside. I got my swag from Bond. In other words, I was fake, pretender. I wanted to be more like Lindsey. But the hood, the jungle wouldn't allow it. Relationships were hard to keep. People you cared about came and went all the time. Not good to get too attached. He was the 3rd good friend to move away. I prayed I'd be next.

Well, I had been searching and I finally found one. My first Black Hero! No, not Lindsey!

CHAPTER 19

THE RULES OF ENGAGEMENT

I sat in O'Dell's twiddling my thumbs. Floor shined, containers cleared, all barbers sat in their chairs; faces buried in the newspaper. TV offered little relief. The rhythm of the air conditioner kept me awake. Its refreshing breeze mixed aftershave and tonics. I searched for signs of life. I perused the magazine rack and there he was. I had heard of him but never saw him. He stood bold, proud on the cover of Sports Magazine. I pulled him closer. A laser stare ensued. It wouldn't relinquish. How could it be? An odd ball recognized for something great! Staggering back to my seat under his spell, he commanded my attention.

Ink covered fingers, doubled vision; I came up for air 2 hours later. Glued to my hands, I couldn't put him down. I was hooked! I asked Mr. O'Dell for the magazine. I took it home, hid it under the sofa. I read the article over and over. I threw it out only after the mice had consumed most of it but not before I had found my first black hero, Muhammad Ali, the World Heavy Weight Boxing Champion. I read everything I could find about him. I watched reruns of his fights on TV.

A chiseled 6'3", 236 lb walnut colored boxing machine. A few freckles remained. Curly black locks combed in the ring after each fight. Ali's mother was white, his father black. I gave him odd ball status on looks and personality. There was no other person on the planet like Muhammad Ali! The most confident man alive! Predicting the round he'd knock out his opponents and delivered! Many whites didn't like him. They called him, "Loud Mouth", "Cocky", "Arrogant", and ended their name for him with the word, "Nigger." They went to his fights hoping he'd lose, but he never loss. I loved this guy!

WHY I LOVED ALI

He was the Heavy Weight Champion of the World, an odd ball doing something great. Mama said, someday I would do great things. I wish I knew what they were. I loved Ali because he stood up for what he believed. They put him in jail because he wouldn't fight in a war he didn't believe in. I loved Ali because he protested against the ills of society. He participated in Civil Rights Marches and spoke out against racism. I loved Ali because he talked trash and backed it up in the ring. I loved Ali because he talked in rhymes. He was quick witted, smart, and crafty. I loved Muhammad Ali because he stood up to bullies. When a kid stole his bike, he learned to box; found the kid and took his bicycle back! *He made me proud to be me!* He became a real life hero! I wish I knew more black odd balls like him. Bond remains my fantasy, action hero. He fed my passion for danger and adventure. I looked to Ali for help with my everyday issues.

Mr. O'Dell was the only black man on the planet that didn't like Ali. He had his reasons. Said he wasn't a Christian. He was also pissed that Ali wouldn't fight in the war. Mr. O'Dell lost a son in the war. He felt Ali was no better than his son. Said he was glad they put Ali in jail for draft evasion. Well, I didn't care if Ali worshipped a goat! He was my hero. I respected both men's stances on their beliefs. I pressed down my feeling for Ali around Mr. Odell because his Barber Shop was my hangout minus my crew. I traded doing odd jobs for TV in the AC.

Mr. Odell was once a boxer himself. A middle weight, he stayed in good shape. But his worn, tattered face told his story. Mini train tracks ran the length of both brows. Small contusions rode his cheek bones. His nose veered right. Arthritic left hand revealed contorted knuckles, digits out of place. A picture of him in his boxing gear hung behind his chair.

He taught me and several other kids in the neighborhood how to box. He scheduled boxing matches between us in the alley next to the shop. I had two or three bouts a month. I must admit, I was pretty good. When I had my man in trouble I did the "Ali Shuffle" to piss off Mr. Odell for not liking my hero.

"All right Lil Ike! Box the way you were taught," he would shout.

He always called me by my Dad's name, Ike or Lil Ike. I didn't know why. He called Lavelle by his name and Casey by his. But me, I was Lil Ike. He gave me a tongue lashing at the end of the round.

"Don't be showing off out there. The goal is to win the fight, not dance around like some girl," he barked.

I nodded yes. But my shuffle was my tribute to my hero. A man I'd grown to admire. When I'm in the alley boxing I transformed into Ali. I copied his every move. I'd windup my left hand as if I was going to hit the kid with it. While he watched my left I'd jab him in the face with my right.

"That's not the way I've taught you to fight! Use your jab!" Mr. Odell would yell.

But the crowd loves it! I also circled my opponent to the left like Ali. Now that, Mr. Odell liked. He taught me to use my left jab while moving to the left.

Sometimes if I'm just hanging out in the barber shop, doing odd jobs, he'd have me beat the stuffing out of a kid that's there to get a haircut. O'Dell baited the kid's father into letting his boy put on the gloves to box me. I think Mr. Odell knew I had anger issues. And he knew I didn't like kids from the Parks, a bunch of uppity fucks who thought they were the greatest thing since sliced bread. None of us Townies liked them. And guess who O'Dell would pick for me to box? Yep, a Parker! I usually beat them to a pulp except this one time.

Mr. Odell had me box one a year older than me. I wasn't sure I wanted to fight him because he was taller and weighed a little more than me. I inquired of Mr. O'Dell.

"Why do you want me to fight this kid? He's older than me,"

"You can take him Lil Ike," he whispered as he laced up my gloves.

In a weird way I needed Mr. Odell's approval. He was kind to me. He believed in me. He coached me in every bout I had. The other barbers coached the other kids. I didn't want to let him down. Therefore, I agreed to fight. I looked over at the older kid. He looked scared, like he didn't want to fight. For a moment I thought, he might be a pussy. My eyes brightened. Then I remembered what Mr. Odell said, "Never under estimate your opponent." A nice crowd has gathered to watch.

As the match began, I did well during the first two rounds. Mr. O'Dell was hyped! He always pumped me up in between the rounds.

"You've got this Lil Ike! Just keep your hands up and use your jab. Don't forget to throw combinations after he throws a punch," he instructed.

We came out for the third and final round. We touched gloves and squared off. I'm moving to the left while throwing my left jab. The kid tried a left hand uppercut. I blocked it with my elbows. As I readied to throw my combination, he nailed me in the face with a hard right. It rang my bell and everything else in my head. I staggered backwards.

"Cover up Lil Ike! Cover up!" Mr. O'Dell yelled.

My will kept me upright. My legs went Jell-O. I wobbled back to the wall. I'd never been hit so hard. Dark spots floated across my gloves. I thought to myself, this kid's gonna knock me out.

"Cover up Lil Ike!" Mr. O'Dell continued to shout.

"Hit him! Hit him!" The crowd chanted.

Dazed and confused, I managed to peek through my gloves. To my surprise the kid was just standing in front of me, his gloves to his chest. I could see his eyes. They were sad. It was as if he was in as much discomfort as I was.

"Hit him again! Knock him out!" The crowd and his corner continued to chant.

In a move I hold in the highest esteem to this day, the kid turned to the crowed and shouted,

"No!"

He walked over to his corner and demanded they take off

his gloves. The bell rang. It was over. He knew he had won. So did I. Our corners took off the gloves. We shook hands. He congratulated me.

"Good fight."

"Thanks. Good fight," I replied.

For the first time I experienced what I had done to other kids. I didn't like it. I learned several things that day.

1. The older kid was better than me. Not as a boxer but as a person. His insides were better. If I had my opponent hurt I would've punched him drunk until he dropped... or they rang the bell.

2. That kid taught me, you don't have to kick a man when he's down to win. If the fight is over, it's over. You don't have to injure or humiliate your opponent. You don't have to dishonor or shame him. You know you've won. So does your opponent. Just walk away and be done with it.

3. The best lesson was when he turned to a crowd of mostly adults and stood up for what he believed in his heart was right. They knew the bout was over. Why injure me, embarrass me for their entertainment? His character was so much better than mine!

After that fight, I never boxed again in the alley at O'Dell's. I didn't stop because I lost. I stopped because the kid made me look at myself. He made me realize I was hurting people for the enjoyment, entertainment of others. It wasn't like I was a professional like my hero Ali. The kid made me feel like a bully. In a way, I was. I hid behind a pair of boxing gloves to take out my anger, rage, frustrations on kids that had nothing to do with my condition.

I continued to have fist fights. Come on, it was the jungle. But after that match, I never hit a kid when he was hurt or down. I didn't inflict more punishment than necessary to win the fight. I never fought because the crowd wanted me to. The kid taught me the Rules of

Engagement in a confrontation. They allowed both parties to walk away with their pride and honor intact.

A true Double-O must have integrity. I gave that kid "Major Double-O" status. I hoped to get there one day. And when that day comes I'd finally be at peace. I wouldn't have to pretend anymore.

CHAPTER 20

PREDATORS

Doc Hilliard, the only black doctor in the county, died...53 years old. He lived in an apartment over top of O'Dell's. His medical office sat across the alley where I once boxed. On occasion, he'd watch our matches, checked the fighters after the bout. A quiet man who drank too much, seen staggered on Franklin, never affected his business though.

Rescue lights flashed near O'Dell's the afternoon of his death. The EMTs were in his apartment. A crowd gathered in the alley. I pressed my way to the front. Police tape impeded my progress. The crowd was buzzing.

"Doc. Hilliard's dead." They gossiped.

My ears perked up. This blood hound Double-O needed intel. How did he die? Why was there police tape? I turned to the man next me,

"How did he die?" I asked.

He looked at me, managed a half smile and said, "You don't want to know."

What did he mean by that, I thought. The EMTs carried Doc's covered body down the steps. The crowd gasped. The police removed the yellow tape momentarily. We parted for clear passage. Carrie Faye, wrapped in a blanket, walked behind the body...escorted by two police officers. I thought *why was she here?*

"Is she the one?" The crowd whispered.

"I guess so," someone answered.

"She's the one that ran out screaming for help without any clothes on," one lady said.

"Yep, said he died while she was on top of him," another woman clarified.

What? Carrie Faye killed Doc Hilliard? Why...? How...? It was as if I stuck my finger in a light socket; my mind stammered and jerked trying to process the intel. I needed more pieces of the puzzle. I turned with the crowd to watch as both she and Doc's body were placed in emergency vehicles. The man across from me spoke out,

"He'd been paying her the past year."

Bingo...a light bulb moment. Wow, I couldn't believe it! Carrie Faye was hooking with Doc Hilliard. She just turned 15 a few months earlier. Her apartment was across from Benny Lee's. She waved often.

Crazy as it seemed...I still found it hard to knock her hustle; but my heart knew hooking at 15 was wrong. The Rescue Wagon pulled away, no siren, just flashing lights. The cop car carrying Carrie Faye sped off in the opposite direction.

As the crowd and I left the alley, a lady continued the gossip.

"She's not the only one! There are others around here he paid for years. They started about her age. Some are 25 or 30 by now."

Wow...Doc Hilliard was a real pervert. I kept quiet, continued to walk. As I came out the alley I saw Benny Lee standing near the street.

"Benny!" I called.

"What's up," he answered turning toward me.

"Wait up!" I walked up to him and whispered, "I guess you saw?"

"Yeah, Doc's dead," he said as we walked toward the apartments.

"Did you know about Carrie Faye?"

"Yeah —I knew. I overheard my sisters gossiping about her. They laugh at her behind her back. Yeah...she's been hooking with Doc for a while."

"Why didn't you tell me?"

"...You never asked"

"…Man that's crazy. I would never think she would do something like that."

"Remember Joseph, we're all pretending! We show people what we want them to see. We hide the real person inside,' he reminded me.

Boy, he wasn't kidding! I nodded yes as we stopped near the big tree in front of the apartments.

"Street lights will be on soon. I gotta go,"

"Yeah – me too," he said.

"Well, see ya later alligator!" I yelled crossing the street.

"After while crocodile," he hollered back.

In the days that followed, the official word on the street was, Doc died from a heart attack while having sex with Carrie Faye. It became a running joke. I didn't find it funny. I mean, I got it. They were making fun of Doc. But every time I heard it, I thought of Carrie Faye. Now everyone in town knew she was a hooker. I couldn't imagine the shame. I wasn't sad Doc died.

Mama always said, "God don't like ugly." Meaning, God doesn't like when you're doing wrong. Doc was definitely doing wrong! It was his fault he was dead. Excuse the pun but, "He shouldn't have screwed with young kids." Boom! Lights out! Good night.

Doc's death seemed to usher in the rain. Showers tapped upon my roof, soaked my spirit. Wolf Man yowls made it worse…I stopped. Trapped in the tiny mazeI called home, I peeked through the curtains. Gray skies frowned back. No relief in sight, I called April. Yes, the same April whose grandma's mulberry tree Adam and I raided.

April was spunky, well developed for her age. A little pudgy in middle but I liked her. Our make-out sessions outside the school dances were epic. She had something she wanted to tell me about her cousin's boyfriend, Bobby Earl. She tried to tell me twice before.

"Just…tell me," I said.

"Don't tell anyone," she pleaded.

"Tell anyone what?" I asked.

"Promise me you won't tell," she demanded.

"Okay! I promise not to tell. What is it?" I begged.

Silence, I heard a deep breath. She whispered, "Bobby Earl had sex with me!

"What? He did what?" I gasped.

"Please don't tell anyone," she implored. "He made me swear not to tell anyone," she confessed.

"April, he's like…18 years old!" I growled in anger.

"I – know," she shamefully admitted.

The manic darkness, the empty place when I screamed at my dad, was back again. Hurt, anger, and jealousy, hit me in my ear at the same time. After throwing me against the ropes, she picked me up and body slammed me with,

"And it wasn't the first time either!"

I grabbed the base of the phone, drew it back, ready to smash it into the wall. I wanted to be her first but we weren't ready. Well, at least one of us wasn't ready. Instead of smashing the phone, I groaned, "Why? Why?"

"Because I let him," she smugly replied.

"You did what?! Why'd you do that?" I asked in anguish.

"Because he's nice to me, he buys me little gifts; bracelets, necklaces, earrings. He says I'm not a little girl anymore," she confessed. She began to tell me about the acts…

"Stop, Stop!" I don't want to hear anymore. That's abuse!"

"He said it's not abuse if I let him."

"It's abuse, April! You should tell your mom. Or tell your cousin what he did."

"The last time was four months ago."

"I'm telling you, your cousin's boyfriend is a molester!" I don't care when he did it."

"It doesn't matter! They won't believe me anyway," she mumbled.

"Yes they will!"

"No – they won't. They love him more than they love me."

Quiet

"I'm sorry you feel that way."

"Me too," she said with a sniffle.

I couldn't talk anymore. My feelings were climbing the ceiling. We said our good-byes but not before she made me promise again not to tell anyone.

I hung up the phone. I lay in bed staring at the ceiling. I needed to calm down. Mama said when I got angry I should take deep breaths and count backwards from 20. Someone needed to know this guy had hurt my friend. It was dumb of me to make that stupid promise. I needed to calm down.

As I continued to lay there I thought about Doc and Carrie Faye. How he had abused her. Bobby Earl did the same to April. He paid her with little gifts instead of cash like Doc. I didn't want April to end up a hooker like Carrie Faye. Then… in a light bulb moment, I thought about myself. What if I grew up to be like Doc and Bobby Earl? Benny Lee and I joke about me being a perv but what if someday I grew up…? What made them do it? When they were young, were they over curious about girls…? No way! I would never be like those criminals. They hurt girls. I liked girls. They lied to them, deceived them. I would never do that.

I needed to leave the rocks. The sooner the better! I was constantly surrounded by pedophiles, drugs, crime, hurt, lose, and broken dreams. If it wasn't for my family and Benny Lee, I would have lost it! I was on life support and suicide watch at the same time. They kept me grounded, but it was hard. I didn't always buy into what they were selling. My Double-O status grew daily, whether I wanted it to or not. The rocks, my neighborhood, the jungle forced me to grow up fast. But my Double-O status had no reference in dealing with April's dilemma. I shouldn't have made that promise to her. The rain finally stopped. I needed to blow off some steam.

CHAPTER 21

THEY STRIKE
WITHOUT WARNING

I told Mama I was going over to Benny Lee's as I hurried out the back door. She never liked when I went over to Franklin Court. I moved quick but she didn't object; anything not to hear me yowl like a wild animal. I'm greeted by puddles, the canal in the street, time to car surf.

Heavy down-pours resulted in beaches in the low-lying areas for us hood rats. We took boards large enough to lie on, found a flooded street, and rode the waves made by the cars. I met up with Bennie Lee and the crew in front of the apartments.

"What's up? Are we going?" I asked.

"Yep, you got here just in time," Benny answered.

"Man, we thought you weren't gonna show," said Otis.

"I was on the phone when the rain stopped. I broke camp as soon as I saw it was clear."

Off came our sneakers, tied strings together, and looped them around a branch. We waded to our favorite spot.

"Booker is my name and car surfing is my game!"

We let out a booming Wolf Man yowl as we strolled down Franklin Street toward our surfing spot, between 11th and 12th Avenue, on 2nd Street.

"We need to hunt for new boards," Booker said.

"Ms. Vivian threw out some old paneling. I saw them on my way to the movies." Duke informed.

"Her house is on the way to our spot. Let's go!" Otis directed.

As we continued to wade through water, I asked Duke, "What movie did you see?"

"Godzilla vs. King Kong," he answered.

He told us about the big fight scene, acting out each blow. He told the best stories.

"Godzilla was spitting fire and shit at Kong. Kong was running, hiding and making weird noises; totally bitching out! Then Godzilla started baseball batting him with his giant tail. Kong played possum and while Godzilla was celebrating the win, Kong grabbed Godzilla's ass by the tail and threw him into the side of the mountain...Boom!" he shouted. "Boulders and shit fell, smashing Godzilla."

We were losing it laughing at Duke as we watch him pretend to be on WWF. He continued, "But Godzilla came back spitting that fire shit and kicked Kong into the rocks. But Kong realized the fire didn't burn anymore because the scientist had sprayed him with a protective coating. Then Kong went off!

Duke reached over and grabbed Benny Lee to act out the final scene.

"Kong gabbed that fire blowing dick, stuck a tree branch down his throat, head butted him, gave him a flying drop kick, ran over to him and gave him a full body slam...Voom!"

Tears were in our eyes from laughing so hard. Side stitches ached. The funniest shit ever! Then he stopped and looked away. We stopped laughing in anticipation.

Silence

More silence

We couldn't take the suspense any longer. Finally Booker screamed, "Who won?"

He slowly looked around at each of us. He let go of Benny's collar and said, "Neither. They both fell into the sea and drowned."

"Ah man!" We groaned as we got back to walking.

We argued over who we thought won the fight as we approached Ms. Vivian's house. We spotted the boards floating near the street curb. Duke, Booker, and I went after one. Benny Lee and Otis went for the other one. We worked to break the panels into equal parts large enough to surf on. As we continued our panel smashing Duke raised his head, looked toward me, and softly said, "Joseph, don't move!"

In the hood you learn early, when someone of authority spoke, you listen! It could be a matter of life or death. So I froze on Duke's command.

"Don't move!" he repeated.

The sternness of his voice spoke volumes. By now Booker is aware of the situation. I looked at him. He gasped and shook his head. Although my lower body was frozen, I managed to turn my head to look back. There, four inches away from my heel was a gigantic scorpion on the board I was standing on. His tail curled upward, waiting to strike.

"Oh No! I'm gonna die!" I said as I turned back to Booker.

Duke knew if I tried to run, I would step back onto the venomous tail with my barefoot. Sweat beaded on my forehead. Suddenly I had to pee. Duke picked up a brick and started toward me.

"Stay still," he ordered.

He circled behind me.

"Hurry Duke, please!" I begged.

I peeked back as Duke brought the brick down full force, "Splat!"

"Oh Shit!" I shouted as I ran forward. "What the fuck man!" I yelled hopping around ringing my hands.

My reaction got the attention of Benny Lee and Otis who were 20 feet to our right.

"It's over. Calm down." Booker tried to settle my nerves.

Benny Lee and Otis came over.

"What's wrong?" Benny asked.

"Where is it? Where is it? Is it dead?" I squirmed.

Benny Lee and Otis were clueless. They looked at me and back at each other.

"Chill out! It's dead. I killed it," Duke said.

"Killed what?" Otis asked.

"There was a large scorpion about to sting Joseph," Booker announced.

Benny Lee's and my eyes met. Paler than normal, I was mute! I could only nod.

"It's dead. Come see for yourself," Duke invited.

He led us to where the scorpion laid, flatter than a pancake.

"Are you alright?" Benny asked.

"You sure it didn't sting you?" Otis inquired.

"I'm okay. It didn't sting me," I reassured them. "Thanks Duke. Thanks Booker for saving me!"

"What are you thanking me for? I didn't do anything. It was all Duke," Booker squealed.

"Well...at least you didn't get in the way," I joked to relieve the tension.

The crew began to laugh.

"What are you trying to say Joseph?" He asked in disgust.

"I'm just kidding Book," I answered

"You wouldn't be joking if that damn scorpion had stung your ass would ya? Nope, we'd be 911ing your monkey ass to the hospital," he stated sarcastically.

With the crew still laughing I conceded. "You're right Booker. You're right," I said with a chuckle.

"Nah... nah. What does he mean by that Duke?" he asked.

"Why did you get him started?" Duke moaned.

Booker was a little self-conscious. I could relate! He also over thought everything. His buttons were easy to push. I wasn't trying to piss him off. Things escalated when the guys laughed. That ticked him off.

"Kinda like some of your classmates pushing my buttons, huh?" I asked Duke.

"Exactly... both of you need to grow up," he barked.

As we went back to work on the boards I felt Booker's heart. It was in my hands. My nervous energy caused me to make fun of him.

"Hey, Booker," I called out loud.

Everyone stopped, looked toward me; waited for me to continue with the jokes.

"What – now," he asked somberly.

I spoke loud enough so everyone could hear me.

"Hey man, I'm sorry...I didn't mean anything by it."

He looked up at me, glanced around; everyone was watching. He looked back at me and said in a low voice,

"It's cool."

I looked over at Duke. He gave a slight smile and a nod. I apologized to Booker in front of everyone. I didn't have to, but I needed to; for the both of us. I really didn't mean anything by the comment. But I could feel his pain. I knew it all too well. The other guys razzed him all the time. I guess he didn't expect that from me. He needed some respect. I tried to give him some earlier by thanking him. Unfortunately, he walked into the comment. My apology gave him his pride back, the Rules of Engagement. We quickly went back to work.

Boards completed, we headed for our surfing spot. It was near Robert's house. The water there was usually 2 1/2 feet deep. So deep we helped several drivers push their stalled cars to safety.

To body surf, we waited for a car to drive through the water. In a mad rush we ran from the shallow waters, dove onto your board, and rode the waves as far as we could. It was dangerous as cars drove through behind us. There was also oncoming traffic and cars turning in from the side streets. Motorist gave us a hard time.

"Get out the road, you little shits! Go home! It's too dangerous! Take your bad asses home before you get hurt!" they shouted.

As they drove pass we'd jump into the middle of the street with our middle fingers exposed. Their mirrors delivered our message. We knew they wouldn't get out in two feet of water to give chase. If it was a car I recognized, I didn't participate.

When it came my turn to surf, instead of diving on my board and riding the waves, I dove out and grabbed the bumper of the car. I held on with one hand and gripped my board with the other. I sailed like a boat. The crew cheered as if I just scored a touchdown! When I finally let go they rushed me, piled on, and under I went. We laughed and cheered as we walked back to our starting point. After my surf, everyone attempted to grab the car bumper to ride the waves longer. The scene was a far cry from an hour earlier when a poisonous arachnid threatened my life. We were the FCC Crew. Dark Angel moments didn't dampen our spirits. Mama always said, "God takes care of babies and fools!" Well, we weren't babies....

After two hours of our water games, we'd had enough, homeward bound. I thought of Robert. He lived only a half block from where we were. But I couldn't leave the crew. It wouldn't be right. Besides, there was no way his mom would allow him to play in dirty canal water. With board in hand, we marched on.

"You think Batman can beat the Green Hornet?" Booker asked.

"The Green Hornet would just shot him!" Duke answered.

"You think the Green Hornet can beat James Bond?" I asked.

"Oh no, there he goes into Bond mode again!" Benny joked.

"You guys know Bond will beat the Green Hornet," I insisted.

"All I know is Kato will kick the brains out all three of them at once!" Otis bragged.

We laughed. They all agreed, except me, that Kato was better. We hid the boards in the bush behind Betty's; tired and hungry, we trudged onward. Upon arrival at the tree we climbed up to retrieve our sneakers. As we descended we made plans for the next day.

"Let's spear eels tomorrow," Duke suggested.

"Don't forget to bring a fork and a stick to make your spear," Benny reminded.

"I have church in the morning. I'll catch up with you guys in the afternoon," I said.

"Catch you tomorrow." Benny said in parting.

"Yep, be good man. See you tomorrow." I hollered back crossing Franklin.

After I got across the street, the scorpion popped into my head. His venomous stinger ready to strike, end me. I couldn't get it out of my mind. I didn't tell my family. They'd freak out. I took a shower, ate and laid down on the sofa.

"Are you okay?" Mama asked.

"I'm okay. I'm just tired," I answered.

Mama could always read me. She suspected something but didn't persist. Thank goodness! If I had told her about the scorpion she would've grounded me for life!

I didn't get much sleep. I wrestled with the scorpion and April. I knew I promised not to tell, but I couldn't allow Bobby Earl to hurt her any longer. I said a prayer for her in church. I wanted to tell Benny Lee about April, but what could he do? I decided to tell Lavelle. He and her brother Mark were friends. I thought if I told Lavelle he would tell Mark, and Mark would tell their mom. After dinner I told Lavelle I needed to talk with him.

"Come with me outside for a minute," I requested.

We walked silently about half way to the street before I turned to face him.

"What do you have to tell me?" he asked.

"You and Mark are friends, right?"

"Yes, but you know that. Is this about Mark?"

"No, it's about his sister, April."

"What about her?"

"She... needs our help."

"And why do you think she needs help?" he inquired.

"Bobby Earl, her cousin's boyfriend...is having sex with her!" I squealed.

Lavelle grabbed me by my shoulders and shook me.

"How do you know this?" he asked.

"She told me. That's how!" I confessed.

"You better not be lying!" he warned with a finger in my face.

"Why would I lie about something like that? She made me promise not to tell anyone.

You're the only person I've told. Will you tell her brother?" I pleaded.

"I'll definitely tell Mark. I always thought Bobby Earl was slime. Now I know he's not only slime, he's a molester as well. Don't tell anyone else, no one!" He demanded.

"I won't. I swear," I assured.

The heaviness was gone. I felt lighter. I was glad I told someone who could help her. I was confident her brother would tell their mom. I'd probably lose April as a friend, but I didn't care. I didn't want her to get hurt again. If I needed help, April would have done the same for me. If I were in trouble, she'd find someone to help me.

I missed April at school the next week. I asked Lavelle about her. He said,

"She went to live with her grandparents in Manopa for a while. They'll get her the help, counseling she needs."

He also said Bobby Earl had to break up with April's cousin or April's mom would report him to the police. Shit! I wanted that bastard locked up. But at least my friend was far away and he couldn't hurt her anymore. Lavelle told me not to ever speak of it again, ever.

In the jungle predators came in all shapes, sizes, ages, and colors. So did bullies. They struck without warning. Their sting, bites, or blows; damaging, even deadly.

CHAPTER 22

PREPARE FOR BATTLE

The Christmas season was upon us. Our tree twinkled in the living room. My skin still tingled in its' presence. The enchanting glow...my magic carpet; sailed me away. I placed my yearly holiday order: a basket and a ball. I was hooked on hoops. But it was difficult practicing on the rocks; too much time lost chasing the ball. I was frustrated until I talked with Lavelle. He said,

"Bend your knees more when you dribbled. That will keep your hand closer to the ball. Then you can control the ball better when it bounced off the rocks."

Success achieved. Lavelle was my personal hoop tutor. My gym teacher, Mr. Daniels, taught me how to shoot a layup and foul shots. The library book also assisted in my evolution. Before the winter break Mr. Daniels announced, "Tryouts for the school basketball team will start after we come back from Winter Vacation."

We had the best team in the league the year before. I wanted to try out but told no one. I knew if I was going to make the team I had to improve my outside shot. My pole, basket at home wasn't the official height. I practiced often at McKenzie.

Sometimes, when I arrived at McKenzie, older boys were there playing 5 on 5 pickup games. When play was at one end of the court I took shots at the basket on the other end. Dribble moves practiced on the sidelines. The older kids would invite me to play with them when they needed another player. That helped the most, like being in an advance class. They gave me pointers every game. Those guys weren't my haters. They wanted me to succeed. My haters didn't play sports.

I couldn't keep it a secret forever. I finally told Benny I was trying out for the team. And of course, he told the rest of the crew. Mama knew because she signed the permission form but I asked her not to tell anyone, just in case I didn't make it. But she secretly told Jeanie to pray that I make it and Jeanie told my brothers to pray as well...some secret, huh?

Well, the final day of tryouts was over. Mr. Daniels congratulated the participants on four good days of hard work. He proceeded to say,

"I'll post the names of those that made the team on the door of the equipment room tomorrow. The list will be posted at the end of the day. Team practice will start on Monday."

I was too nervous to sleep. All I thought about was what would I say to everyone if I didn't make it? I had worked so hard to improve. I wanted to make Lavelle proud of me. He was the best athlete around. I secretly wanted to be like him in basketball. I didn't say much in school all day. I gave fake smiles to the guys' jokes at lunch. Benny Lee knew I was worried but gave no pep talk. He gave me my space, choosing instead to give me a "cornball look", a smirk and a nod of approval. They made me smile, a real smile for a moment.

After school I did a "Dead man walking" stroll toward the equipment room. Benny Lee caught up to me.

"What do you think?" he asked.

I raised my shoulder, brows, and slightly shook my head. As to say, I don't know.

We were joined by Elijah and Booker on my death march. A crowd of kids was gathered in front of the door.

"I can't do it..." I said. I turned to Benny. "You go Benny. See if I made it."

Benny knocked kids aside as he made his way to the front. He looked at the list. His back was to us for what seemed like forever.

"Shoot, I didn't make it," I grumbled.

Putting his hand on my shoulder Elijah said, "Don't doubt yourself."

Benny finally turned back toward us, smirked and shouted for the world to hear, "Joseph Graham, #5 on the list!"

"See, I told you not to worry," Elijah encouraged shaking my shoulder from behind.

"That's awesome bro, Congrats!" Booker said with a pat on my back.

"Don't jive me man. Am I really on there?"

"Come see for yourself."

I worked my way through the crowd,

"Excuse me, excuse me!"

"Check it out brutha-man," he said as he stepped aside.

I started at the top and there it was, in black and white, Joseph Graham at #5. I turned to Benny and smiled. I didn't want to celebrate in front of the kids that didn't make it. But Benny didn't care. He hugged my shoulders, gave me nuggies on my head, and shouted,

"You did it! You made it. Give me some skin."

We slapped five and started for home. The crew asked me a ton of questions. When will the games start? What jersey number will I choose to wear? Will the school give me new sneakers? My friends were as excited as I was. At one point the joy over took me.

"I made it! I made it!" I shouted as I stopped and bounced on my toes.

"Ah Joseph... you found that out about 10 minutes ago," Elijah said in his calm manner.

"I know Lijah but I'm so happy! I need a piggyback ride!"

I jumped on Elijah's back.

"Yee Haw! I made the team!" I shouted while riding his back.

The crew, now joined by Otis began to laugh and chant, "Joseph! Joseph! Joseph!

"Get off my back you fool," Elijah chuckled.

I climbed down. I confessed how much I wanted to make that team. It was the first sports team I had tried out for. Mr. Daniels kept only 12 of the 31 kids that tried out.

I told my family the night before about the list being posted. When

I walked into the house everyone was there except Daddy. He didn't get home from work until 5:30 pm. I couldn't believe it. No one said anything when I walked in. They only stared. Finally Lavelle broke the silence.

"Well?" He asked in anticipation.

Silence

I squinted as I looked around at them. I turned my mouth to one side and said,

"I made it!"

I was mobbed by my family!

"I knew you could do it!" Lavelle said as he put me in a headlock and gave me nuggies.

"Good job, little bro!" Casey congratulated with a pat on the back.

"Congratulations Joseph! Jeanie said with a hug and a kiss on the forehead.

Mama broke into song as she entered from the kitchen carrying a cake!

"This little light of mine, I'm gonna let it shine," she sang.

My siblings joined her in song. It was one of the happiest moments of my life. I wanted to cry but I wouldn't allow myself. I hugged Jeanie as they sang. Mama lit the one candle on top of the cake. That moment made up for all the birthday parties I never had.

"Congratulations baby! Blow out the candle," Mama said.

"Thanks Mama," I said with a hug.

I blew out the candle to cheers. Mama made my favorite cake, the one with strawberry jelly for icing. Lavelle brought the milk to the table and the celebration began; cake before dinner. That was one of the best days ever!

"Joseph, you prepare for war during peace time!" Jeanie warned.

"What?" I sighed

"If an army trained its' troops after the war has begun they would lose every time! No, they train the troops when there's no war. Once war is declared they are ready at a moment's notice for battle. This gives an army or team a better chance of winning. Last night you said if you made the team the games would start in three weeks, right?" She asked.

"Right."

"You have three weeks of peace time before your battles begin. You must work hard in practice so you'll play well in the games! Tell your teammates to do the same," she encouraged.

"Amen!" "Here, here!" Casey and Lavelle approved Jeanie's advice.

I expected my brothers to give me the pep talk. Instead it was my sister who did the honors. Jeanie never played sports but was second only to Mama in knowledge and insight. Whenever Casey wanted to get smart and override Jeanie, she'd say, "Quiet, I used to give you a bath." Bam! Shut him down!

"I promise I'll work hard. I want to be good. I also want to win!" I announced.

CHAPTER 23

GUILT BY ASSOCIATION

Three weeks went by fast. I worked hard in practice as Jeanie suggested. Mr. Daniels had to tell me several times to ease up. I took charges, dove for loose balls, all on the concrete court. I was used to it. I learned to play the game on rocks! Skinned knees were a part of the game. No one got an easy layup on me either, a hard foul every time... lesson learned from the older kids.

I was in a fog the day of our first game. My focus meter bounced like a ball. My mind swirled in space as the teacher spoke. At lunch, I sat next to Benny Lee, staring into my milk carton.

"Are you okay?" Benny asked.

"I'm okay. I'm hyped about our first game today."

"Calm down. You'll do fine. The guys and I are coming to the game."

"You are? Yo, thanks guys," I said scanning the table.

My legs pumped underneath like fingers on a typewriter. I couldn't stop them. I had earned the position of starting point guard. My job was to set up the team and run all the offensive plays. I was also named team co-captain. I had a lot of responsibility but I wasn't afraid. I had played with much older and better kids. I was just anxious to show what I could do.

The opponent was J.C. Shelton, a neighboring school. We had only four teams in our league. The white schools had eight teams in theirs. They wouldn't let the black schools join their league, and of course, none of them wanted to join ours. That was how it worked in the Deep South. Blacks had only half of what the whites had, but Society said, "Make it work!" I had half of the Black's half and was told, "Make it work". My crew had half of my half and told the same thing.

Both teams were on the court for warm up. Mama and Lavelle had arrived. The crew was also in attendance. I wanted to do well. I wanted to show Lavelle how much I had improved. The crew was clowning around laughing, joking and calling my name. Without warning, the Hula Poolas walked underneath our basket! I thought, *"What are they doing here? They don't have a member of their crew on the team."*

They were there to cause trouble. It started as soon as they sat down. They began to make fun of the opposing team. The refs and Mr. Daniels warned them to cut it out or they had to leave. Butterflies circled in my stomach.

The ball was tapped and the game began. The crowd was deafening. I couldn't hear myself think. But we were prepared. Mr. Daniels brought a stereo and played loud music the last two practices. I couldn't believe how well my team played. We were up by 6 points at half-time. We were leading by10 points after three quarters. Mama was smiling. Lavelle and the crew cheered on each basket I scored. We won the game 32-24. The fans erupted into applauds and celebration. I scored 10 points on four made baskets and two foul shots.

The two teams lined up to shake hands in a show of good sportsmanship. As I went through the hand shake line I spotted Lavelle in the crowd. He smiled, winked, and nodded. I winked, smiled, and nodded back. He made me feel ten feet tall! At the conclusion of the hand shake gesture I was mobbed by my crew. Elijah grabbed me in a bear hug and spun me around. We celebrated in grand style yelling, chanting, and giving our wolf man yowl in a circle. I caught Mama's eyes as we ballyhooed. Her smile had vanished. Mr. Daniels called the team together for a post-game talk and cheer.

On the way home Mama asked, "Who were those boys?"

"They're my friends and classmates. You know Benny Lee," I answered.

"Do all of them live in Franklin Court?" she inquired.

"Yes Mama, but they're good kids. We look out for each other," I replied.

I did my best to assure her my friends where okay kids. She continued,

"You watch your back around them," she warned.

Wow! I was shook. Where did that come from? Mama was spooky like that at times. She called it a "Long Seeing Eye." She said she could see into certain things. It scared the shit out of me and my siblings when she talked like that. But we always heeded her warnings!

"I will Mama," I reassured her.

She cautioned, "An association brings assimilation!"

"What does that mean?"

"When you hang around people you start to act like them," she explained.

Boom! Mama just dropped the mic. She shut me down completely! Her words had never been truer.

At school the next day I received nothing but love from the students and the teachers. Even the custodians spoke my name when I walked past them. My mind was made up. I would work hard and win a basketball scholarship to attend college. I would use the game to help me fulfill my promise to Mama.

Around 9:30 am, I was called to the front office. I thought, "Wow! The Principal wants to show me love too, awesome." When I arrived at the front office the crew was there.

"What are you guys doing here?" I asked.

"I guess you didn't hear?" Otis said.

"Hear what?"

"You better tell him Benny. I'm too ticked off," he growled.

Booker and Elijah sat clenched lipped. They looked angrier than a swarm of bees on a hot day.

"You better sit down. You're not going to like it," Benny warned.

"What's going on?" I asked with bated breath as I took a seat.

"Last night after the game someone spray painted our tag, "FCC" on the bleachers and at one corner of the basketball court. The maintenance men reported it to Principal Johnson. She's been interviewing kids all morning. She knows those letters are our tag. She called us down here to find out which one of us did it," he summarized.

"Which one did it? Did any of us do it?" I inquired in a slightly raised voice.

"No! We left shortly after you and your mom. There were parents and players still here taking pictures when we left," he explained.

"Well who did it? We don't tag things. Duke would have a fit. So who did?" I asked.

"Take one guess?" Booker offered.

"You've got to be kidding me?" I replied.

"Nope, we're not. It had to be them," Benny disclosed.

"I'm going to punch their faces in!" I growled.

"There won't be anything left for you after I'm done with them. I going to catch each one of them and beat the living shit out of them," Otis promised.

The secretary cleared her throat.

"Just leave Rosco for me. I owe him an ass whooping for Lindsey," I whispered.

"Man, screw those punks. My mom's gonna kill me!" Elijah moaned.

"Ya'll know Duke won't let us fight them! Especially, since we have no proof they actually did it," Benny reminded us. "He's always defending them dicks."

Benny was right. They did it but we had no proof. As a crew we decided not to rat on the Hula Poolas to Principal Johnson. We had no evidence of their guilt anyway. All we could do was proclaim our innocence. Mr. Daniels was paged to the front office. The crew looked over at me. I shook my head in disgust. He walked in, looked at me, and kept moving. When he gave me that look, I knew I was toast.

I'm the first of the crew to be called into the Principal's Office. She knew I couldn't have done it because I played in the game. Everyone saw me leave with my mom. But Mrs. Johnson and Mr. Daniels had devised a plan. They believed one of my crew members did it and wanted me to snitch. They got angry when I wouldn't give them a name. No crew member gave up the other. Even if we did it, we'd never snitch on each other.

We were sentenced to three after school detentions, during which time we had to clean up the paint. Mr. Daniels gave me a one game suspension. I wasn't allowed to go to practice while serving the detentions. We were also ordered to help the custodians clean the bath rooms. At 8:00 am that day, I was a god! My light was finally shining. For once I felt hope. But by 10:00 am I was a criminal, Vandalizing School Property was the official charge. In two hours I had gone from "Sugar to Shit!" My light, my shine taken, and I had nothing to do with it. I was disciplined for running with my crew.

Elijah was right. This wouldn't go over well at home. I never got in trouble at school. I didn't want to hear my dad. Even if Mama and Lavelle vouched for me, he would grumble and gripe anyway. He didn't want any negative reports from school. One of his favorite lines "You go to school to learn, not act like a fool!" Mama would be angry as well. The boys she warned me about were named in the vandalism with me. Excuse the pun and redundancy, but that "Shit really stunk!" I was screwed and EVERYONE knew I was innocent! The Hula Poolas ran their game on us, got us good. They stole my moment.

After processing the intel I came up with a plan. The telephone at my house was turned off. Principal Johnson couldn't call my parents. She'd have to send them a letter. That could take a day or two. Our mail was delivered to the post office. It could take another two days before the letter was picked up from the mailbox. My practice and game schedule was on the refrigerator. No one would know I was serving detentions. They would think I'm at practice. Lastly, my next game was away. My family told me they would only attend my home games. If I could get to the following week without my parents finding out, I would be in the clear. But I still needed to intercept that letter to be safe.

A week went by. No word from my parents about the detentions. They didn't ask and I didn't tell! I had served the detentions and was back playing on the team. We went on to win the league championship.

In late April a banquet was held in the school cafeteria in our honor. The cheerleaders were invited as well. Awards were given. I had waited for that moment for some time. I received my first trophy! Casey and Lavelle had a bookshelf full of them. Now I could add mine to the family collection.

I floated on air as Mama and I walked home. My feet hadn't touched the ground since Mr. Daniels gave me that trophy.

"Congratulations Joseph! You and your team did well this year," Mama applauded.

"Thanks Mama. I had a great time playing. All my teammates were cool too. Someday I hope to win a scholarship and play basketball in college," I confessed.

"Now you're talking! Keep thinking like that. You can do anything if you put your mind to it," she encouraged.

"Like Lavelle when he's running over people trying to score a touchdown," I added.

"It's the same when he plays basketball too! He's so stubborn, determined not to let anyone stop him. It's part of his gift; determination and will," she proclaimed.

"What are my gifts Mama?" I asked.

She paused, looked at me, and said,"Your gifts are passion and compassion. You are driven by wonderment; excitement, passion. You also see the good in people! You want them to do right by each other. You must be very careful with your gifts. Continue to use them for good. They could be easily drawn to the dark side. Oh by the way, a letter came from Principal Johnson some time ago," she divulged.

No! I had forgotten to intercept the letter. There I was learning the meaning of my life according to Mama's "Long Seeing Eye", hoping she would tell me the great things I would do in the future. Then paw! Out of the blue I was struck with a blow harder than Ali hit Liston. She stopped, turned to me and asked, "Why didn't you tell me?"

"I knew you would get angry and Daddy would hit the roof. Plus I didn't do it. I couldn't have done it. I played in the game that day. Everyone saw me," I recalled.

"I know you didn't do it! Remember, I was at that game too. We walked home together"

"They thought my friends did it. But they didn't. Another group of kids did it," I squealed.

"Who did it?" she asked.

"A group of kids that run around with Jonny T," I ratted.

"Why didn't you tell the Principal?" she inquired.

"We had no proof. But they had no proof my friend did it either. Jonny T and his friends were at the game. They were the kids making fun at the other team. They're nothing but trouble makers," I explained.

"Well, I know you didn't do it. That's why I didn't tell your father about the letter. But you still should've told us. You know you can talk to us about anything. We always want to hear your side of the story first," she comforted.

"I know I should've told you. I'm sorry. It won't happen again."

"It better not!" she warned.

"Mrs. Johnson and Mr. Daniels knew I didn't do it. They told me so themselves. They wanted me to give up my friends. But my friends didn't do it. So they became angry and gave me a discipline as well. I was blamed for something I didn't do all because I pal around with my friends from Franklin Court. That made no sense to me at all," I complained.

She grabbed my shoulders and turned me to her. Facing each other she said,

"Son, don't forget this. You're known by the company you keep! In other words, make good friends. Your friends can get you in trouble! You were innocent, but because you pal around with those kids, you were found guilty."

CHAPTER 24

RUN FOR YOUR LIFE

I didn't see much of the crew the second half of the school year. Basketball practice, homework and the games took up most of my time. Mr. Daniels also held Saturday practices. They were the key to us winning the championship. Rumor had it, none of the other schools held Saturday practices. Well, summer vacation had arrived. It felt good to chill with the crew again. No hunts, hustles, or adventures today. We were off to Fountain Park, named for the huge water fountain in the center of the playground.

Fountain Park was next to West Side High School, the only secondary school on the west side of the tracks. On the east side there was a Junior High and a High School. Once again, we were given half and told to make it work. I asked Jeanie, why was it that way?

Jeanie said, "They passed a law called, "Separate but equal."

Really! Equal! Where? In reality, it was just more bullying. Prove to me it wasn't.

The playground and West Side High was halfway between the Black Ritzy Community known as the Parks and the Townies of Franklin Street. Both were also one block away from the church I attend. The crew teases me every time we past Mount Union Church. They'd say things like,

"Hey Joseph, the Reverend's calling you." Or, "You better get in there and recite your Easter Speech!"

They always made some smart comment. I laughed it off. None of my crew attended church regularly. They only went on Christmas, Easter, and funerals. Although they joked with me about church, most wanted their families to attend more often. The subject came up several times in Crew Therapy Sessions.

Arriving at the playground we spread out to pass the football. The sun was high, a gentle breeze; the aroma of hotdogs on the grill; a ghetto fabulous day. We played a game of 2 on 2 Football with Duke as the all-time quarterback. Elijah had to babysit again. After our catch and run scrimmage, we migrated over to the basketball courts.

"Look who's on the far court," Benny announced.

We spied the court to find the Hula Poolas. Steam shot from my ears as I stomped and snorted. It was time for revenge.

"Let's get'em Duke," Otis pleaded.

"Why? They aren't bothering us," he answered casually.

"What do you mean? Those bastards cost me a game. Did you forget we got three detentions for the shit they pulled?" I fired back.

"Can you prove they did it?" he smugly asked.

Silence.

"Then stop your bitchin! To use your own words, "Let a sleeping dog lay." Besides, this is not the place for a rumble, too many people watching. The cops will be called for sure. I hate those guys just as much as you do," he said.

"Well, you have a funny way of showing it. You give those corn holes way too much respect," Benny firmly stated.

That took Duke by surprise. Benny Lee was his first cousin. He didn't expect Benny to come at him like that. But we had taken enough from those fake thugs. Every time we wanted to fight them Duke said no. Well, enough was enough! It was time for Duke to come clean with us; time for him to fess up or shut up.

"Okay Benny and the rest of you little dicks, you want to know why I won't rumble with them. Well for starters, one of us here can't fight his way out of a wet paper bag!" He barked and glared at Booker.

"Why are you looking at me bitch? You don't have to worry about me. I can protect myself!" Booker barked back.

"Yeah, what are you going to do? Tell some of ya jokes or try your double talk bullshit to make'em stop beating your face in? Well, that shit don't fly in a rumble. I don't want to see you get your face broken and I have to explain to your aunt how it happened," Duke countered.

"We got Booker's back!" Otis spoke up.

"Yeah, we got Book," the rest of us concurred and nodded.

"Okay you smart asses! You don't even know the rules of a rumble. It starts one on one with the two leaders squaring off first. That means I would have to fight Jonny T, my teammate! Now Mr. Big Words Joseph, since you played on a team, please explain to me how I can beat the shit out of my teammate then call him brother when we take the football field together?" he questioned.

"Then why did your teammate allow his crew to get us in trouble at school?" I countered.

"I asked him and Johnny T said he didn't know anything about it," Duke answered.

"Bullshit! He knew. That fucker probably put'em up to it," Benny fired back.

"Well Duke, you may not have to make a rumble invite. Looks like those pussies will invite themselves to an ass whoopin. Look whose coming over?" Otis alerted.

We turned to see the Hula Poolas coming our way. I channeled Ali instantly.

"Don't bitch out Duke! Teammate or not, kick his ass if he talks any shit," Benny insisted.

"Leave Rosco to me! I owe him two ass whoopins," I snarled.

"I'll take Jamal," Otis voted.

"Give me Leon," Benny chimed in.

"I got Mikey," Booker manned up.

"Stand and punch Book. Don't let him get you on the ground," Otis instructed.

"Got'cha!" Booker agreed.

"You guys are so stupid," Duke said with a headshake in disgust.

That was easy for him to say. He didn't clean toilets for three days after school! We each had our man marked, a before the bout stare down given as they approached. Here we go! Let's get ready to rumble.

"What's up Duke?" Johnny T greeted.

"What's up?" Duke answered.

"You guys want to play 5 on 5? We have a court on the far end," he invited.

I wanted to shout, "Hell Yeah!" But it wasn't my call. I bit my tongue and continued to stare down Rosco. Duke turned to us.

"You guys want to play?" he asked.

"Sure. Yep. Uh-huh!" we answered with vengeful eyes on the opposition.

This would be better than a rumble. We could get our shots in during the game without anyone calling the cops. Trust me neither crew would play by the rules. We must be on guard when they try to retaliate. We also needed to keep an eye on Booker. This was perfect! Duke could play nicey, nicey with his teammate while we got our revenge. I promised myself I would knock the taste out of Rosco's mouth the first chance I got.

As both crews walked to the far court to prepare for battle, "Dan the Man," in his rolling jukebox, turns into the park. His speakers were at 100. All heads turned. Dan was a local DJ who did house parties and school dances. He came to the playground often to start dance parties. As Dan pulled onto the grass, kids rushed toward his van. Within minutes his turntables was setup outside the van. Music littered the airwaves. Both crews fell victim to the soulful sounds. We zombie walked to join the crowd.

And just like that, without warning, our perfect chance to smash the Hula Poola's faces in was gone. I heard it said, music soothes the savage beast. Well, in this case, it did. When that beat dropped….

Kids came from all directions to dance and socialize. Some brought blankets to sit on and take in the sights and sounds. The older kids crowded the front near the speakers. A constant flow of cars paraded through Fountain Park, each driver drawn by the music, which could be heard all over the west side.

There were girls all over the place! At that moment, I wished I wasn't with my crew. I wanted to dance with this girl across from me. We had eyed each other from head to toe, twice. But, none of my crew liked to dance. And none would dare try while the Hula Poolas were around. So, I had to settle for talking to her. I went over and introduced myself. She asked if I wanted to dance. I lied. I told her I couldn't dance. I remembered Lindsey saying, "It can't be that great if you can't be your true self around them."

The music stopped. "DJ Dan" got on the mic.

"Quiet! Quiet! I have an announcement," he said.

He waited until the chatter calmed. He continued, "I was just told Mr. Roland slapped a black boy in his store about 10 minutes ago!"

The crowd gasped!

"Oh no, he didn't!" shouted the girl I was talking with.

Mr. Roland was the white owner of Roland's Super Market on Franklin Street. The store was a block from my house and a half block from Franklin Court. As fast as the playground filled it emptied. The same kids that ran to DJ Dan's van were now running at break neck speed toward Roland Super Market. The crew and I joined the race, sprinting to catch up. Cars burned rubber as they speeded toward Franklin Street. The kids unleashed their wrath of racist language as they ran full throttle. I had to keep pace. If I fell, I wouldn't survive the trampling.

When we arrived at the store it looked as if all of the west side had gotten the word. The mega crowd was yelling for Mr. Roland to come out and take it like a man. He had locked himself inside. He peeked out at the crowd from time to time through the glass door, which was now covered with paper. There were three cops standing in front of the doors. A small section of the crowd ran around back to the service entrance. They were met by three cops with hands on their guns.

I panned the scene to gather as much intel as possible. I noticed all the white owned businesses were closed. It was 3:30, prime time business hours on a Saturday afternoon. The buzz was they closed in fear of the crowd. Hundreds stood in protest. Cars detoured down side streets to avoid the scene.

The crowd grew restless. They shouted racist obscenities.

"Bring your white ass out here so we can slap you! Come on out here Cracker! Why did you hit Kerry you white devil!"

Ah, he slapped Kerry. I knew Kerry.

More cop cars arrived on the scene. One of the cars was Car 313! The crowd went berserk! Car 313 was one of the cars that patrolled the area. No one liked the officers in that car! They treated us like scum. Rude and very disrespectful they were. As the officers vacated car 313 rocks and bottles were thrown at them. Mr. Roland unlocked the door to let the officers inside.

"There you are! I've been looking all over for you," Casey yelled as he grabbed my upper arm. "Have you seen Lavelle?"

"No I haven't," I answered.

"Mama sent me to find you. Let's go!" he demanded.

"No! I want to see what's going on," I yelled, pulling my arm out of his grasp.

Pop! He smacked me in the back of my head with an open hand.

"I said, let's go!" he repeated

He spun me around by my arm and pushed me in front of him. Casey didn't talk much but I could tell I had pissed him off. So I complied and started walking. When we were half way home I asked,"Why did Mr. Roland slap Kerry?"

Casey explained, "My friend Debra said Roland accused Kerry of stealing. Kerry denied it. Roland told him he was lying and slapped him. Kerry ran across the street to Soul City Clothing Store where Debra works. He told them what happened. Mr. Burke, the white owner of Soul City told Kerry to call his mom. They locked the door and kept Kerry inside until his mom came to get him. Mr. Burke closed his store sensing trouble."

With that incident, race relations in Reservoir City dropped to an all-time low. The same was true across the country. Civil Rights leaders were assassinated by white gunmen. Racist Whites firebombed black homes and churches. There had been race riots in Detroit and Philadelphia. Blacks held Freedom Marches in the south. The Klan held rallies to intimidate, bully black protesters. White cops allowed their police dogs to bite black women and children while they spray black men with high pressure water hoses. Those stories headlined the news daily. My parents made me go to the bedroom when the horror show began. They tried to shield me from the ugliness of racism. I obeyed long enough to peek through the sheet hanging in the doorway to see the hatred unfold on national TV.

This was my life. Blacks in the south were humiliated every day with racial intimidation, bullied by whites. We were taught to say to them, "Yes Sir, no Sir. Yes Ma'am No Ma'am, while they called us degrading names. They treated us like little servants. We were taught not to look them in the eyes. They rubbed the heads of little black boys thinking it would bring them good luck. I hated it! It was so humiliating. They'd say,

"He's so cute. What's your name? How old are you? What grade are you in?"

They pretended to care but the entire time they talked they rubbed my head. When I got older I would shout,"Strangers don't touch!"

That startled them and they'd walk away.

Now Mr. Roland, a white man had slapped a little black boy! Knowing Kerry like I did, he probably did steal something. But that didn't give Roland the right to slap him. Armed with years of built up frustration and resentment, the community was ready to retaliate. Roland threw gasoline on a burning fire. The incident gave the community an excuse to go on a rampage against every white person in sight. That wasn't right either, but tempers were out of control.

As my family and I sat down for dinner, the chants from the crowd grew louder, "Freedom! Freedom! No justice, no peace! We shall not be moved!" As night fell, the crowd turned into an angry mob. White motorists felt their rage. Their cars were pelted with rocks, bottles, and bricks. They apparently didn't get the memo, "Don't go down Franklin Street!" We had a decent view of the street from our backyard but couldn't see Roland's Super Market. The neighbor's large trees blocked our view in that direction. My parents made Lavelle and me stay inside. Lavelle could lose his scholarship if he got involved. Mama knew my passion for excitement might cause me to leave their side, so she told

Lavelle to keep an eye on me. We watched from the bedroom window until my Double-O nature kicked in.

"I'm going to the roof," I told Lavelle.

"Don't! Daddy will beat you with the electric cord," he warned.

"No he won't! He never whips me," I boasted.

He thought for a second, smiled, and nodded in agreement.

"Okay, but hurry back. I don't want to get in trouble," he said.

I snuck out the front door, climbed onto the roof, and crawled to the back of the house. The rest of my family was standing in the backyard. They had no idea I was behind them. The roof was still warm from the afternoon sun. I crawled back about 10 feet as not to be seen by them. I had to sit on my butt to endure the heat. The roof offered a much better view than the window, but I still couldn't see the supermarket.

The mob darted around looting and destroying property along Franklin Street. Kaboom! A massive flash of light radiated through the trees, a loud roar from the mob. It came from the direction of the supermarket. Kaboom! This time flames shot skyward above the tree line. My Double-O meter couldn't take the suspense any longer. I crawled back to the front of the house, jumped down, and bolted toward Roland's.

Dashing through the field where the Tent Meetings were held, I neared the back of the small shopping plaza on the far end from the supermarket. Franklin Street resembled a war zone. From the wash house to the red light at 7th Avenue was on fire. The area lit as bright as day! All the white owned businesses were ablaze. Crash! The mob continued throwing fire bombs at stores and the police. It was a full scale riot. Oh the rush! I locked into Bond mode.

Thump...thump... thump, the rocking of an abandon car until finally it was pushed onto its roof; a game winning cheer from the crowd. Crack, a fire boom tossed into the car window, a mad scramble for cover by the mob. Baboom! The gas tank exploded sending the car airborne. All I needed was a bag of popcorn and a seat. Unbelievable for sure, but it was real.

Roland's Market was at the other end of the plaza. The end where

I stood was black owned and operated, out of the line of fire. I dared not go onto the street if I valued my life. I was secluded, undetected by the cops and robbers. Ironic; during all the violence I hid at the corner of a funeral home.

Flashing lights appeared in the sky behind me, a loud flapping noise above. A beam of light cut a path through the night sky. I turned to gather intel. Two helicopters descended 100 yards from me. The operators quieted the engines. A loud humming sound approached. I turned back to the street to find a huge army tank turning onto Franklin from 7th Avenue, the National Guard. The troops marched in line behind the weapon. Simultaneously turning onto 7th from the opposite direction were about 100 cops and canines plus the Korn County State Troopers. They fell in behind the Guard. I left the movie in a rush. I didn't want to see the ending. The rioters reign was over.

I ran home in a flash. Lavelle was at the front door waiting for me.

"Where have you been? Mama was just looking for you. I turned on the water and told her you were in the shower," he said.

"Thanks for covering for me but please get back inside," I begged.

"Why? What's going on?"

"There's a tank coming, the army, about 100 cops with dogs, and troopers. The rioters don't stand a chance."

I ran through the house to the back door to warn the rest of the family.

"Mama, Daddy, guys, please come inside. It's going to get bad!" I pleaded.

"How do you know?" Daddy asked.

I explained in about 15 seconds what I saw and ran back inside. I loved action but I had no desires to be beaten to death by the cops. I turned back to look through the screen door as the tank and the National Guard came into view. Mama, Daddy, Jeanie, and Casey rushed inside. Daddy closed and locked both storm doors. We watched the horror from the windows. Once again, Mama tried to shield me from the trauma, demanding that I go to the far bedroom. Of course she sent Lavelle with me. We weren't going to be denied our view of the action. We opened the screen part of the window wide enough to see Franklin Street. Gunfire, sirens, barking, explosions, resonated through the Quarters. It was official. Franklin Street had become a real war zone.

We closed the window and moved into the living room to watch the 11pm news. Mama stayed in the bedroom to pray. I watched the newscast from beneath the sheet once again. After Casey adjusted the antenna, there it was on TV; the fires, the tank, the Guard, the cops, State Troopers. The rioters were running to keep from being caught, beaten, and arrested. They showed the rioters being placed in the emergency vehicles. streams of blood covered their head, face, and clothes. There was little life left in them!

Two days later, after it was over, the final count; three dead, 54 injured, and 26 arrested. The white owned businesses in the area of Roland's were destroyed. White owned Ray's Groceries, which wasn't in the line of fire, was spared. Several cars rested on their roof tops. Others were burned beyond recognition. There was trash scattered everywhere. It looked as if someone dropped a massive bomb on the area. This was by far the worst thing I had witnessed in my life! The pungent odor of smoke, ash, burnt rubber and gasoline lingered. The anger and rage I saw from the crowd made me ask, "If blacks were in control would we practice the same racial hatred toward whites as they do toward us?" I didn't know. But what I did know was, racial anger and hatred lived on both sides of the railroad track.

After being shut in for two days as looters were chased, beaten, and arrested, I was wound tight. Once the streets were cleared, it was time to find my crew to see if all were okay. I caught up with them in front of O'Dell's.

"Glad to see all you pussies in one piece," I greeted.

"Man it's been crazy around here the last couple of days," Benny said.

"Man… when I saw shit blowing up, I thought you bitches were a goner," I joked.

"Nah man…I saw'em throw a fire bomb through Roland's window… blew the whole damn roof off that sucka," Benny said.

We laughed.

"Yo, that must have been what I saw through the trees from my house. Fire shot up like a 100 feet!" I added.

"Yep, my dad and I were standing in front of the apartments watching. But when he saw that tank coming down Franklin he said, "What the fuck! It's time to get inside," Benny joked in his dad's voice.

We continued laughing.

"I was watching the youngins when my mom ran inside screaming! Said she heard bullets whizzing past her head when the cops started shooting. One missed her by inches!" Elijah reported.

The laughter stopped.

"Man, I saw the worst beat downs. I was coming back from the soda machine at the beauty shop. I looked across the street to see a cop's dog tackle this guy. Within two seconds, the cop jumped on the man's back and beat him to the ground with his night stick. He must have hit him 20 straight times; in the head, on his back, shoulders, arms, all over!" Otis squirmed.

"Yo man, that's crazy. I hope he didn't die. Hey, where's Duke?" I asked.

"He went to work with his dad," Benny confirmed.

"Here comes Booker," Otis announced.

Booker came toward us with his head down kicking stones.

"Hey Book! What's up?" Benny greeted.

"What's up Book? We all echoed.

"What's up?" He answered with his head hung low.

"What's wrong Book?" Benny asked.

With his head still down, he answered, "Did you hear about the three guys that was killed?

His voice starting to crack, he continued, "Well...one of them was my favorite cousin, Malik. He was only 18.

He could hold back the tears no longer. He sobbed openly. We put our arms around him. We tried to console him as we walked toward the creek. A Crew Therapy Session needed to decompress. To process what we all had witnessed, endured in our neighborhood.

We sat on the bank flipping rocks into the creek. We rambled on about what we saw, heard, and witnessed during the riot. We cried with Booker over the death of his cousin, Malik.

"They didn't have to kill him. The people that saw it said all Malik had was a brick in his hand. When the cop called to him, he ran. The cop ran after him with a police dog. He let the dog go. The dog tackled Malik, and the cop jumped on top of him and started beating him everywhere: the head, back, face, arms…everywhere. He died in the hospital from the injuries. He was my favorite cousin," Booker cried as Elijah hugged him.

Benny Lee, Elijah, and I cut our eyes over to Otis. He looked back. At that moment we all realized the beat down Otis saw was Booker's cousin Malik. Otis started to speak. I cut him off; afraid he would say something stupid.

"Book, man I'm sorry about your cousin. Those cops and state troopers went crazy! They chased people all through the Quarters too. Some of them were just watching, not participating in the riot, and they got a beat down for nothing too," I offered.

Otis tried to speak again, Elijah spoke louder, "Yeah Book, they were shooting at my mom, and she hadn't done nothing either. Two bullets flew past her head as she was running home from the front of the apartment."

As Elijah spoke Benny Lee and I gave Otis that look. You know the one. That look your parents give you when they want you to shut your pie hole or they'll smack you silly. When Elijah was done Benny Lee spoke. Elijah joined me in a stare down of Otis. We also gave him a slight side to side head shake as if to say, "Don't say anything about what you saw." Otis could be crass, insensitive at times and we all knew it. This was not the time for jokes or put downs.

Benny Lee said, "Book, your cousin was an alright guy, everybody liked him. I bet it was Car 313. Those dicks are always dissing black people. They're supposed to help you not hurt you,"

"At first all my relatives thought the same thing. It was a cop from Car 313. But police Car 313 doesn't carry a K-9 dog," Booker told us still looking down drawing in the sand with a stick.

And he was right; Car 313 didn't carry a K-9. Three sets of eyes turned to Otis. They said *if you fuck this up you will get punched!* He got the message. Otis offered his sympathy,

"I'm sorry too, Book. Your cousin was a good guy. He never hurt nobody."

Elijah, Benny Lee, and I nodded and smirked slightly at Otis. He nodded back. Booker perked up a little.

"Thanks guys. I don't know why these white people have to come in our part of town and start trouble. If Mr. Roland would've slapped Kerry my cousin would still be alive," Booker said as he stood. We stood with him.

"Yep, you right, uh-huh," we agreed with Booker as we brushed the sand from our clothes. We walked Booker home and parted ways.

A few days later a vicious rumor was spread about Don's BBQ Shop. Don's shop was one of two white owned businesses still operating on the west side. Because of its' downtown location it wasn't targeted during the riot. Don had the best ribs in three counties. It was the Friday night hangout after West Side High sporting events. The shop was the Saturday night spot before and after the movies. People came to Don's for his famous ribs and "Foot Long Hotdogs." The rumor was: Don was selling road kill.

My gag reflex wouldn't stop when I heard the rumor. I didn't believe it, but I felt sick anyway. I loved Don's food as did most in Black Town. The rumor spread like wild fire, "Don's BBQ Shop was selling Road Kill!" Although the rumor was never proven it was enough to damage Don's business beyond repair. He closed a few weeks after the rumor began. Discrimination lived on both sides of the tracks.

It had been a month since the riot, and still no charges had been filed against Mr. Roland. The neighborhood organized a march to protest the treatment of blacks in Reservoir City. They also wanted to protest the lack of good wage paying jobs, poor housing conditions, and better schools in the black community. The march was designed to shed light on the racism and discrimination that existed in our city. Reverend Samuels, the pastor of my church, would lead the march.

My parents chose not to participate. Instead, they stood road side with signs in support of the protest. My siblings prepared for the march. Mama didn't want me to march. She said I was too young and excitable.

"Please Mama! I promise I won't run away from the family," I begged.

"No!" She stated.

"But there are other kids from my school marching. Why can't I?" I protested.

"There could be trouble. I can't risk it," she replied with arms folded.

I dove onto the sofa and buried my face in a pillow. Casey was in the hallway between the two bedrooms. He heard my plea. Seeing my disappointment he vouched for me.

"I'll keep an eye on him Mama," he offered.

Fighting back the hurt I raised my head from the pillow and look back at Casey. He continued, "I'll keep him by my side the whole time," he stated.

"Don't play with me Casey! Don't let anything happen to my baby!" she demanded.

"I won't let anything happen to him. And he hasn't been a baby for some time now," he answered with a smile.

The rest of the family laughed as they joined us in the living room. My lips were sealed.

"I don't care what you say. He's still my baby and don't you let anything happen to him," She smirked.

"I won't. I promise. Get dressed Joseph," he ordered.

With a resuscitated heart, I sprang from the sofa.

"Thanks Casey!" I whispered walking into the bedroom.

"Just make sure you stay at my side the entire march," he demanded.

"I will. I promise," I assured.

Mama knew Casey was responsible, reliable. If I strayed, he'd find me and smack me around good. She trusted Casey to look after me.

We prepared for the march. My sibling and I put on African attire. We donned ourselves in African shirts, hats made of Kente cloth, and other African garb. The African flag waved across my T-shirt. Afros picked as high as possible, we were ready to go.

We arrived at Mt. Union Baptist Church at 12:30 pm, nearly 150 people had gathered. The march was scheduled to start at 1:00 pm. Over 500 protesters were expected! We were given signs and our lineup position. We waited with the crowd in the shirt soaking heat. Robert and Matt were in the crowd. Robert was with his mom and two older brothers. Matt was three rows in front of Robert. He stood next to his older brother. Booker had arrived with his aunt and uncle. They were moved to the front. He told the crew his family would help lead the protest since his cousin was one of the killed in the riot. Kerry and his family were also moved to the front. Reverend Samuels raised the blow horn. He greeted the crowd and proceeded to announce why we were there and the etiquette to follow during the march.

"We want a peaceful march. If the police attempt to harass you, stay calm!" he instructed. "Let's show them we're not the problem, they are!"

He went over the March route and told the crowd to move into position. I stood between my brothers. Jeanie was to the left of Casey. I was elated to be there with my family as we prepared to protest the injustices. But inside I was torn. I thought to myself, *do I belong here? Am I black enough? No one has ever offered me "Five on the black-hand side." Could I sing, 'Say it Loud, I'm Black and I'm Proud'?" Or did they see me as Casper, Kimba, or Howdy Doody?*

I looked to my right to find Robert. We smiled and nodded to each other. He was singing away. Why couldn't I do that? I looked the part. I was all spruced up in my African attire. My curly afro stood tall. But the truth was…the bullying had affected my ability to express my blackness. I looked to my left at Jeanie. Her skin was lighter than mine, but she sang louder than most. Lavelle looked over at me.

"Why aren't you singing, Mr. Chorus?" he chuckled.

We laughed. I slowly began to sing, "Say it Loud, I'm Black and I'm Proud." We sang that and other songs until we reached the front of what was once, Roland's Super Market.

I had never felt so black before. Knowing you're black is one thing. Feeling black is another. I knew I was black. My mom was black with light skin. My dad was black with brown skin. Look, I wasn't stupid. I knew I had white blood in me. So did my siblings.

It came from my mom's side of the family. Her grandfather was white and married a light skinned black women; one of those that could pass for white. Her dad married a light skinned black woman as well. My siblings and I had Indian blood too. It came from my dad's side of the family. His mother was a full blood Creek Indian who married a brown skin black man. We are black! I am black! That I knew.

But knowing and feeling are two different things! Knowing, knowledge comes from your head. It's what you've been taught. Feelings come from your core, your heart. Therefore, feeling black comes from within. It's the acceptance of knowing you're black. That acceptance allows you to freely express your blackness. The bullying had affected my ability to feel black. It interfered with my capacity to freely accept and express who I was. The wounds of bullying went to that place Mama always told me to protect, my heart. It wasn't fair. I was there to protest against the injustices white society casted down upon us as a people; all while facing some of those same injustices for my own black brothers. I couldn't win for losing.

We put the signs down as we stood in front of the ruins once known as Rolland's Super Market. We crossed our arms and took the hand of the person next to us. We began to sing, "We Shall Overcome." We stood in solidarity against; racism, prejudice, bigotry, discrimination, the tools used to bully blacks. Not all whites used them, just a significant amount. Because of white bullying, Blacks weren't allowed to freely express their freedoms as Americans citizens. Their verbal beat downs and discriminatory practices made it hard to accept yourself as worthy individuals. It was double-painful for me as I fought some of those same battles within my own black community! So I began to sing to some of the very people I marched with.

Oh, oh, oh deep in my heart
I do believe

"I" shall overcome someday!

My siblings looked at me with the weirdest glare. I changed the words in the song from, "We Shall Overcome Someday" to "I Shall Overcome Someday." I gave no apology!

CHAPTERS 25

SHOE SHINE BOY

The March brought the community together but no charges were ever filed against Mr. Roland. They said it was Kerry's word against Mr. Roland. Although there were several witnesses to the slap, they would never get a chance to testify. Bullied! So Roland got away with it. The community got no justice for a white man slapping a black boy accused of stealing a piece of candy. Roland decided not to reopen the supermarket. No one saw him again.

The crew and I had to find a new hustle. Since the riot, no kids were allowed in White Town without a parent. So our mango hustle was over. We didn't sell soda bottles and hunt for coins anymore. Those hustles were good enough to buy kiddy stuff! Our wants and needs had grown with our age. We needed to make more to attend the movies, go roller skating, or buy the clothes we liked.

The crew was always two steps ahead of me. They were more street savvy. They showed me the ropes. I understood the crew did some things out of necessity. Me, well I was along for the ride, the thrill, the adventure. Don't get me wrong, I needed the money from the hustles as well. But I mainly tagged along for the camaraderie. I needed their friendship, acceptance. They didn't need mine! I brought nothing to the table except my loyalty and guts. It was my ticket into the group or so I thought. Duke often said, "Joseph, I have to hand it to ya, you got guts!"

He meant I was tough. They respected my courage. So I performed accordingly. They also protected me from their ultra-extreme capers. They often left the apartments without me. They didn't want me involved if they were caught. I'm sure it was Benny Lee who told them to leave without me. We vowed not to let anything bad happen to the other.

I met up with the crew in from of the apartments. They each had a strange looking box.

"What's that?" I asked.

They looked at each other and laughed. They did that often when I asked questions.

"What's so funny?" I asked with squinted eyes.

"Haven't you seen a shoe shine box before?" Duke chuckled.

Casey has a shoe shine box but it looked nothing like theirs'. He had the store bought kind he got from Goodwill. I continued the naive act to find out what was going on.

"No I haven't. How does it work?" I inquired.

They all shook their heads in disbelief. Benny Lee briefly explained, "You put your shoe polish and rags inside here. You ask the man for a shine. If he says yes, you tell him to put his foot on top of the box here. And you shine his shoes. We're going to make some money."

The rest of the crew cheered his announcement. When I heard "Make Money," my circuit board lit up like the 4th of July! My bond skills awoke. They searched my Double-O status for a frame of reference. Okay, I had it. I shined Casey's shoes sometimes and he paid me. They're going to shine other people's shoes for money.

"Hey, I want to go!" I pleaded as I grabbed Benny's arm.

"You don't have a box," Duke said.

"I'll get one! Tell me where I can get one?" I begged.

"No stupid, you don't buy one. You have to make one!" Duke scolded.

"Okay, then show me how to make one!" I pleaded.

My plea was met with moans and groans. They were ready to go.

"We don't have time right now. I'll show you how to make one later. Look, you can shine with me today. I'll show you how it's done," Benny replied.

"Thanks," I said.

There was a strut in my step, a pride in my glide. Off to a new hunt, a new hustle. Benny and I walked a stride or two behind the others. Booker and Otis verbally joisted with each other as usual while Duke refereed.

"You do know how to shine shoes don't cha?" he smirked.

"Yeah, I know how to shine," I assured him as we kept pace.

He raised his shoe shine box and began to pull things out to show me.

"Here's what we have to work with. We have 4 colors of polish; black, brown, cordovan, and neutral. Use the neutral if the shoes are green, blue, or gray. This is a bottle of black sole dressing for the heel. We only have one rag to apply the polish but you can also apply with your fingers. There are two brushes and 2 finishing rags to remove the polish."

Man, Benny knew his stuff. I never imagined all that was in the box.

"So where are we off to?" I asked.

"We're going to Jake's Bar. It's one of the best spots to get shines," he replied.

"Cool! I know where Jake's is. My dad hangs out there sometimes on the weekends," I confessed.

"Yeah, my dad does too. That's why I come up here early, leave before my dad gets there. You should do the same," he suggested.

"I'm with you partner. When you leave, I leave," I confirmed.

"Okay, we're almost there. Here's how you ask for a shine. You walk up to him and say, "Excuse me Sir, would you like a shoe shine?' If he asks, how much, you tell him 25 cents. If he's wearing boots it's 50 cents. Now if he doesn't want a shine, you ask him if you can bush off the dust for 10 cents. Once you get a shine, before you finish, ask if he wants sole dressing; that's an extra 10 cents added to the price of the shine. You got that?" He asked with skepticism.

"I got it," I assured him as I rattled off the services and the different prices.

"You and that damn Booker. It took me a half day to learn all that when Duke taught me. Hell, Otis still has trouble with it. He makes it up as he goes along," he confessed.

"What about Booker?" Booker asked after hearing his name.

"We were just talking about how well you remember things," I answered.

"Smart, Tart, smell my fart!" Booker joked.

We laughed while Duke just rolled his eyes and shook his head. As we approached the corner of Jake's the crew split up. Booker already had a shine. He posted at Larry's, a food joint across the side street before Jake's. Duke walked a half block over to The Big Top, another bar in the area. Otis continued with me and Benny Lee to Jake's. He parked at one corner of the building while Benny and I took the other end.

Benny made me watch as he shined his first couple pair of shoes. He allowed me to practice on his second customer. He went over the spots I missed. I was a quick study.

"This sure beats falling out of 30 foot high mango trees!" I joked.

"Or digging through rotten food and roaches to find coins," he added.

"Yep, this is guaranteed easy money," I said.

"I think you're ready for your own customers. Ask that guy right there," he encouraged. "If you get a shine come back and get the box. If I'm using the box come get a brush, a rag and some paste to get started. I'll bring the box to you when I'm done."

We worked like that the rest of the afternoon into the evening. There were times I had the box and Benny had to come get materials to start his shine. At the end of my first night he asked, "How much did you make?"

"I made three bucks! How about you?"

"I made $6. Okay, here's $1.50 to even up our take," he offered.

"Not this time Benny! I weaseled in on your hustle. This $3.00 should be yours."

"But that's not how we roll…now is it?"

"I know but I used up all your polish. Keep it to buy more polish," I insisted.

"Buy polish!" He laughed. "Well, you do have a point. I guess I'll hang on to it for now. Let's get a sandwich from Larry's on the way home."

"Now you're talking! I'm starved. I smelled their food all afternoon."

I made $3.00 my first day as a Shoe Shine Boy. It was the most money I had made in one day. Three men paid me 50 cents for a regular shine. If I didn't beg to tag along, I would have been out of the money. We all needed money!

On the way home Benny Lee paid for my hamburger and soda. The cost, you guessed it, $1.50. I should have known he'd find a way to even our take. He told me not to worry about the polish. He'd get some later. We were joined by the rest of the crew inside Larry's Sandwich Shop. We all bought burgers and sodas. The sky darkened as we walked homeward. The street lights were shining bright; a half hour past my curfew. I'd hear it when I got home but the hunt was worth it. Following Duke's lead, we took a detour.

"Where are we going now? I got to get home!" I complained.

"We have to hide the boxes," Duke said.

"We never take the boxes home. We don't want to run the risk of our parents finding them," Benny explained.

"Yep, out of sight, out of mind." Booker added

They hid them in the high bush behind the wash house.

I got it about hiding the boxes. You walk in the house with it and the questions would fly: "What is this? Where did you get it from? Where did you get the money to buy all the stuff inside?" You'd rather get a whippin for coming home late than giving up your money maker.

By the following weekend I had my own shoe shine box courtesy of my crew. I couldn't thank them enough. Each crew member had donated items from their box. I had everything but polish. The guys retrieved their boxes from the bush. We moved out.

"Don't worry about polish. We all need polish," Benny said.

"Yep, time for a polish run," Duke added.

"Will someone loan me some money to buy polish? I'll pay you back at the end of the night," I asked.

I got that look again from everyone.

"Don't worry Joseph, we got you," Duke assured as we continued to walk.

"You ask too many questions," Otis said with an eerie grin.

"Ask too many questions!" I growled. "Excuse me, Otis! I just wanted to borrow some money to buy some polish," I barked.

The crew skidded to a halt! They gave me that, "What the fuck are you talking about" look again. They burst into laughter. Oh boy, what had I said now? As we picked up the pace Duke picked up a conversation.

"We're going to the drug store on Beanville Highway to get our supplies," he stated.

"Just know I'll pay back whoever buys my polish," I interrupted.

Laughter!

"None of us have money Joseph. That's why the guys are laughing. You don't' have to pay anyone back. We need you to stay outside and watch the boxes," Duke explained.

Okay, the light bulb over my head was on! They were going to steal the supplies. They knew I wouldn't participate. They didn't ask me either. Mama had burned it into my brain, "Don't steal!"

"Okay, I got it. I'll watch the boxes," I agreed.

"It's about time you finally get it," Booker smirked.

"Shut up before I grab your throat ya scrawny little runt!" I fired back.

"Scrawny? That's funny. And Joseph thought we all had money," he busted with a rhyme.

The crew laughed out of control as we approached the drug store. Even I managed a smile before Duke got us back on task.

"Okay, what do you guys need?" he asked.

"I need a brush and a can of black polish," Otis reported

"I'm out of black and brown," Benny announced.

"A can of brown and a shine rag," Booker revealed.

"And I need sole dressing and black. Joseph needs one can of each color. So here we go. Benny you get three cans of brown. Otis, you get a can of neutral and cordovan. Booker, you grab three cans of blacks. I'll get the brush, sole dressing, and a can of black. You know the routine. Let's go," he ordered.

They entered the store a minute apart from each other. They left the same way. Their abrupt pace indicated they had scored. Each grabbed their box recognized by their initials. We pressed on for two blocks before we stopped to divide the take.

"By stealing the supplies we get to keep all the money we make," Booker proclaimed.

"Right on! Yep! You got that right! The crew agreed.

Booker and that mouth, but he was right. It would take each of us a half day of shines to pay for the supplies we just got for free. Although I didn't participate I still felt a little bad about the theft. From that day forward I bought my own supplies. I used money from my phone message hustle to help me purchase what I needed. Sometimes I bought supplies for Benny Lee so he wouldn't have to steal them. If they planned it out they wouldn't have to steal polish. Just buy a can of polish a week at 50 cents a can! It would take only two shines to pay for the polish. But my friends, street kids didn't think that way. They'd tell you, "Why pay for it when we can get it for free!" Living poor was tough. You developed the mentality, "By any means necessary." Survival was the name of the game in the jungle.

We worked a two block radius. Within that area was three bars, two restaurants, a service station, a fish market, and three small stores. Men will get a shoe shine in the most unlikely places. The owners wouldn't let us set up inside their establishments. We addressed our potential customers 10 to 15 feet from the entrance. We rotated between the businesses. There were times when two or three of us were shining next to each other. We had a contest to see which shine was the best. The customers admired the competition. It was good for a 10 cent tip. I learned to pop the rag and chant to the beat as I shined.

"Ham Bone, Ham Bone where you been?"

Then I'd pop the shining rag on the surface of the shoe.

"Around the corner and going again!"

I'd pop the rag again between each verse. It was good for a 10 cent tip every time.

The goal was to make 50 cents for a regular shine. Some gave me all the change in their pocket! I made between $6 and $8 dollars every Friday and Saturday evening. Mama became suspicious.

"Where did you get all this money?" she asked.

"I made it selling mangoes!" I said.

That was the first time I lied to Mama. It worked for awhile until the money started to accumulate. She asked again,

"Where are you getting this money from?"

"I told you I made it selling mangoes!"

She stepped to me and said,

"Mango season was over two weeks ago! Now tell me the truth, where are you getting this money?"

Oh boy, I was busted! Mama knew all along I was lying. She was trying to give me a chance to come clean about the money.

"I made the money shining shoes. I have a shoe shine box, and I shine shoes," I confessed.

"Where is this shoe shine box?" she asked.

Because I had lied to her twice, she demanded to see the box. Oh boy, another dilemma! The rule was, never take your box home. I was already in enough trouble for lying. If I brought the box home the crew would be angry at me for snitching. It sucked, but what should I do? Well the crew would just have to be angry. This was my mom! I'd choose her love and loyalty over theirs any day of the week and twice on Sunday. I lived with her, not them! It's time to come clean. I went to get my box and brought it home to Mama. She was seated in the living room when I returned. She examined the box.

"Where did you get these products?" she asked.

"I bought them with my phone message money," I answered.

She raised one brow as she looked up at me.

"And where do you shine shoes at?"

I pause for a moment knowing my answer would cause a disturbance in the solar system.

"I shine at Jake's Bar,"

"What? I don't ever want you up there again!" She screamed as she stood to her feet.

"Why not Mama?" I whined.

"Those drunken heathens might hurt you son!" she belted.

Humm, Mama did have a point. I never thought of the danger. I was too busy making money and hanging out with my friends. In the words of Lavelle, "If you really want to do something don't let nothing or no one stop you." I asked my dad for help. He was in the kitchen listening. I scurried over to him.

"Daddy, can I please shine at Jake's? That's where all the money is!"

He knew I was desperate. Me asking him for permission! He knew I would rather die than live in that moment. My sunken shoulders told the story. He walked forward forcing me back into the living room. He turns me around to face Mama. He stood behind me with his hands on my shoulders.

"Babe, I'll be up there. I'll keep an eye on him. He's doing something honest to earn his own money." He advocated on my behalf.

"You can't watch him every moment Ike!" She snapped back him.

"I know most of the guys up there. I'll have them keep an eye on him too. I'll send him home at 8:00 pm," he assured.

Holy Guacamole! He negotiated an extra hour too! My heart beamed rays of joy.

"Please Mama!" I begged.

With hands on her hips, she reluctantly agreed.

"If you come through that door a minute pass 8:15 it's over," she declared, wagging her finger.

"Thank you Mama!" I said with a hug.

It was the first time she didn't hug me back. I turned to dad.

"Thanks Daddy!"

He gave me a smile and a slight nod. He knew the majority of the men didn't get to Jake's until after 7:00 pm. By giving me more time he knew I could make more money. I grabbed the box which was sitting on the floor, and hurried out the backdoor.

I met up with the crew at Jake's.

"Where have you been? We waited for you at the wash house," Benny asked

"You guys aren't going to believe this," I spouted.

"Believe what?" Duke asked.

"I got busted!" I said.

"By the cops?" Otis whispered.

"No, you dip stick! If the cops had busted me I'd be in Juvie right now," I said.

"Then who busted you?" Booker asked.

"My parents, I had to show them the box," I confessed.

"We told you not to take it home you knuckle head!" Duke shouted.

"What happened?" Benny asked.

"My mom asked me where I got all the money from three weeks ago. I lied to her. I told her I made it selling mangos. She asked me again. When I tried to use the same lie she told me, Mango season was over two weeks ago and she wanted the truth," I spilled.

"Man, she busted you good," Benny said.

"Yep, so I had to fess up. I told her I had a shoe shine box and I made the money shining shoes. She didn't believe me since I had lied to her twice. She asked to see the box. I'm sorry guys but I had to take it home. I know I promised but I was already in enough trouble for lying."

"Well, what happened?" Duke asked.

"She looked into the box and asked where did I get all the supplies from? I told her I bought them with my phone message money."

"Smooth! Thanks for not selling us out," Otis mocked.

"Go on," Benny encouraged.

"Well, when I told her where I was shining, that's when the shit hit the fan! I thought she was going to tear my head off. She told me not to ever come up here again. But it's cool. As you can see I'm here," I bragged

"How did that happened?" Booker inquired.

"My dad came to my rescue. I begged him to let me shine at Jake's. He talked to my mom and they worked it out. He even gave me an extra hour to shine. I don't have to leave until 8:00!" I bragged.

My announcement was Novocain. Its effects took hold. They stood with gaped mouths, drool started to run. I knew I had scored major points.

"He did what?" Duke blurted coming out of his coma.

"Yep! Don't have to be home until 8:15," I said with a smile.

"What did you do to earn that?" Benny asked.

"Nothing, I didn't even ask for the extra hour!" I answered.

"Wait, I thought you didn't like your dad?" Otis asked.

"Ah...I like him today," I joked.

The crew laughed with me.

"You lucky dog, my ass is burnt toast if I'm caught with this box," Duke confessed.

"Yep, I'll get chopped down to the root if I'm caught, Benny confessed. My mom love to bitch at me anyway. She'd have a field day if she found this box."

"Lucky-ducky, Joseph...you schmucky! Stop bragging about your extra time cause brothers it's time to shine!" Booker joked with a rhyme.

There were congratulatory pats on my back. They knew I had won the day in Bond style. You should never count out a Double-O.

My crew had hit the big times. We had the best hustle in town. No kid would dare try to weasel in on it. Once I was up and running, Benny and I didn't share our earnings. He had his customers and I had mine. We all borrowed from each other when we ran out of supplies. And if one crew member was having a slow day, we shared our shines with him. Customers didn't like to wait.

My dad was right. The crowd grew much larger after 7:00 pm. He came toward me shaking hands with those he greeted.

"Are you alright?" he asked as he neared.

"Yeah, I'm okay."

"How's it going?"

"Pretty good, but it's picking up now."

"You keep your eyes open around here and don't forget to leave by 8:00," he warned.

"I will," I assured him.

He turned to his left.

"Hey Bill, come over here and let my boy shine your shoes?" he yelled.

"That's your boy Ike?" Bill asked as he walked toward us.

"Yeah, that's my baby boy. The last shot in the gun," he joked.

"He's no baby anymore Ike," Bill replied as he placed his foot on top of my box.

"I guess you're right," Daddy conceded.

"Don't forget, 8:00!" He gave a final reminder.

"I won't," I confirmed as I began to shine Bill's shoes.

As he turned and walked away, he told all those he met I was his son and to let me shine their shoes. I had customers for the next hour, one after the other. This was also his way of asking them to keep an eye on me.

CHAPTER 26

THE MAN FROM DETROIT

I made enough money from the shoe shine hustle to buy and do whatever I wanted. One thing I enjoyed was going to the movies on Saturday afternoon. Sometimes Benny would come with me to the Heart Beat Theatre. It was a dirty, dingy place with roaches and rats. But they made the best sausage sandwiches in town! We sat with our feet up against the back of the seat in front of us; laughing, eating, and threw popcorn at each other all afternoon. The first movie was always a rerun. I must have seen Hercules, Planet of the Apes, Jason and the Argonauts three times each. My all-time favorite was, "Ski Party" featuring James Brown. I saw it four times. I also enjoyed "To Sir with Love." Don't tell anyone, but I cried at the end.

The Heart Beat was next to the "Triple T Bar." It was the roughest bar in town. They bagged them and tagged them out of there every weekend. I always left the movies by 4:00 pm. before the crowd gathered at Triple T's. That place gave me the creeps. Black paint coated the outer layer; dark gray and green trim; a cold, sinister vibe given off. I passed on the other side of the street, as I entered and left the theatre.

Whenever I went to the movies I met the crew at Jake's around 5:00. One Saturday the crew wasn't there! I checked everywhere. Not like the crew to miss out on making money. I worked that night by myself. I made $14, the most money I ever made in my life! Three paid me a dollar for a regular shine and several paid 50 cents. Plus I had two boot shines. If you really hustle you could shine 10 to 12 pair of shoes in an hour. It only took five minutes per shine. The money was great but I worried about my crew?

After church and dinner the next day I went to find them. I wanted to know what happened the them. A pale quiet occupied the front of the apartments. I went around to Benny Lee's crib. I knocked; one of his sisters answered.

"Is Benny home?"

"Just a minute," she said.

I waited at the door. A moment later, Benny appeared. We exchanged greetings and walked to the front of the apartments. We never talked crew business in the company of others. We climbed up the big shade tree to have some privacy.

"What happened to you guys last night? I went to shine at Jake's after the movies and no one was there," I asked.

"I guess you didn't hear," he replied.

"Hear what?" I questioned.

"We got busted. Our parents found out about the boxes," he answered.

"Ah man, how did it happen?" I moaned.

"My sisters saw my money and tried to take it. I fought them off. They said they would tell our mom if I didn't tell them where I got it from. I made them both swear not to tell. They swore so I told them. But they lied and squealed on me anyway."

"Man, that's messed up!"

"Straight witches! All three of them! My mom squealed to Duke's mom and Booker's aunt. They made us bring them the boxes because they didn't believe us," he continued.

"The same shit I went through with my mom."

"Yep, but at least you got to keep your box. They took ours, destroyed them, and threw away the supplies. They don't want us up at Jake's anymore. They said it's too dangerous."

"That's messed up!"

"Yes it is. So that's why we weren't there last night."

We sat there quiet for a while. The conversation moved to favorite football teams.

So for a while, it was just Otis and I holding down the shoe shine hustle. For whatever reason they didn't tell Otis's Grandmother. The night no one showed up, Otis had to take care of his sick Grandma. When his grandmother became ill again, he had to stay at home more often until she was better.

The month that followed, I had the shoe shine hustle all to myself. I took Benny Lee with me a couple of times. We shined out of my box. The very same way I started out. He and I were back to old times sharing our take 50/50. But he got tired of running back and forth for the box and lost interest.

With the shoe shine hustle all mine, I became addicted to it! I would sneak out on Sunday evenings when Mama went back to church for night service. I'd shine for an hour and a half and run home before she returned. My earnings were increased! My best weekend was $28.00! I tried to give Mama some of the money. She never took a penny! She didn't approve of me being at Jake's. I used the money to buy sneakers, dress shirts, and slacks. I wanted to dress like Casey and James Bond. Casey dressed well. I learned to put outfits, colors together by watching him. I bought my first full dress suit with shoe shine money.

Jeanie took me to Anderson's Department Store to buy the suit. While she shopped I went to the suit area. I had my eye on a brown Double-Breasted suit for weeks. On Mondays I had enough money to buy it, by Friday I didn't. But once the shine business was all mine....

The price was $15.99. When I reached the suit section, there were two suits on display. The brown one I adored and a blue one I liked just as well. I looked at both for a half hour. I couldn't decide. When Jeanie had all her items she came over to get me.

"So which one have you decided on?" she asked.

"I don't know. I like them both. I can't decide," I confessed.

"Well hurry up! I'm ready to go."

I stood stoically as I eyed both suits, which by now I had taken off the rack and tried the jackets on three or four times each.

"I can't decide. Which one do you like best?" I asked her.

"It's your money. It's your choice. You buy the one you like the most."

After standing for another five minutes frozen in ice, Jeanie could wait any longer.

"Come on! I have to go. Bring them both. I'll buy the other one for you!" she ordered.

"Really, thanks Jeanie!" I radiated as I walked beside her to the cash register.

"You've been working hard this summer. To make that much money from shining shoes for only 25 cents a pair is a big accomplishment," she complimented.

"Thanks Jeanie. I'll pay you back."

"You're welcome. You don't have to pay me back. Just remember to always work hard for the things you want!" She encouraged.

"I will. I promise."

After shopping it was back to the hustle. Jake's was what we called an "Open Air Bar." A roof covered the raised sidewalk in front of the place; a countertop extended outside the bar to the sidewalk. A patron could step right up from the sidewalk to a large window-like opening and be served. You could stand outside, enjoy your beverage, and take in the atmosphere of the bar without entering. It was awesome. The roof shaded me from the blistering sun while I made my money. Jake didn't allow me to shine a customer's shoes while he or she was at the counter. So I asked before they got there or went inside. If I missed someone before they reached the counter I would wait until the bartender went to make their drink to ask for the shine. My approach was,

"Excuse me Sir/Ma'am, would you like to have a shine after you're done with your drink?"

Some replied, "Sure, come on; you can give me one now."

I'd answer, "I can't. I'm not allowed. Mr. Jake doesn't want me shining at the counter.

Some would get angry at Jake. "What do you mean you're not allowed," they'd yell. To calm them down, I would quickly reassure them it was okay, and I would wait until they were done, no problem. It had only been a couple months after the riot. Mr. Jake was white, so they didn't want to hear anything about another white owner ordering around a black kid. Any way...

The bar was jumping. I was perched 12 feet away from the front door all night. The music was hot! Playing on the jukebox was. "Who's Making Love" by Johnny Taylor. It was one of my favorites. I'd made close to $12 dollars. It was getting late. I wanted to squeeze in one last shine.

"Excuse me Sir, would you like a shoe shine?" I asked one well-dressed men.

"Sure kid. Don't get any polish on the suede," he said.

Man, he wore the nicest pair of shoes I'd ever seen! They had light brown lather, dark brown suede, and a gold buckle on the side.

"You aren't from around here are you Mister? Where are you from?"

"How do you know that?" he replied.

"Mister, I've shined every pair of men's shoes in this town and I've never seen a pair as nice as these!" I complimented.

"You're a smart kid. I'm from Detroit," he said.

"Wow, that's a big city and a long ways away. What's it like there?"

"There's a lot of big buildings. Detroit has a lot of people. There's also a lot of night life too. At least 100 places like Jake's."

"My dad said they make cars in Detroit."

"Yes they do. Some of the best cars in the world are made there."

As soon as he finished his sentence a loud crash came from the bar. The needle on the jukebox scratched across the record. Voices shouted from inside, "Stop", "Cut it out", "Come on man." Another crash, a loud thud and the front doors swung open. Two guys were going at it! Spectators were trying to break it up. The Man from Detroit and I froze in disbelief as we looked on. Once the two men were separated the guy with his back to us pulled out a gun! He fired several times at the guy he was fighting. The man from Detroit ran and ducked behind a parked car. I ran to the corner of the building to take cover. I peeked around the building. People were scrambling to get back inside as the other guy was now shooting back from the other corner of the building.

The man from Detroit was kneeling about 10 feet away from me. The dim light overhead, revealed a long scare on his neck. He reached under his suit coat and pulled out his gun! A big sucker! Looked like a 45. I could hear Mama's voice, "Those heathens might hurt you." I kept thinking all I had to do was leave before this last shine like I started to do. I had made enough money for the night, but no...I had to be greedy and get one more shine. Now my life was in jeopardy.

The Man from Detroit saw me peeking around the corner.

"Stay back!" he yelled to me.

I drew my head back and nodded yes. I shook like a leaf on a tree. Several more rounds were fired. I was trapped, no place to go! Finally, the gun fire ceased. I stayed put until the cops arrived. The man from Detroit put his gun away and stood.

"Get out of here!" He said as he tossed me a 50 cent piece.

I stepped from behind the building clutching my box. I briskly moved in the opposite direction from the action. I watched the man from Detroit cross the street. I glanced back to see paramedics kneeling over a body. I scurried to the next block and made a left. I took the long way home to avoid the danger and being questioned by the cops. The fight, the shootout, and the long route home made me miss my curfew.

Dad wasn't at Jake's that night. He went to work to help with a cookout for the guests. By the time I got home at 8:35 he was there. He had driven past Jake's and saw all the emergency vehicles out front. He did a spot check and didn't see me. Looking at the time, he assumed I was home. He was shocked when I wasn't there. Mama was beside herself. She knew about the shooting at Jake's. As I opened the backdoor she was reeling.

"Go find my baby Ike! Those heathens better not have hurt my boy! I told you not to let him go up there. Now go find him now!" she insisted.

"I'm here!" I interrupted as I stepped from the shadows.

Both breathed a sigh of relief. I could tell Mama wanted to give me a hug, but instead she started in on me.

"Where have you been? You're late. You had me worried to death. There was a shooting at Jake's. Where were you?" she demanded.

I hated lying to my parents, but in this case...

"I had walked up a block to the store to get a soda. When I came out, I saw all the emergency cars in front of Jake's. I asked a man standing in front of the store what was going on. He said there was a shooting at Jake's. So I took the long way home to avoid the danger. That's why I'm late."

"So that's why I didn't see you when I drove through. You were in the store?" Daddy asked.

"I guess so," I answered.

"That's it! No more shining shoes at Jake's," Mama declared as she gave a hard glare at my dad.

Her stare was piercing! It said, "You better not object!" Daddy nodded in agreement, forbidding me to shine shoes ever again at Jake's. It was a great run but my life as a shoeshine boy was over. Word on the street was the guy lying on the sidewalk was shot in the shoulder. He would make it. The cops arrested the guy that shot him.

I met the crew after Sunday dinner under the big shade tree. They lounged about.

"Well, who is this, a new member of the crew?" I joked as I approached and saw Elijah.

"Shut your pie hole Joseph! Don't forget, I'm an original member," he bragged.

"Well, you got me there," I admitted.

"We're surprised to see you," Duke said.

"Why is that?" I asked.

"Well, we figured if you didn't get killed at the shootout last night, your mom probably killed you and your dad for letting you shine up at Jake's," he smirked.

The crew chuckled.

"Yo, she was ticked! She made my dad agree not to ever let me shine up there again. I never saw her so upset! I had to lie to them when they asked me where I was during the shootout. But yo, the shootout was the wildest shit ever! I thought the riot was crazy but the shootout was insane," I motor mouthed.

I proceeded to tell them everything I saw. I told them about the man from Detroit, his gun, and his boss ass kicks! I explained how he was ready to protect us. Booker, with the death of his cousin fresh in his mind, jumped to his feet. His voice cracked."You're a damn fool! You should've run. Got the hell out of there as fast as you could," he scolded me.

"Did the guy have a mark on his neck?" Duke asked.

"Yeah, how'd you know that?" I questioned.

"That was Detroit Slim. He's Dwight's cousin. Dwight's a kid in my grade. He said his cousin was once a gangster in Detroit. The mark was the work of a guy trying to cut his throat in a fight!" Duke informed.

"You could have been killed man. Don't play around like that," Benny warned me.

"I wanted to run Booker but I couldn't. Bullets were flying all over the place. And yes Benny, I could have bit dust but the man from Detroit had my back. If anyone tried to harm us he would've taken them out," I assured.

"My mom said it's the scariest feeling in the world to hear bullets whizzing past your head," Elijah recalled.

"Yo man, if any shit like that jumps off again, you run and don't look back until you're safe. You and that James Bond bullshit's gonna get you killed!" Duke warned.

Otis was quiet the whole time. On occasion he gave a Bellview, home for the insane type snicker. But it wasn't a funny conversation.

"You're right Duke. All of you are right. But you must understand...

I positioned my index, middle finger, and thumb to look like a gun. I bent my knees and slowly spun around humming the James Bond theme song and said, "You can't kill a Double-O!"

"Oh man! There he goes again!" "He'll never learn!" "He really thinks he's James Bond!"

They sighed in disgust as they pelted me with their trash.

There we go. That's more like it, enough with all the sappy stuff. But I heard them...I heard them good. I must be more cautious with my life.

CHAPTER 27

KNOW WHEN TO WALK AWAY

The Parkers were snobby Sons of Bitches. Several attended my church. You would think people came together in church; not true. The Parkers sat on the left side of the church. The Townies sat on the right. My brothers and I sat in the middle. We took stats on the Parker girls. Whenever I caught one eyeing me they'd point their nose to the ceiling, turned their head, pretending like they weren't scoping me out; snobby little twitches. After church, they'd cling to their mama's skirt.

Around these parts there were preconceived ideas about Townies and Parkers.

Townies	Parkers
Townies live in the jungle	Parkers live in the suburbs
Townies were tough	Parkers were pussies
Townies were poor	Parkers had money
Townies were dumb	Parkers were smart
Townies worked with their hands	Parkers worked with their brain
Townies were cool, uninhibited	Parkers were stuck up nerds
Townies had morals	Parkers had better morals

Townies didn't care about their reputation	Parkers protect their reputation
Townies were niggers	Parkers were blacks
Townies planned for today	Parkers planned for their future
Townies wanted to live like Parkers	On the weekend Parkers lived like Townies

This labeling added to my identity crisis. I was a Townie but I wasn't dumb! I had good morals! Well, most of the time. I cared about my reputation. Ah…well, most of the time. And I made plans for my future. My goal was to win a basketball scholarship and go to college. So where did I fit? I was hammered with criticism from all directions. The other day a kid called me a mulatto. He said, "Where are you going you fucking mulatto." The kid knew both my parents were black but to score points with his friend, he made a joke of me. I wasn't black enough for the blacks. I wasn't white enough for the whites. I wasn't rich enough for the Parkers. I wasn't poor enough for some of the Townies. When would it end?

None of it made sense to me. Why must you have a particular shade of skin to be accepted? Why must you live in a certain neighborhood to gain respect? Why must I be called a Nigger, a Mulatto, or an Albino? I didn't make fun of anyone unless provoked. I didn't try to bring anyone down until they start with me. I was taught, "If you get hit, you better hit back!" It was the law of the jungle. But I was out numbered. It stung when they branded me with labels. The burn went deeper when my own kind did it to me.

It was easier pretending to be James Bond. How messed up was that? I lived my life through a Hollywood character and a professional boxer. But when I took on their persona I felt invincible. I could block out the noise of racism, poverty, and the black on black prejudice. When I was them, I felt insulated from the shame and rejection. I could hide in the light, in broad daylight and no one could see my life gushing from my wounds. I could let the hate, anger and bullying roll off my back when I was Bond. The problem was I couldn't pretend to be Bond or Ali all the time.

I considered all of them bullies: whites, cops, the Parkers, and the black name callers. If I bought into their critism they would suck the life out of me. Through their degradation they were telling me, "I was nothing! I'd never amount to anything! I wasn't good enough! I was ugly!" Wait, that's a new one. I'm ugly? Well, that wasn't what your little sister called me when I had my hand… Stop! Cool out!

My days were filled with images of lesser. I didn't need any of them to remind me. Eating beans and pork scraps every day. Living on rocks where slave laborers once lived. And I looked, spoke, and thought different. With each of their labels and insults they drove that "Not Good Enough" nail further into me. They'd reached the place Mama said not to ever let anyone or anything touch; that place being, my heart, my joy. *"That's what bullies do. They find your sores of life and rip the scabs off! They make you hurt, bleed, pain. Mama said, "Joseph, don't let the world change you. Always be yourself!" But it's so hard Mama. The people and the conditions won't allow me to be myself. They make me question myself every day. Who am I? What am I? How did I end up here? Will I ever get out of here? Will I live past 16? Why do I exist? I tried to remember what my Daddy said, Joseph, keep your head up! The world would love to see you standing around with your head down, broken. Don't do it. Keep your head up!*

Dealing with bullies took away my positive energy, my good intentions, lost innocence. They kept picking at my sores of life, their scabs until I became angry, bitter, and jealous. They wouldn't allow me to heal. They tried to force me to keep my head down, something my father told me never to do! They kept picking until I began to lose myself.

Living on the rocks was a jungle within the jungle. If I stood on the rocks for any length of time my ambitions, my productivity, my creativity was stifled. The rocks grinded me into a cloud of dust and spat me out, torn and dejected, left for dead. I'd cough, spit, and fight my way back to life; finding a glimmer of light to keep my dreams alive. Later I realized that tiny light was only a placebo. A false indicator to make me think things were getting better. In other words it was false hope. Yep, poverty on the rocks could only offer me false hope.

So every day I sat on the edge waiting! I didn't need the bullies to push me or tell me to jump. I knew my options. I became dependent on my alter egos to help me survive; to help me hide in plain sight as I endured the suffering. They allowed me to hope, to dream, and hold on for another day. Even in the face of death, I held onto James Bond until it became clear; Bond couldn't save me. I had to save myself.

The crew and I picked up a bad habit when we had the shoe shine hustle. We started to gamble! We played cards for money. We mirrored the adult behavior at the apartments. They played card games outside in back of Franklin Court. Their games were 25 cents a hand with 25 cents bet on High Spade. On occasion, their games grow to 50 cents a hand. The crew's games were held in front of the complex underneath the big shade tree. If you wanted in, the games were 10 cents a hand and 5 cents bet on High Spade. The games were usually in progress when I arrived. There were four seats at the table. I would often wait to get in the game. If you're not in the game you're responsible for keeping an eye out for car 313. I learned to get into the game when no seats were available by betting on a player's High Spade. If he wasn't betting on his spade I'd ask if I could. If he agreed, I would move next to him and bet. If I won the High Spade bet I would slide him 5 cents to help keep him in the game so I could repeat my bet. If I lost, he got nothing.

I became very good at counting cards! I won far more times than I lost. The gambling addiction overtook me. When the crew wasn't having a card game I would venture to the back to watch the adult's gamble. At first I'd watch from a distance. The players were usually the parents of the crew. Knowing they would lose their seat if they left the table, they began to send me to the store on food and cigarette runs. That got me closer to their table. The regulars were; Mrs. Rivers, who was Benny's mom, Ms. Walters, who was Elijah's mom, and Black Coat, who talked funny and wore a long black coat year round. Everyone knew he carried a gun underneath it. He flipped his coat back from time to time to reveal it. He wasn't a mean man but hated to lose. The fourth seat was held by several guest players. I once asked if I could have the open seat. Ms. Walters bitched so loud! She made it clear it would never happen as long as she was at the table. I wasn't deterred.

One day after a store run I noticed Mrs. Rivers, Benny's mom wasn't betting on her High Spade. I whispered in her ear,

"Can I bet on your spade?"

She paused, kept her eyes glued on the table. Seconds later she said,

"Sure, if you spot me when you win!"

"Not a problem!" I replied.

"Then go ahead, place your bet," she invited.

That was an awesome move! Like Bond in "Dr. No" or "Thunderball", I was in the game! I had earned the trust of the group with the store runs. And I wasn't breaking Elijah's mom's rule about sitting at the table. I won $2.00 my first day.

I repeated the process many times over. I'd do the store runs and work my way into the game. It wasn't long until I preferred the adult game over the crew's game; more money in the pot in the adult game. Plus, I earned money on the food and cigarette runs. To get to the game I would cross the street at Ray's, jump on the path behind Betty's, and take the McKenzie Bridge to reach the back of the apartments; undetected by the crew. When Elijah's mom wasn't at the table I was allowed to sit and play as long as I wanted. I won more days than I lost in the adults games. But the adults would get pissed when I won and had to leave. It was amazing how they could sit there all afternoon and not have to pee.

My Dad found out I was gambling. I wonder who told. Well, take one guess. Yep, I was sure it was Elijah's mom, Ms. Walters. Daddy told Mama. They double-teamed me when I came home. They had an Ultimate Tag Team match on my ass that left me brain warped for hours. Daddy was barking while Mama was crying and pleading.

"You have no idea the danger you're in gambling with adults!" Daddy warned.

"Joseph, God is not pleased with you for doing that!" Mama cried.

"If I hear of you gambling across that street again, your ass is mine! You hear me boy." he declared.

Out of all the warnings my Dad had given me somehow I felt he meant this one, something about the tone in his voice. His glare sent chills through me.

"I'm sorry, I won't do it again!" I promised.

"I'm not playing with you!" he reinforced.

"I know! I won't gamble anymore," I reassured them.

I was grounded for a week. I should've gotten an ass whippin, but I was the baby. You get away with a lot of shit when you're the youngest. I was glad none of my siblings were home. All three would've smacked me around good. Well, maybe not Lavelle.

My parent's talk lasted eight days. I was back to doing store runs, betting on spades, and sitting at the card table with the adults. One day I was waiting to get into the game when Black Coat asked me to go to Ray's to get change for a $20 bill. He told me I could keep $1.00. I bought a pack of cookies and played a game of Pinball. As I left Ray's I stopped at the red light before crossing the street. I checked my pocket and the $19…it wasn't there!

Oh no! I turned each pocket inside out…nothing! I found a hole in my left front pocket. The money must have fallen out. I traced my steps as I rushed back to the store. Eyes glued to the ground. Nothing! Upon entering I dashed to the counter.

"Did you find the change you gave me?' I asked the clerk.

"No. What happen?" he inquired.

My voice cracked. "I have a hole in my pocket; the change must have fallen out."

"You played a game of Pinball. Go look around the machine," he suggested.

With tears streaming down my face, I feared for my life! Black Coat had a gun. We all had seen it. There was no way I could go back to the game and tell him I lost his money. He'd never believe me. He'd see me as some punk kid trying to steal his money and put a slug in me sure as day! Then go to my house and put holes in each of my family for revenge. I had signed mine and my family's death warrants! I was a dead man walking.

I didn't have enough money at home to replace the $19. I couldn't go to my parents, they had warned me about gambling. With tears flooding my face, I frantically looked around the Pinball machine. Nothing! Every word my parents spoke about gambling came back to haunt me. They clawed the walls of my brain.

"Go in the back and ask Mr. Ray. Maybe he saw the money," the store clerk yelled.

Wiping my face to no avail I moved to the back of the store. Mr. Ray was standing at the post office window. Ray's also serves as the local postal office. He was a big white man who towered at 6 foot 3 inches, 250 lbs. He spoke with a deep, southern accent. My broken spirit advanced closer. I shook, wobbled; the thought of Black Coat's cold, dark face took my equilibrium.

"Mr. Ray did you find any money?" I sobbed.

"Who datmuneybelone to?" he asked?

"It's Black Coat's money," I sniffled.

"Whatayadoinwid his muney?" he inquired.

"He needed change to play in the card game. He sent me to the store to get change. Now I've lost his $19, and I don't have any money to replace it. I'm dead for sure. Everyone knows he carries a gun," I explained.

"Why ya at a card game wid grown folks? Ya know yo daddy don't want ya around no gambling boy!" He scolded me.

"I know Mr. Ray. I know," I confessed as drops streamed again.

His demeanor changed quickly, like he didn't care. He began to speak in a solemn tone.

"Come-a-round to the door," he ordered.

I walked three paces to the door. He unlocked the upper half and pulled it back. He grabbed a stool and sat. His steel blue eyes dressed me down! I stood naked with guilt and fear.

"Joseph, I found da muney! But if I give it back you must promise me you'll never, ever go around dat gambling table again," he demanded.

"I promise Mr. Ray! I promise!" I cried.

"Don't you lie to me? Cause you know if you go back to that game without his money you could get hurt real bad!"

"Mr. Ray if you give me the money I promise I'll never gamble again. I'm not lying! I promise!" I begged.

"Okay! I better not hear about you at dat table again. If I do, I'matell your parents," he warned as he stood.

"Never again Mr. Ray, Never!" I promised.

Mr. Ray reached into his pocket and counted out $19. As he handed it to me he grabbed my wrist.

"No Mo!" he insisted with a tight squeeze.

"No more Mr. Ray," I assured.

I took the money, gave a colossal thank you, and hurried for the door. The tension, stress descended with each step! My eyes cleared. I was alive again. I gave the clerk a nod. I flashed the money as I shuffled past. He nodded back with a wink. I held the money as though my life depended on it. I crossed the street and broke into a trot. I gave one last face wipe before I turned the corner to the card game.

"Here you go!" I said to Black Coat, handing him his money.

"Wattookcha so long?" he asked.

"Ah, I had to use the toilet," I answered walking away.

"Ju not playinjaday?" he asked.

"Nah, not today," I said never looking back.

I went home nonstop. The episode made me nauseous. A weighted heaviness came upon me. My hands shook. A dark cloud followed me. No rain overhead but a monsoon crashed within me. I had never been so afraid! It was time to make some changes.

I enter the backdoor to my house. I gave Mama a weak greeting as she stood at the stove. I dove onto the sofa. My face pressed into the pillow. I couldn't move. Jeanie's favorite song was playing, "A Change Gonna Come," by Sam Cooke. She sang her favorite part:

"It's been too hard living and I'm afraid to die.

Cause I don't know what's up there, up there beyond the sky.

It's been a long, a long time coming, but I know a change gone come."

That verse was where I was in my life. It had been too hard trying to balance my pretending, the bullying, and my thrill seeking nature. A change must come. I worried Mr. Ray would tell my parents about the episode of me and Black Coat's money, exposing me for the lying, risk taking gambler I had become. I didn't know if Mr. Ray had actually found the money or he saw a scared shitless kid in serious trouble and decided to help. Either way, he saved my life! Not all white people were racist, prejudice, or bigoted. The neighborhood knew that about Mr. Ray. His store was spared during the riot.

Duke and the crew had warned me to get a grip, to dial it back a notch or two, or I could get seriously hurt. The time had come for me to take inventory. I asked myself, *was I controlling Bond or was he controlling me? In the beginning it was all make believe. Now it was out of control. I was buried so deep into the character, I didn't recognize myself anymore.* Yes Jeanie, a change was gonna come. It had to if I was going to survive and keep the promise I made to Mama.

CHAPTER 28

TEARS IN THE SAND

I avoided my crew and Franklin Court for a while; afraid I might venture over to the card table. I needed to make good on my promise to my parents and Mr. Ray about gambling. I hadn't heard anything from my parents about Black Coat's money. Mr. Ray was a man of his word. Now it was my turn to hold up my end of the deal. Mama once said,

"If you don't feed it, it'll die!"

She said it was a physical and spiritual principle. I understand the physical. I needed to stop feeding my passion, urges for reckless behavior. Gambling was first on the list. It, like shining at Jakes, nearly closed my curtains for good. But how could I completely give up the hunts? They feed something inside me I couldn't explain. When I roamed the streets with my crew I had; energy, substance, self-worth. The lion was out the cage. Change would mean casting aside my alter ego, James bond. Without whom, I was nothing more than those terrible names they called me. But I was determined to dial it back. I just didn't know how.

During my hiatus from the apartments I talked to Matt on the phone. He'd just returned from his family reunion in Sea Garden. He shared some decent stories. I chilled a day with Robert; we sat on his back steps rating movies we saw at the Heart Beat. His German shepherd was the main attraction. He chased us. We wrestled him and played fetch. I even killed some time in the Quarters with Marques and Chanson. They lived four and five houses down from me. Both were boring but safe. They weren't allowed to leave the house until their mom came home from work.

Benny had been gone for three days. That made it easier to stay away from the apartments. He and his family went to visit relatives in Rising Tide. I couldn't wait for his return. I was burdened with thoughts of change. He knew how to bring me back. I didn't want to talk to my family about it. They, like myself, had found comfort in pretending; hiding our wounds of life right under your nose. We had become experts at hiding in the light. But none of their coping mechanisms sought danger as an outlet, only mine. Benny was due to return the next day.

Dying a slow death in the Quarters, I needed some release. Restless beyond compare, I played Pinball at Ray's four or five times over the past two days. I shot baskets for hours. The crew spotted me from the street. They let out a Wolf Man yowl. I yowled back. Man, it was good to see them. I yelled, "What time is Benny coming back?"

"Around 6:00!" Booker belted out.

"Okay, thanks," I shouted as I went back to shooting baskets.

That was too late to visit. Plus they needed to rest. I delayed my visit until the next day.

Only four days of summer vacation remained. The crew and I will finally attend West Side High! We had waited all our lives to be Jaguars! This will be Duke's third year. He told the crew all about it. But I needed to talk to Benny Lee first.

"Joseph!" Mama called from the backdoor.

"Yes!"

"I need you to go to the store for me."

"Okay!" I confirmed as I took my last shot.

I brushed off the dust as I approached her. She handed me a list and $3.00.

"Here are the things I need from Ray's. Get white rice not brown rice," she instructed.

"Beans, White rice, Bread, Flour, and corn meal," I read the list to her.

"Oh, and get self-rising flour!" She reminded.

"I got it Mama," I assured her as I walked away.

On the way to Ray's I was haunted by an incident that occurred the week before. A kid called me an "Albino." He bumped into me on purpose and said, "Watch where you're going you Damn Albino." He and his friend laughed. Those encounters would pop up in my head when I was alone, quiet. My family said, ignore it. That was easy for them to say. Words hurt! It was very hard for me to let kids get away with disrespecting me. They would think I was soft. You couldn't be soft in the jungle.

As I left Ray's with the groceries, Cray and one of his friends was outside. I didn't care for Cray. He was one of my biggest haters. I looked away when I passed them. Hoping he wouldn't start with me. I was about eight feet beyond them when I noticed I had too much change in my hand. I looked into the bag and discovered I had forgotten to buy an item. I walked passed them again. I quickly grabbed the handle of the door.

"So what did the little Mutt forget?" He blurted out to amuse his friend.

A bazooka blast exploded in my head. Shrapnel pierced my brain on all sides. I tried to tell my feet to keep moving. They wouldn't listen. As I battled to control the effects of the blast I could vaguely hear Mama, Lindsey, Duke saying, "Don't let them push your buttons!"

My mind flashed back to the time I caught Casey cleaning his gun. He has a silver .32 caliber pistol with a white pearl handle; only Lavelle and I knew he had it. He bought it after a run-in with a guy at the Triple T. The guys' girl was making eyes at Casey. He accused Casey of flirting with her and wanted to fight him. Casey said he just walked away but later bought the gun for protection if it ever happened again.

"Come in! Close the curtain," he ordered. "You want to hold it?"

My eyes stretched wide to match my smile. I had never held a gun before. The handle caught my eye, drew me toward it, the chance to be a real live Double-O.

"Sure! Is it loaded?" I asked.

"Nah, I took the bullets out," he said.

He put his arms around me, gave instructions on how to aim and shoot. I visualize Cray's face in front of me as I pulled the trigger. Oh no! What's going on in my head? My thoughts had become dangerous! Someone opened the door; I moved aside. That brought me back from that dark, dangerous place in my head. During my anger blackout, I must have turned to Cray. I stared him in the face. My mouth was loaded to fire off swear words at world record pace.

"So what are you going to do, cry?" He asked as his friend continued to laugh.

I heard Mama again, "Don't do it! Don't say it!" For once I listened. Not because I wanted to; I had to. I couldn't run holding a bag of groceries. I walked over to him. My eyes, fixed on his. I wanted to punch him in the gut so hard he'd shit blood for a week!

"So what are you going to do now, hit me?" He joked as he turned to his friend.

"Say it again Cray! Call me another name. And if you do, I promise you my brother will beat your ass so bad your mama won't recognize you! Say it again," I suggested sarcastically.

His friend laughed hysterically. Not smiling, I cut my eyes over at him. I didn't flinch.

"Cray, don't say nothing. His brother's a beast!" His friend warned.

"Why you got to bring your brother into it?" he asked apologetically.

"Yeah...I didn't think so!" I fired back at him as I opened the door.

I bought the missed item and played a game of Pinball to cool off. How long must I put up with this shit? When I exited the store, they were gone. Thank goodness! I took the dirt path home feeling proud. It was the first time I didn't swear or talk about someone's mama when they called me a name. But I couldn't keep threatening people with my brother. The vision of the gun was disturbing! Although I had done risky things, this marked the first time I had dangerous thoughts. My teacher said, "Thoughts lead to actions!" I wished it would stop. That day I was a Mutt, the week before an Albino. What would I be the next day? I needed to talk to Benny Lee.

I opened the backdoor, placed the bag on the tiny table. Lavelle and a couple of his friends were in the living room: Ed, Steve, Fred, and Louis. I liked hanging out with him and his friends. Mama read me as soon as I walked through the door. I began to take items from the bag. Our eyes met. She gave me that look; a code only she and I understood. We developed it to communicate around Daddy when he was on his drunken rant. Lavelle and his friends were in ear shot of us. She turned her head, tilted it slightly to the left, and raised her eyebrows. I shook my head side to side while I continued to remove items out the bag. She reached into the bag and grabbed my hand. I looked up. She gave me the same look with wider eyes. Underneath Lavelle and his friend's conversation I whispered, "A name." She threw her head and shoulders back while pushing out her lip. As if to say, "And what did you do?" I lowered my head. I shook it side to side again to indicate; nothing. She gently squeezed my hand inside the bag. I looked up once more. She leaned back in a staggered stance with the same look. I gave her a smile and whispered, "Nothing!" She smiled and gave me a hug with her free hand.

"I'm proud of you!" she whispered as she hugged me.

I didn't tell her I threatened to have Lavelle beat the life out of the kid. I didn't want to rain on her parade. It was a victory for both of us. Once the bag was emptied I joined Lavelle and his friends in the living room. After greeting everyone, I sat on the floor. I pretended to watch TV. They tried to talk around me. I kept my head forward.

After some time had passed, Lavelle asked. "Joseph, why don't you go to the bedroom?"

"Why?" I questioned.

"We want to talk," he answered.

"Then talk! I want to watch this show," I suggested.

"Go to the room!" he ordered.

"No! And you can't make me!"

I stood and went into the kitchen to make my favorite sandwich, peanut butter and jelly. I returned with my sandwich and a glass of milk. As usual I put too much jelly on the sandwich. I tease Lavelle and his friends by taking long, slow bites from my sandwich in front of them. I ate the sandwich like I was on a TV commercial for some tasty product. Mama walked through.

"Joseph, wipe your mouth. You look like a little Jelly Gobbler or something."

Lavelle and his friends fell on the floor laughing! They couldn't stop. Then they started to tease me.

"Joseph the: Jelly Gobbler, Jelly Goon, Jelly Head, Jelly Bread, Jelly Belly, Jelly Joseph, J.G. the Jelly Goon."

They kept it going for awhile. Finally, they decided on JG The Jelly Goon for their nickname for me. It was their way of getting back at me for not giving them any privacy. I laughed it off with them. I liked those guys, and I could take a joke. At least, JG was better than the names the other kids called me. I didn't say anything, but I liked it. Plus, JG was the initials of my name, Joseph Graham. Within a week all of my brother's friends called me by my new nickname, JG. I liked to spell it: Jay Gee.

It was Friday. I had given Benny Lee enough time to recover from his trip. I needed to talk with him, just the two of us. Maybe we could go to the creek, skim some rocks, and talk. I had a lot on my mind.

He was hard to track down! He wasn't at home. I checked the apartments, the wash house, and the McKenzie Recess Fields. He was nowhere to be found. Although I chilled with some of my other friends earlier in the week, I didn't feel comfortable discussing with them what was on my mind. I ran into Elijah as I passed through Franklin Court one last time.

"Have you seen Benny Lee?" I asked.

"I saw him earlier in front of the apartments but I don't know where he went."

"Okay, if you see him tell him I'm looking for him."

"Roger that."

I had grown hot and tired. Not ready to go home I headed for my second favorite hangout, O'Dell's Barber Shop. Maybe I'd sweep the floor for a few coins and listen to the old heads for a while. They talked about everything in the barber shop; money, cars, politics, sports, and race issues. I took in as much as I could. Some of the talk was over my head. My Double-O status had no skill to reference, so I filed and stored as much as possible; it could come in handy someday. Mr. O'Dell ran a clean shop. No cussing, no swearing. No dirty talk about women. The only arguments were about sports. Who had the best team or which athlete was the best? Back in the day when business was slow, he gave me boxing lessons. Now my boxing days were in the rear view mirror.

I must admit I enjoyed boxing. It gave me the opportunity to release my anger, aggression, frustration. I got great satisfaction from boxing. I'd unload all my baggage upon my opponents; the name calling, my dad's weekend rants, my inferior feeling, and the embarrassment of living on rocks in a 25 x 22 foot box. With each punch I unleashed my wrath, my fury. But boxing was over. Mr. O'Dell often asked if I wanted to put on the gloves again. I respectfully declined. I told him they made me feel like a bully, and I didn't like bullies. He'd smiled at my answer but never persisted. I did need to find another safe outlet though.

As I neared the barber shop I passed the "New Do for You" Beauty Shop. It's where Jeanie worked. She wasn't due to come in to work until later, so I kept moving. The building had an office on one side and the beauty shop next door. The doors were separated by a large soda machine. Both doors were usually open to allow workers in the shop to answer the telephone in the office. I never understood why they wouldn't get a phone on the parlor side! I cruised pass the soda machine and glanced into the window of the office. There, standing behind the desk was Benny Lee! I backed up and entered the office.

"Benny! Where have you been? I've been looking all over for you!" I said.

He looked dazed, stunned; eyes were in a panic. He put his index finger to his lips. He scampered over to me, grabbed my arm, and whisked me into the alley.

"What's going on?" I asked as I pulled my arm away.

"I need you to do me a favor!" he requested.

"Okay, what is it?" I inquired.

"I need you to stand by the soda machine and let me know when Mrs. Walker is coming. Here's a quarter. Buy a soda and drink it slow," he instructed. "If Mrs. Walker is coming, tap hard on the side of the machine next to the office door," he concluded.

"Sure! But what's going on? I insisted.

"I'll explain it to you later," he said.

Leave it to Benny to take us on a secret hunt. I was game, played along. I bought the bottle of soda and took my position. Benny slipped back into the office. I occasionally glance into the shop. Mrs. Walker pressed hair and flapped her gums with the customers. I turned to check on Benny. I gagged on my soda! He was rambling through a large purse and pulled out a huge money bag; he was robbing the place!

That was the madness of the hunt. You never knew what could happen. You went with the flow. I promised myself I would never forgive Benny if we got caught. But if I did my job that would never happen.

It was defiantly a Bond type adventure. My Double-O skills sprung into action. I got hyped. I couldn't let Bond go now. I needed him. I turned back to check on Mrs. Walker.

"Hi Joseph, I thought that was you. That soda looks good. Think I'll have me one too."

Oh god no, it was Mrs. Walker! She crept up on me like a theft in the night. I felt a strong urge to pee. Something ran down my leg; condensation from the soda bottle or.... Bond took over.

"Hi Mrs. Walker, yes, this is a mighty fine soda; definitely needed on a hot day like today.

I talked loud enough so Benny could hear me. I moved in front of the office door to reveal the soda machine and shield Benny from sight. I continued the loud, awkward, conversation.

"I stopped by to say hi to Jeanie and forgot she was coming in later."

"Your sister is one of our best beauticians. The customers love her. You tell her I said so and we'll see her this afternoon," she said as she put her coins in the machine and pulled out her soda.

"I certainly will Mrs. Walker."

"Thanks. Keep cool," she said as she went back into the beauty parlor.

The drip stopped running down my leg. I took the last swallow of my soda. Benny tugged my shirt.

"Let's go," he commanded.

We jetted through the alley between the beauty shop and the record store. We were like two speed boats hydroplaning. The coins clanged like cymbals in Benny's pocket. I pitched the soda bottle in the bush. We didn't stop until we were at the McKenzie Bridge. We crossed and settled at the upper end of the creek, on the school side, away from our normal hangout.

"Why didn't you tell me you were going to rob the place?" I asked as we caught our breath.

"Remember…you don't steal,"

"Well yeah, but at least I would have known what you were doing."

"Why? So you could back out or try to stop me?"

"Maybe," I said with doubt.

"Well, ya didn't! And look." He pulled a sock from each pocket filled with coins.

"Man, how much is it?" I asked in awe.

"I don't know. Let's count it. Why is the front of your pants wet?"

"Long story: don't ask."

Benny took off his shirt and laid it on the bank. We dumped the coins onto it and put our backs to the apartment so no one could spy on us.

"What did you do when you heard me talking to Mrs. Walker? I tried to talk loud enough so you could hear me."

"I heard you. What happened to tapping on the machine?"

"While I was checking on you, she snuck up on me like a vampire; could've bit my neck and sucked all the blood out of me, and I wouldn't have known it."

"Well, once I heard you call her name I hide under the desk. I had loaded the socks and was ready to go when you started talking.

I took one pile and he the other. The count was on; final tally; $31.50. Benny drew a division equation in the sand.

"$15.75," I said.

He looked at me and squinted.

"How do you do that?" he asked softly.

I smiled but gave no response. He stared, shook his head, and continued.

"Okay! Count out your $15.75," he ordered.

"I can't take that much money home! Remember what happened with the shoe boxes? Just give me $5.00 and you keep the rest," I suggested.

"Yeah, you're right I can't take that much home either. Okay, I'll give you $5.00 and I'll take $10.00. There's something I want to buy. I'll bury the rest. We'll come get it later," he decided.

"Good Idea," I said.

With his head down he began to dig a hole with his hands.

"Benny!" I called.

"What?" he responded while digging.

"What if your mom found out you robbed the beauty parlor?" I asked.

"Correction, you and I robbed the soda money," he clarified.

"Either way…what if she finds out? What will she say?" I asked.

He paused, turned to me, and said softly, "Man, she doesn't care about me!"

"What do you mean, she doesn't care? What if Mrs. Walker, the owner called the cops on you? Then you'll have to lie to her and your mom."

"It wouldn't be the first time," he answered as he continued to dig.

'What are you talking about?" I asked

"She never listens to me anyway! She doesn't care about me! And she doesn't love me either!" he stated with certainty.

"Benny, don't say that? Sure she loves you," I encouraged.

"No she doesn't! She told me she didn't. She said, 'I can't stand you. You remind me of your daddy, and I can't stand him either.'" He confessed choking on his words.

He began weeping gently! Drops trickled into the hole he was digging.

"She was just angry at your dad for something. That's all," I consoled him.

"I would love to believe that, but it wasn't the first time she said it. Whenever she's angry at me she says, "I can't stand you! You remind me of your no good, lazy daddy!" he admitted.

I had no words. This was what he tried to say many times but stopped short. He had carried this inside for years. The weight of it finally broke him. Why didn't I see it? How could a mother say that to her son? My Double-O files had no frame of reference. Sure, he stole to get the things he needed. Yes, he lied to her to protect himself from her verbal assaults. Other than that he was one of the nicest kids I knew. He never got in trouble at school. He didn't start fights. And he shared everything with me. He was my brother, I felt him. My innards became a hollowed pit. I was in the well with him, trying to climb out.

In silence we counted out our take. With the coins back inside the socks, Benny placed them in the hole. He buried the coins along with his tears, marking the spot with stones and twigs. He put on his shirt. A refreshing breeze circled. The creek was serene. Clouds danced by as we laid on the bank. Our forearms served as visors. His agony still evaporating, I soaked it in. He wanted, needed his mother's love. The vision of Casey's gun appeared again. The pearl handle felt so good in my hand. He was telling me to steady my aim. I had Benny's mom in my sight.

"Now squeeze the trigger," a voice said.

"Ouch!" Damn mosquito. The sting brought the clouds back into view. I needed to control my anger, my thoughts. I was having the gun vision too often. I jumped up and grabbed Benny by the shirt.

"Come on! I know what you need," I said.

"What?" he asked.

"Ah, I need you to do me a favor. I'll explain it to you later," I joked. We both forced weak smiles as I looked him in the eyes.

We whisked the sand from our bodies as we stood. We hopped on the path behind Betty's to get to Franklin Street. Crossing at the red light, we entered Ray's; straight to the Pinball Machine.

"This is what you need! The loser pays for the next game," I wagered.

I put the first two quarters in. We played the game until our hurt was gone. I bought snacks and sodas between the games. I spent most of my take. I didn't want Benny to spend his money. He wanted to buy something, probably for school; it was starting in three days. He got angry at me for spending my money.

I joked, "You can pay me back; you're rich."

We laughed away even more of the hot wax dripping inside of us.

The money didn't matter to me. Seeing my friend happy meant more. I put my concerns aside. He needed a friend. He would have done it for me. Besides, the crew's Annual Fish and Swim was the next day. We did it every year on the last Saturday before the start of school. I planned to talk with Benny Lee then.

It was a long night. I coughed and wheezed from the cold I had. Benny's break down dogged me. The thought of him not feeling loved at home overwhelmed me. I may have been bullied on the streets but at home...I was loved. But his quandary wasn't the base of the iceberg.

I was spiraling out of control; feelings, thoughts, behavior, at titanic level; promiscuity, violence, criminal acts. Mama, Duke, Lindsey, and Benny Lee danced in my head at once; 'They're just jealous." "Ignore them." "Don't let them push your buttons." "Dial it back."

I was only 12 years old trying to make sense of it all; the bullying, Daddy's rants, near death by scorpion, the shootout at Jake's, gambled with Black Coat and his gun, and running toward a full scale riot for enjoyment. Now add robbery to the list. I had become a thief. Something I swore I'd never do. The worst part about it, I helped rob the place where my sister worked! How low was that?

As I laid there coughing, blood poured from my wounds. For some time I had been bleeding but few noticed. I had become a master at hiding in the light. Maybe it was the cold, but I was tired... aged... empty. I knew if I didn't control my urges, impulses, and passions, I wouldn't make it to 14. I needed to let Bond go... cut back on the hunts too. I had to talk with Benny Lee. I didn't want to lose his friendship, he was my brother, but the beauty shop hunt was way over the top.

Mama said, "Don't feed it and it'll die." But how do you kill something that gives you life? I had no idea, but I had to try. Benny needed to know that the Annual Fish and Swim would be my last hunt for a while.

CHAPTER 29

SINKING TO RISE NO MORE

Kids and parents flew around everywhere buying last minute items for school. My parents got up with the chickens, dragged me out the house. It seemed as if half the community was in Discount City Department Store. I thought we'd never get out of there. The next stop: Piggly Wiggly, to buy groceries. Both stores were a block east of the railroad tracks. I would pass both again later that day as the crew walked to the Intracoastal for our Annual End of the Summer Fish and Swim. Our meeting time was set for 2 o'clock at the wash house.

Most of the neighborhood kids spent their last Saturday at the Fountain Park Pool. We chose not to participate. For starters, none of the crew had swimming trunks except me. I lied, told them I didn't have any either. There was a 15 cents entry fee. We'd rather buy food with our money. Plus, the pool was a hangout for the Parkers. Swimming in the Intracoastal was ten times better; never crowded. We swam, fished, and played with the Manatees, a huge mammal that looked like a giant seal or a baby hippo, gentle and playful.

I was the last to arrive at the wash house, had to convince Mama to let me go. The cold and coughing gave her concern. I begged her to let me see my friends as it was the last Saturday of summer vacation. She reluctantly agreed. She wasn't a fan of my Franklin Court friends.

I told her we might go shoot baskets at McKenzie. The key word was might! She gave her approval if I wore long pants and a shirt. I secretly put on my shorts and T-shirt underneath. Duke, Benny, and Booker stood with their fishing rods. Otis was holding the bait

"Where are you going, to church?" Benny joked.

"Ah, school starts on Monday," Otis added.

"Well, the Troll can speak," I busted on Otis.

"No offense Joseph, but you look pretty silly wearing those clothes to go swimming." Booker politely piled on.

I unbuttoned my shirt and kicked off my sneakers.

I hummed the James Bond theme song.

"Oh no, there he goes again with that Bond shit! Give it a rest Joseph," Duke moaned.

That tune had become a reflex. It's so cool and timely, but it had to go too.

"Now what you got to say, bitches?" I boasted, as I revealed my T-shirt and shorts.

"That's a lot better than that preacher outfit you came up here wearing," Otis busted.

"Yo, when did the gargoyle learn to speak?" I busted back.

"He got, Hooked on Phonics. Now he can spell too! Booker piled on.

"Keep it up Booker! One of these days I'm gonna put you in a bear hug so tight your nut sack's gonna pop!" Otis retaliated.

We laugh hysterically.

"Easy Otis; don't ruin his manhood before he gets a chance to use it," Duke teased.

Before we ventured out, I hid my clothes behind the wash house. The 25 minute walk commenced. We took Reservoir Boulevard across the tracks so as not to be seen by any relatives.

"Did you guys get all your stuff for school yet?" Booker asked.

"Yeah! Yep! Got mine this morning!" We answered.

"I can't believe you little dicks are going to be at West Side High this year!" Duke joked.

"Yeah, finally!" Benny responded.

"Seemed like forever," Otis added.

"Well, that's because you failed a couple grades," Booker joked.

"Only one, you tadpole. I'm doing to squeeze the life out of you, you little bastard. Come here," Otis growled, chasing after Booker.

"Now now Otis, we don't want the little fool to miss the best part of his life; attending West Side High." Duke hinted.

"Tell us again about the best parts Duke," Benny pleaded.

"Well…the best part about West Side is…the senior girls. Their tits are the size of softballs. Their lipstick and makeup… perfect. After taking one look at them, your pole will be as straight as this fishing rod!" Duke divulged.

"Tits as big as softballs? Oh my God!" Benny relished.

"Yep, so you better keep your "Tighty-Whities" pulled up and fix your pole pointed toward your belly button. That way they won't see your hard-on! Everyone laughs at newbies when they walk around with a hard-on," Duke warned.

"Man, we're going to be in Heaven! Every day we get to see softballs bouncing right in front of us," Booker drooled

"Some days the fast girls wear mini-skirts. The principal usually catches up to them by lunch time; make them change. Every boy in school stops to watch them walk by, even the newbies," Duke informed.

"What? …Mini-skirts in school? You lying Duke," Otis said.

"I swear on my dead grandmother's grave. It's all true," Duke assured.

"You mighty quiet today Joseph. What's up?" Benny asked."I figured all this girl talk would have you all fired up!"

"I got a cold, coughed most of the night, throat's a little sore," I answered.

"Well you better heal fast cause we're gonna be Jaguars in 2 days!" Benny announced.

The crew cheered as we reached our destination. We took the path from the bridge to reach the bank of the water. I peered across. It glistened. The salty air cleared my sinuses. Sneakers, T-shirts tossed. Fishing rods set aside. One after the other we plunged in. Ah, nothing better on a summer day! We swam to the middle and waited for our friends. On cue, they popped up around us, one for each of us. I swam beside my Manatee friend, petting him gently. We submerged together. I was saddened by the long marks tattooed on his back, carved by speedboats racing through the water. The mammals were too large, too slow to avoid the propellers. We played with our friends for an hour or so. Climbing out the water, we shared stories about our time with the sea animals. We gathered our things and walked 30 yards to our favorite fishing spot.

My teeth began to chatter. My shoulders shook. I needed my long sleeved shirt! The crew collected worms the day before. A hard rain two nights ago brought the worms to the surface of the soil. We also used bread ends to bait the line. I shared Benny's fishing rod. Booker shares with Otis. On a good day, we caught five or six. I never took my catch home. I gave them to Benny Lee. My parents would have a fit if they knew I was in White Town fishing.

"Cough, Cough, Cough, Cough…"

Another coughing spell. I threw up, chunks of phlegm geysered.

"Yo man, get away! What you got some kind of disease?" Otis complained.

"Can't you see he's sick?" Benny defended.

"Otis, spell disease? As I thought…don't use words you can't spell," Booker scolded.

"Man, are you alright?" Duke asked me with concern.

"Yeah, I'm okay. I've had this cold the past couple days. That's why I had on all those warm clothes. My mom wouldn't let me go unless I wore them. I had one of those coughing spells last night," I confessed as I wiped my mouth.

"Well if Joseph's good, let's go get our last dip of the summer," Duke suggested.

We packed up the rods and the bait. Benny Lee and Duke each caught a fish but threw it back, too small. We had to be home in an hour. A 30 minute splash party awaited us. We swam a couple relay races. Of course, Benny and I were on teams. Otis and Booker made up team #2. Duke served as the official. He parked in the middle treading. Each team member had to swim out to him, swim around him, and back to tag their teammate. My team won the challenge, two races to one. Duke swam in. We were about to put on our shirts.

"One last dare of the summer. Let's race to the other side," Duke offered.

"I'm in," Benny agreed

"Me too!" Booker seconded.

"I'm out," Otis spoke up.

"I'm out too. I'm tired," I said.

Otis and I acted as the official starters for the race.

"On your marks, get set, go!" we shouted.

And they were off! Otis and I sat and watched from the bank. Duke, Benny, Booker was the order of finish.

"Come on you wimps! Get over here. Don't be a pussy all your life!" they yelled to us.

Otis wasn't a very strong swimmer.

"You want to try it?" I asked.

"I will if you will!" he answered.

"You sure?" I asked with concern.

"Okay, let's race," he challenged.

"Give us a count down!" I shouted to the crew on the other side.

The distance was about 65 yards across. Not an impossible task at all.

"3, 2, 1, go!" Duke shouted.

Splash! We dashed toward our comrades cheering on the other side. Holding a half body lead at the mid-point, I glanced to my left; Otis vanished, turned back. I swam on. Without warning, a fog covered the screaming maniacs in front of me. I swam another 10 yards before my lungs caught fire; vaporizing my oxygen. Suddenly, I was carrying 10 pound weights in both hands. I franticly tried to press on but my legs wouldn't respond.

"Help! Help!" I shouted before I went under.

I fought to get back to the surface. I heard the crew laughing.

"Stop playing. Hurry up, we don't have all day," they shouted.

"Help!" I bellowed before I went under again.

The crew thought I was faking. Where were the manatees when I needed one?

My mind raced at the speed of light. The Reaper's chill gave chase. Faster and faster went the drumming in my chest; its' cadence pressed the back of my throat. Slipping into the world of shadows I held onto hope...tied a knot at the end of its rope. A flurry of images passed in a blur; my family, friends, coach, my crew. With anxiety at zenith, I pleaded with God, "Don't let me go out like this!"

Oxygen depleting, pilot light faint, my life-force diminished. All struggling ceased. A peace, calm enveloped me. Only Mama mattered. Her love seized my final thoughts. The promise made to her cradled my heart. Fading deeper and deeper into the murk, I imagined her disappointment when they told her I was with a group of guys she warned against. I envisioned her reaction when she learned I was in a forbidden section of town. The tears when she got the news, "Her youngest son was dead." Our bond, our love, separated forever...the promise broken.

I felt a tug at my legs, my arms. I had become fish bait.

Stillness.

Quiet.

"Breathe! Breathe!"

Smack! A firm hit to the back.

"Breathe," the voice repeated.

"Cough, cough, cough..."

Air, water, phlegm propelled from my lungs. Duke, Benny Lee and Booker had lifted me from the depths. Duke swam behind me, a handful of my shorts. Benny and Booker each held an arm. After a couple breaths...I was back to life.

"I'm good. You can let go now," I said.

"You sure?" Benny asked.

"Yeah, I'm okay. Just swim with me;" I said.

I swam the remaining 20 yards to the other side. After I reassured them I was okay, they helped me climb onto a boat dock. I sprinted through several backyards on my way to the bridge. I dashed across and returned to the area where our clothes and Otis sat.

"What were you trying to do, kill yourself out there?" He asked with creepy laughter.

"No Otis, you dick; I was drowning!" I snapped.

"Oh! For real?" he mumbled.

I thought, *what an idiot!* But I was too unnerved to verbally joust with him. I dressed to ease my shivers. The guys asked for a countdown to race back across. Otis did the honors while I sat pondering another close call. Tremors over took me, goose bumps surfaced.

This near miss wasn't like the others. This one forced my acquaintance with death. He shook my hand. His grip pulled me under, even though, I was sinking long before we met. The Reaper spoke loud that day but Life spoke louder; issuing a warning, "Slow your roll. This isn't fantasy. Nor is it make-believe. This is life and you only get one." I finally got it, but life had to teach me.

Mama use to say, "Listen to me son. Learn from me. Don't wait for life to teach you. His lessons are much harder."

No truer words. I was done with adventures for a while. I needed to breathe. Seeing my life flash before me, on my way to the great beyond, was enough. It squashed my last resolve. I planned to talk to Benny Lee on the way home.

I was so lost in thought I didn't see the order of finish in the race. To be honest, I really didn't care. Coming out of the water they came toward me.

"Are you alright?" Duke asked.

"Yeah, I'm good. Thanks guys for coming to get me. I guessed this cold caused me to run out of gas. I had no strength. I couldn't move," I answered, trying to hide my shakes.

"Man, when you didn't come up that last time, we thought you were a goner. I've never swam so fast!" Booker expressed.

Benny Lee didn't say a word. He grabbed his things and sat next to me. Our eyes meet. He was visibly shaken. I gave a slight nod. His face was stern. Pulling his T-shirt over his head, he reached for his sneakers. I tossed sand into them. He looked up.

"Don't do that again," he whispered.

"Don't do what? Toss sand in your sneaks or almost drown?" I whispered with a smirk.

"Neither!" he answered shaking sand from his shoes.

"Neither! Whoa, what a word. You sound like Joseph," I joked.

"Yeah, I guess I've been hanging around his crazy ass too much," he said with a smirk and a shove to my shoulder.

"I guess now is a good time to tell y'all. I have some bad news guys," Duke announced.

"What bad news?" Benny asked.

"Well Benny, your aunt and uncle pulled the plug. I won't be going to West Side this year or any year after. They've made me quit school. I start my job on Wednesday," he said.

A sand storm gust swept through, clouds rolled in, the sun faded. His parents made good on their threats, his worst nightmare. He continued.

"This means I won't be around much anymore. I work most Saturdays and a half day on some Sundays as well," he concluded.

Our stunned hush was deafening. The glue that held us together was gone. I didn't know how to react. At 14, Duke had to take a job to help pay bills; adult responsibilities. No more kid. Gone were his hunts, his carefree adventures. The guy that saved my life twice was moving on. In a way, so was I. We donned our clothes in silence. We stood to leave. Still searching for words, I went over to Duke.

"Thanks," I said and hugged him as a line formed behind me.

He knew what I meant. I needed to say no more.

"You taught me a lot Duke," Otis said and hugged as well.

"You were a great leader Duke. I'm gonna miss you," Booker confessed hugging tight.

The show of friendship, gratitude, and respect got to Duke.

"I'm gonna miss you guys too. His voiced cracked a little as he encouraged and cautioned. "Just remember to look out for each other. And stay away from the Hula Poolas. I know y'all want revenge but they aren't worth going to Juvie over!"

Benny Lee stood before him.

"I'm sorry they made you quit. That's really messed up. I know how much you looked forward to playing football this year," Benny spoke with regret laden words.

Duke playfully put him in a headlock, gave him nuggies, and said. "I know li'l cuz but we still got each other. Keep these guys safe for me, okay?

"Sure Duke…sure," Benny answered.

We gathered the fishing rods and tracked homeward. Not much talk in route. A brisk pace replaced our words. An overcast of anguish hovered. The FCC Crew would never be the same.

As we crossed the tracks into Black Town, our spirits lifted a little.

"Duke, at least you don't have to do school work anymore. I gotta pass four classes this year?" Otis complained.

"Don't worry Otis. I'll help you," Booker volunteered.

"Me too, I got your back," I reassured him.

"We all got your back Otis," Benny proclaimed.

"That's what I like to hear. Keep looking out for each other," Duke stated as his last request as leader of The Franklin Court Crew.

He waved farewell as he took the path from Reservoir Boulevard to The Heights Apartments.

"I'm really gonna miss Duke. He looked out for me," Booker reminisced.

"He looked out for all of us," Benny said.

"He saved my life twice," I confessed.

"Oh damn Joseph, I had forgotten about the scorpion!" Otis offered.

"My family has no idea…I wouldn't be alive if it wasn't for Duke. Well, if it wasn't for all you guys," I praised.

After thanking Booker and Benny Lee again, I veered off toward home. I took the path behind the now closed Roland Super Market. Again, I didn't get a chance to talk with Benny Lee. Duke's announcement took all the air. After which, I couldn't bring myself to tell him I had decided to back off the hunts. I'm sure he would've understood, especially after the near drowning incident. It was defiantly the last straw. It was time for me to value my life more. But there was more, much more I needed to discuss with Benny.

CHAPTER 30

GOOD-BYE BENNY

Sunday morning. The aroma pulled me out of bed. Mama and Jeanie were at it again; chicken, collard greens, cornbread, potato salad, and corn on the cob. I wished we ate like this every day! I got dressed and hopped in the car with Jeanie for Sunday school.

"You have a big day tomorrow, huh?" she asked.

"Yeah – I guess," I said, staring out the window.

"You don't sound too excited. Come on, you're finally going to be a Jaguar!" She cheered.

"Yep – the Gold and Black," I said still staring out the window.

"That's right, my alma mater," she bragged.

"It's everyone's alma mater, big school though," I added.

"Don't worry, you'll learn your way around there in no time," she encouraged.

There were several Parkers in my Sunday school class. The class was all boys. Most were okay. Tyrone was the only Parker I talked to. He went to school at Titan Prep in Rising Tide. He was a year older. He wasn't a dick like the other Parkers.

Church service was long. It ended with Pastor Samuels calling all students, teachers, and school support staff to the altar. The students kneeled in front. Teachers and staff stood behind. I prayed for myself, my situation, and the crew. We were dismissed from the altar to the sound of a standing ovation.

Mama and Jeanie set the table. I brought glasses in from the kitchen. We took our places. Oh, I forgot to tell you, Casey got married! He met his bride at a house party last year. She worked at the Pepsi Cola Company. They were married in May. He and his bride lived in Sea Garden. He'd finally made it out the quarters. It was Lavelle's turn to bless the table.

"Good bread, good meat, good God let's eat!" he joked.

I snickered. Jean tossed her cornbread at him.

"Stop playing!" she demanded.

Mama's frown smacked him hard. Daddy never raised his head.

"Okay, okay, I'm sorry. I'll say a real prayer," he chuckled.

"The Lord is our shepherd; we thank him for this food. Amen"

"Thank you!" Mama said with a smile.

"That's more like it," Jeanie complimented.

Plates were made. The dinner chit-chat commenced. I became the center piece.

"Well guess who's going to finally be a Jaguar?" Jeanie said.

"So what are you wearing on your first day," Lavelle asked.

"I'm wearing my gold and black T-shirt with my khakis," I answered.

"Good choice. Wearing the school colors is cool on the first day," Lavelle approved.

"Don't you go up there and embarrass your brother! You and that mouth of yours! You get your work done and don't cause trouble for him," Daddy warned.

Clink, my fork dropped against my plate. I couldn't swallow. My gut fizzled. I glared in his direction. How dare he? There I sat with all kinds of crazy thoughts in my head about going to high school and he was worried about Lavelle. Everyone knew he was wrong. Mama quickly intervened.

"Oh, he's going to do fine. Did you look over your schedule yet?"

Pause.

"Joseph!" she called.

I turned to her, speechless, wearing the same glare.

"Can I be excused?" I asked.

"But you haven't finished your plate!" Mama said.

"Finish your plate," Daddy demanded.

No one spoke. Tension replaced the food's aroma. I ate as fast as I could. I put my plate in the sink and went to the bathroom. After washing my face and hands I darted for the back door.

"Where are you going?" Mama asked.

"I'm going over to Benny's," I answered in a huff.

"Don't be gone long," she said.

I didn't answer. I closed the door. Lavelle ran out behind me.

"Wait. He didn't mean it!" Lavelle consoled.

"Sure he did! But it's cool. I won't embarrass you," I assured.

"You could never embarrass me! You're my little brother!" He said with a smile.

"Thanks Lavelle."

I turned toward Ray's still dressed in church clothes. The dirt path was clear. I ran into Booker and Otis in the store. We exchanged greetings. I asked for their help as they were leaving.

"Tell Benny to meet me at the creek. I have something for him."

'He was at the apartments when we left. I'll tell him," Booker agreed.

I bought a soda and left. My destination was the McKenzie side of the embankment. I took the path behind Betty's. I settled opposite from the crew's usual spot. The sun was unkind. I shed garments for relief. The creek was unusually high, four feet or better. I tossed stones to fill the void. Each ripple pulled me further away. My father's comment accompanied me. He showed no concern about me going to school with my heaters. In fact, no one did! No one asked me how I felt. They all thought I was happy to be a Jaguar. That was the furthest thing from the truth.

"There you are! What are you doing over there?" Benny asked.

"I was beginning to think you weren't coming," I answered. "I was over here saying good-bye to McKenzie. We had some great times here."

"Yes we did! But we're Jaguars now. Are you ready for tomorrow?" he asked.

"Yeah, but I'm not going!" I answered as I took a sip of soda.

"Not going…why not?"

"I'm never going to that school!"

"Why not, are you moving? Is that why you called me down here; to tell me you're moving?" he barked at me.

"No Benny, I'm not moving. I'm just never going to school there."

"Then what are you talking about? We've be waiting to be Jaguars forever. You can't get cold feet now."

"I would love to be a Jaguar, but its' never going to happen."

"And why not? …Oh, I get it. Your parents are sending you to that shitty private school. That's just great!" He stated in anger.

"No, I'm not going to Titan Prep. But if my parents could afford to send me, I'd go in a heartbeat!"

"What? You wanna go to Prep with the Parkers?"

"If my parents could afford it, I would. I'm not worried about the Parkers my age. I've kicked most of their butts when I boxed at O'Dell's. It's the older kids at West Side, my haters, that concerns me."

"Ah man, don't worry about them. They're just being dicks."

"Benny, they're going to make a fool of me! You know how I get when they call me names."

"We'll be at school. Just tell the principal. Get'em in trouble."

"They'll hate me even more for ratting them out. They'll say, "There goes that Lil Mulatto, Mutt rat"!"

"Then just do what you always do, have Lavelle beat the shit outtta 'em."

"You don't understand. The name calling dicks have me right where they want me. I can't run away from them. I have to see them all day every day: in the halls, the cafeteria, at my locker. I can't take that. They've won Benny. I'm tired of fighting them."

"You don't know if it's going to be that way or not. You can't just give up! That's not the Joseph, James Bond I know," he praised.

"How am I going to survive? I can't flip out cussing and fussing like on the streets. I'll get in trouble which means my dad will flip out on me. I can't embarrass Lavelle and ruin his good reputation. If I flip out all my high school years are ruined. Kids will say, "Hey look, there goes Lavelle's Lil Albino, nuts job brother." I won't get an invite to nothing ever again; not a party, dance, or a sporting event. Yep they've won."

"So whatta you gonna do? You wanna hook tomorrow? I'll hook with you, but we can't hook school every day. They'll put us in Juvie for sure if we do," he warned.

"I'm not going to hook. Hey, I have something for you," I said as I reached into my shirt pocket.

"What is it?"

"I wrote this last week when you were away. It's called, "Blood Brothers Forever." You want to hear it?"

"Sure! Okay!"

I read:

"We met in gym class several years ago.

Your friendship means more to me than you'll ever know.

When others make fun of me you're always by my side.

You stand up for me when I want to run and hide.

We've stuck together through many battles.

Brave, strong, never rattled.

You are my brother tried and true.

I wish everyone had a friend and a brother like you."

I looked up and asked, "Well, what do you think?"

"You wrote that?" he asked.

"Yep, I want you to have it." I said as I folded it and placed it back into my pocket.

"That's great! Thanks! I'll come around and get it."

"You can get it later. Let's sit and talk some more."

"Okay, what do you wanna talk about?" he asked.

"You remember that time you fell out the mango tree and I prayed and you were better?"

"Yeah…I remember. What a day that was."

"Well, you weren't half dead! I asked Lavelle about it. He said you got the wind knocked out of you when you hit the ground. That's why you couldn't move. He said it happens to guys on the football field all the time."

"Yeah, I talked with Duke. He told me the same thing. Why do you bring that up?"

"Well, I didn't want you to think I had some super power or something," I answered as I reached into my pants pocket.

"Nah, I wouldn't think that. What's that?"

"These are my mom's pain pills for her back. I'm never going to that school, Benny," I said as I dumped the pills into the soda bottle.

"What are you doing?" he yelled.

"It's okay Benny. It won't hurt. All my worries will be over."

"Please don't Joseph! Please!" he begged.

"You were right. We all pretend. I pretended I was James Bond. Thinking he could save me from the bullies, thinking he could make them accept me. I thought he could rescue me from the rocks. I was wrong! He only made it worst. I'm tired of pretending."

"We'll figure something out. Please don't drink that. Help!" he yelled as he stood.

"It's okay. I prayed about it in church today. Maybe my near drowning yesterday was a sign. There was a moment…just before you guys came to get me…I stopped struggling. There was peace. I need to feel that again. I can't risk the bullies calling me names all day, every day, at school. It's too much."

"Help! Help! I'm coming over there right now. Don't do it Joseph." He pleaded as he jumped into the water.

"Good-bye Benny. You were the best friend I ever had."

I threw the bottle up to my mouth. Twelve or more pills tumbled down the back of my throat.

"No!" He screamed. "Don't drink that. Please don't Joseph." he cried as he swam across.

"Be good Benny. Don't rob the beauty parlor anymore. Be good."

"Why did you do that? Help! Please somebody, Help!" He yelled rising from the water.

He took the bottle from my hand, threw it aside. He continued to yell for help.

"I'm glad you're here Benny. I'm glad your...."

I slumped into his lap, clouds were in view; showers sprinkled my face.

"Get up Joseph! Please get up. Don't leave me."

CHAPTER 31

LAID TO REST

A faint siren, cool air circled my nose, alternating pressure against my chest.

"What's his named?" someone asked.

"Joseph! Joseph Graham."

The muffled siren was over head now. Beep...beep in my ear; a familiar squeeze against my hand.

"Don't die Joseph. Get up! Please get up. Don't leave me."

"Be good Ben...."

Beeeeeeeeeee

"He's crashing!"

"Move back! Clear!"

"We're losing him!"

Beeeeeeeeeeeeeeeeeeeee!

I was cold. I flew up toward the sun. Up and up I went; bright lights all around. I landed on a street of....

"Ouch! Why'd you do that!"

"I've been calling you for five minutes to get up!" Lavelle barked.

"Well you didn't have to pull my ear off!" I complained.

"Come on, get up! You don't want to be late your first day of high school," he said.

I jumped out the bed Casey once occupied. I ran to the mirror. It

was true. I was alive. That dream was too real, but writing a poem…
really? I needed to concentrate. What was I going to do? My problem
still existed.

"What were you dreaming about? You kept saying, "Be good
Benny. Be good," Lavelle asked.

I couldn't tell him or anyone about that dream. They'd lock me
away for sure. If the doctor questioned me and I told him all the shit
I'd done, he'd throw me in the loony bin for sure. But what was I to do?
My problem still excited. I grabbed Lavelle by the arm.

"I can't go to West Side Lavelle! I can't!" I groaned.

"Why not?" he asked.

"You know why! Those name callers. They're going to use me for
their punching bag all day, every day," I answered.

"Well you can't hook school every day. Remember what I told you,
if you really want to do it. If you really want to be a Jaguar don't let
nothing or no one stop you. And you know I got your back. So get
dressed," he commanded.

"Okay – If you say so!" I reluctantly agreed.

"Let me see your schedule. What time are you meeting your
friends?" he asked.

"We're meeting at 7:15 at Betty's," I answered as I handed him my
schedule.

"Well you've got 15 minutes. You better hurry." He said returning
my schedule.

"Okay, I gotta go. I'm meeting my friends at Ray's. You better not
hook! I'll see you at school," he said as he walked out the back door.

I'd dreaded that day for some time. I never told a soul until it was
upon me. How could I? I was the great James Bond, a Double-0. Bull!
I was scared to death to go to West Side High. The problem with
pretending is it only works if you can pull it off. How was I going to
pull off avoiding haters at school all day every day? Casey once told me
I had to face my fears if I was to overcome them!

A knock at the front door,

"You ready?" yelled my cousin Mae.

Yes, the same cousin Mae, Mama and I went to visit across the field the night I flipped out on Daddy during my first anger blackout. She and I were the same age, in the same grade. She had asked to walk to school with me. I told her sure if she didn't mind walking with my friends. She agreed. I think she liked Booker but you didn't hear that from me.

"Almost, come in! Let me grab my things," I yelled back.

"Come here Joseph!" Mama called to me.

"Yes," I answered.

"You look nice. Why the troubled face. Don't worry. Everything will be fine. Give me your hand," she said.

I extended my hand. And like every year before she took it, placed her other hand on my forehead and prayed. But this was the first time I really listened to her words.

Mae and I approached the crosswalk between Ray's and Betty's. The crew was waiting across the street. As we crossed I saw Booker and Mae's eyes meet. I kept it to myself. We greeted each other and pressed our pedals forward; PF flyers, Converse, Keds covered our wheels. Benny, Otis, and I took the lead. Mae kept pace just behind with Elijah and Booker. PB & J, Bologna, and Pickled Loaf seeped from their brown paper prisons. We compared schedules. It took my mind off the tidal waves rolling inside. We all, including Mae, had at least two classes together. Elijah, Benny, and I also had gym together. All newbies had lunch at the same time.

The only other time we conversed was at Crew Therapy. We tried to hide our anxiety about our first day of high school. With a block to go, the conversation changed to the Parkers. For Mae and the crew, it would be their first prolonged encounter with them. I had witnessed their arrogance in Sunday school and church. We decided we weren't going to put up with any of their smug, condescending bullshit. Townie Pride ruled!

Entering the front gate to West Side High, my heart thumped faster than the pistons in a car engine. My carburetor choked for air. My palms dripped clutching my folders! We broke off but vowed to see each other at lunch. Mae and I were in the same homeroom, we searched in awe; the school was huge! Kids were racing around everywhere. There were so many big bodies! Duke was right; the older girls did have softballs protruding from their chest. Mae and I found our Homeroom just before the bell. So far, so good, didn't cross paths with any bullies…yet.

I began to feel sick about a minute to go before the bell rang, dismissing us to first period class. My stomach bubbled, my head spun, my brow dampened. Then the bell rang. I was dead meat! I met Mae at the door and we braved the crowded hallway.

Five steps into the melee, "What's up Jay Gee?"

"Hi Ed, not much."

"You're a Jaguar now Jay Gee?"

"Hey Mark, yep, finally!

"Welcome to West Side Jay Gee."

"Thanks Melt."

"Jay Gee, what's cracking?"

"Not much Steve".

"Jay Gee, what's happening? Are you all right?"

"I'm good Fred. Thanks."

That went on all day! No less than three of Lavelle's friends greeted me with a high five between each class. By the end of the day half the school knew me by my nickname, Jay Gee. My fellow 7th graders would stop and look at me. As to say, "Who is this kid? He knows everybody!" It was one of the best days ever! I met up with the crew and Mae at the front gate after school. We celebrated our first day on the walk home.

"Man Joseph, I didn't know you knew all those guys!" Benny said.

"Yeah, and all of them were stars on the football and basketball team too," Booker added.

"I still can't believe Melt Spencer, the varsity quarterback, walked us to class!" Elijah spoke in awe.

"And he's cute too!" Mae added. Booker turned to her with raise brows.

"I can't believe how all of them treated us like their little brothers. That was cool!" Otis added.

"Today was crazy! Totally unexpected! I met all those guys when I was a junior towel boy for the football and basketball teams. Most of them hang out with Lavelle," I explained.

"Why do they call you Jay Gee?" Booker asked.

"It's a nickname they gave me at my house one day when I was being a pain. Thanks to them, now everybody knows me as Jay Gee!" I beamed.

"Jay Gee ha…I like it," Benny said nodding. "Jay Gee…and Benny Lee. Cool, but you're still Joseph to me," Benny said with a punch to my shoulder.

"I know. I'll always be Joseph to my Blood Brother!" I answered as I gave him a massive titty-twister.

"Ouch! You cootie catcher!" he screamed in laughter punching me in the arm again.

"Oh my, there's too much male bonding going on around here for me!" Mae smirked.

"And you better watch it Mae. Booker would like to do some bonding with you," Otis joked.

"See, you're always starting something Otis!" Booker growled as he shoved him.

"Well he didn't lie on you Book!" Elijah added laughing.

"Here Lijah, I found your nose. Now keep it out of my business," Booker said.

We laughed. I looked back at Mae. Her shyness showed. A soft smile covered her lips. The crew took the McKenzie Bridge home. Mae and I continued to my house. Once there she picked up her little brother and sister who my mom babysat during the day.

"How was your first day?" Mama asked.

"It was great! The school is humongous! And Lavelle's friends made me and my friends feel like kings! They gave us high fives all day. They helped us with our schedules, walked us to class. My haters didn't stand a chance! Now the whole school knows me as Jay Gee!" I spouted.

"And you were worried," she said with a smile.

I had verbal diarrhea that wouldn't quit! Mama sat and listened to every word. The night before, I dreamt of destroying myself. When morning came I was scared to leave my house. Now I was king of my class! I was glad I told someone, an older person, what was going on. I did my homework waiting for Lavelle to come home from football practice.

"I hear there's a Junior Jaguar in this house!" a shout came from the kitchen.

It was Lavelle. I ran to him, almost knocked him over.

"Thanks Lavelle! I greeted with a big hug.

"Thanks? Oh yeah, I heard you ran into some of the guys at school. How was it?" he asked.

My mouth still had the runs as words poured like water from a spigot. I couldn't get them out fast enough.

"Slow down! I'm not going anywhere. Finish your homework and tell me the rest at dinner," he suggested.

"Okay!" I agreed.

"We're back together again! Just like at McKenzie," he remembered.

"Yep, just like McKenzie," I said with a big smile.

As I went back to doing my homework, I heard him and Mama talking.

"That was great what you did for him," Mama expressed.

"Well, Casey did the same for me my first day. I floated on air the whole day. It's a family tradition now," he confessed.

Things went well the first three weeks. No haters approached me. The Parkers didn't bother us, and we ignored them. My favorite subjects; Gym, History, and Science. My favorite teacher was Mr. Thompson, my History teacher. I swore he was the smartest man alive! He could recall names, dates, and events without ever looking in the text book. He talked with us at the start of each class. I enjoyed his openness. I felt like I knew him. And then it happened! Books flew, empty desks tossed.

"Fight," someone yelled.

I looked over my right shoulder to find Otis and one of the Parkers going at it! I swung my feet into the aisle. I readied to go help Otis, but he didn't need it. He was pounding the smug out that Parker. Never the less I needed to be there to make sure no one jumped in to help that kid. As soon as I went to stand, Mr. Thompson put his hand on my shoulder and forced me back into my seat.

"Sit!" he commanded.

He rushed to the back and with one shove he separated the fighters. Both went flying five feet in the opposite direction. Holy shit, Mr. Thompson was a Ninja! Otis was a fairly big, strong kid. Mr. Thompson dislodged them like a piece of lint from his sports coat. Impressive!

After separating the two he demanded each go to separate corners of the room as he called the front office to report the fight. Shortly after the call, the dean of students arrived to escort both kids to the office. They were sentenced to a five day suspension. That was nothing new for Otis. He got two or three of those each school year. I was told the Parker kid got smart with Otis and called him a name. Mr. Thompson knew Otis was my friend. He intentionally came down my row to get to the fight. Sensing I might get involved he stopped me in my tracks. He kept me from getting suspended. He cared. He had earned my respect!

The day for the mile run had arrived. It was part of our physical fitness test, required by the state. We practiced for weeks in gym class. Mr. Prince, our teacher was demanding. The crew and I didn't care for him. He made bad jokes about kids as they left the showers. Some kids laughed. We didn't find him funny at all! Benny, Elijah and I ran out the locker room for attendance.

"This is not a race! I will call out the elapsed time as you pass by me. Your grade will depend on how long it takes you to finish the four laps. This grade will be averaged in with the rest of your physical fitness grades," Mr. Prince announced.

A loud "Pop" from the gun and we were off. Four kids took off like rockets. After 20 yards Elijah took off after them!

"What is he doing?" Benny asked.

"I don't know!" I replied.

We chuckled as we kept our pace. We were holding steady in the middle of the pack. Elijah was a big, well, heavy kid. It seemed odd to us and most of the class that he was sprinting. He, Benny, and I never sprinted during practice sessions. Elijah had a half track lead on us as we made the first turn. He seemed to slow down. Good, he wouldn't last three more laps at that pace. As we continued to run, I kept an eye on him. He had slowed to a snail's pace. Benny and I made the second turn. I looked across the football field to find Elijah. He wobbled, did a 360 degree spin, and collapsed!

"Benny...Lijah," I said.

"I saw it too," he answered.

We raced across the field to his aid. From 10 yards out, I saw he wasn't moving. The students called for Mr. Prince. When Benny and I arrived Elijah was lying on his back motionless! A couple Parker kids laughed. One threw a stone and hit him.

"What are you laughing at? Are you laughing at my friend?" I barked as Benny and I stepped to them.

"Hey, cut it out!" Mr. Prince yelled as he arrived on the scene.

"You tell them to stop laughing at my friend!" I fired back at him.

"That's enough out of you Graham!" he snapped back.

My blood pressure rose and it wasn't from the blazing sun. How dare he correct me while those Parker pussies were making fun of my friend? I needed to stay under control. I must stay under.... Too late! I was back in that dark place again. The vision of Casey's gun was in my hand and it was pointed at you know who!

"Joseph! Joseph, don't worry about it. Let's help Lijah," Benny said as he pulled my arm.

"Huh? Oh...okay," I answered, falling back to earth.

"Move back!" Mr. Prince commanded.

"I'm alright," Elijah moaned.

He tried to stand but couldn't!

"Give me a hand. Help me get him out of the sun," Mr. Prince requested.

He supported Elijah's head and shoulders. Benny and I had a leg each while two other kids supported his waist. The rest of the class paraded behind us to the locker room. As we carried him I thought, *if he dies I will never forgive Mr. Prince. I will flatten his tires every month until I graduate!*

Once we were inside the paramedics were called. Mr. Prince told us to get dressed and take a seat.

"He'll be okay. We'll take the test another day," he said.

He began ripping into the kids who were laughing.

"Some of you need to grow up! Stop acting like little kids! What if it was you lying there. Would you want someone laughing at you?" he pounced. "Thank you to the ones that called for me. Also thanks to those that helped me get him inside," he said with sincerity.

Wow! He did care! He really did! I changed my mind about slashing his tires. But he needed to stop the bad jokes. The paramedics arrived as we were leaving for our next class. Elijah was carried out on a stretcher. An oxygen mask covered portions of his face. I looked at Benny. We didn't speak. Concern blanketed our face. As the emergency vehicle pulled away we took a slow walk to the cafeteria.

"I hope Lijah's okay," Benny mumbled.

"Me too! Why did he start out sprinting? I asked.

"I don't know! He's has way too much weight to try that," he answered.

"You're telling me!" I agreed.

We walked to the cafeteria where we met the rest of the crew. We told them what happened to Elijah. None of us spoke much after that. Our minds were on our friend. After eating Benny and I lied to the teacher on duty so we could leave early. Benny went to the library. I went to Mr. Thompson's room. He always brought his lunch from home, ate in his classroom.

I peeked through the window on the door. He sat at his desk eating his lunch. I knocked to get his attention. He looked toward the door and smiled when he recognized me. He rose from his seat and stroll toward the door. I backed away to allow it to swing open.

"Hi Joseph, can I help you?" he asked.

"Can I talk to you?" I requested.

"Sure I have a couple minutes. Come in," he invited.

He left the door open. I sat at the desk in front of his. Like waves in the ocean, in rapid succession, I unloaded sea weed at his feet. I told him about Elijah and what happened in gym class; how the Parker kids were laughing, my anger visions, and the name callers. My haters! I told him how I reacted when they called me names. I told him everything. I was drained.

When I finished he calmly rose from his seat.

"What's your friend's name, the one that was taken to the hospital?" he asked

"Elijah Walters," I answered.

He walked over to the intercom system. He pressed the button to call the front office.

"Yes Mr. Thompson!" A voice answered.

"Do you have an update on Elijah Walter, the kid that was taken to the hospital from gym class this morning?" he asked.

"Yes Thompson, It was heat exhaustion and dehydration. He's breathing on his own. He's doing fine. His mom is there with him." The voice informed.

"Thank you!" He turned to me." There, you see, your friend's okay. Now you don't have to slash anyone's tires." He said with a smile.

I couldn't believe I told him that.

He continued, "Why do you argue and cuss at those kids?"

"To get my respect," I answered.

"Well, it seems as if you already have their respect," he replied.

"How's that?" I asked.

"They go out of their way to address you. To call you names. Try to hurt you. That's a lot of respect right there. They don't do that to everyone. It's all in how you look at it! It's surely not the kind of respect you want. But it's respect just the same. So respect is not what you're looking for from them. You have that! What do you really want from them?" he asked.

"I want them to accept me. To like me or just leave me alone!" I answered.

"You can't make people like you or accept you. Neither can you control what people think or say about you. So stop letting them manipulate you. You're better than that! Stop stooping to their level with the cussing and busting! Most of those kids are jealous of you for some reason. Some may not know your name. They're just following what they saw someone else do. Try this; the next time someone calls you a name introduce yourself to them. Don't let them define you! You define yourself," he advised.

"They know my name!"

"That's not the point. Did he call you by your name?"

"No!"

"Most people would ignore a person if they didn't call them by their name! So why do you react to those terrible names?" he questioned, staring at me from behind his desk.

Oh man, another light bulb moment. It was as if he'd opened my head and poured in truth. Light radiated from my eyes. I could see clearly. For years I had reacted to names other than my own. The haters had used them to wind me up like a little toy and watched me dance for their pleasure. Duke, Lindsey, Mama, they all warned me. Why didn't I listen? I didn't listen because the creed on the streets was, "Get your respect!" I followed that motto for years. It caused me to make a fool of myself, but no more. No more!

"Now you get it?" he asked.

I nodded yes.

"By introducing yourself you are defining you, not the kid that called you a name. Plus you took the fun out of it for him by not flying off the handle. Or you can ignore him all together. Either way, stop letting them manipulate you. It's time to put that to bed. Lay it to rest. Stop responding to those names. If you do anything, tell them your name as if they didn't know it. You define yourself," he insisted.

"It's going to be hard, but I'll try," I said as the bell rang for me to go to class.

"Remember, you can't make people like or accept you. Neither can you control what they say and think about you. But you can control how you react to it!" he said as I headed for the door.

"Thanks Mr. Thompson," I said as I stopped to look back.

"You're welcome," he responded.

As I shuffled through the crowded hallway I saw Booker and Mae. They were holding hands. They released them when they saw me. I ignored their display of mutual affection.

"Elijah is okay. Mr. Thompson called the office and they said he was breathing on his own. His mom was at the hospital with him," I informed.

"Man that's great!" Booker said, exhaling.

"Tell Benny when you see him," I said as I bolted to class.

"Alright!" he yelled back through the crowded mess.

That day couldn't end fast enough. On the way home we stopped by Elijah's to check on him. He was back to himself. The doctor told him to take tomorrow off from school and drink lots of fluids. He laughed and joked with us, reassuring us he was fine.

I was as exhausted as my friend when I turned off the light for bed. All the excitement had drained me; Elijah collapsing, me spilling my guts to Mr. Thompson, and him giving me the advice of a lifetime. I laid there processing what he said. I knew I wasn't out of the woods yet. Lavelle and his friends had done a great job giving me an identity that the kids admired, but I knew it was just a matter of time before one of the bullies struck. And when he did, would I be able to control myself? Or would I embarrass myself and Lavelle? Would I be able to apply the strategies Mr. Thompson suggested? Or would I fly off the handle and ruin it for my brother and myself? I dreaded the possibilities. If I went psycho, I would commit social suicide. I would wear the label: "Psycho" until I graduated! Mr. Thompson said, "It's time to lay the cussing and busting to rest." The uncertainty was unbearable!

CHAPTER 32

THE SMARTEST MAN ALIVE

I had done well curtailing my extremeness, but it wasn't easy. "Don't feed it and it will die." I shot baskets to control the impulses. My wounds were slowly healing; no gambling, stealing, or running toward the fire. I kept my hands where all could see. But a few scabs of life still remained.

I chilled with Benny Lee on Saturday afternoons, when I could catch up with him; and for a bit on Sundays after dinner. He had built another shoe shinebox. His new place to shine was the Framers' Market, the place where he and I once dug in the filth for money. I went with him a couple of times, for old time sake. The truth was I never threw away my box! I and my bothers used the supplies to shine our shoes for church. I hid my box, once again, in the bush behind the wash house. I told Booker and Otis they could use it.

Although I wasn't a physical threat to myself anymore, I was still concerned about how I would react to a hater coming at me in school. I talked with Mae and the crew about it. They told me to cool it. They said that's all behind me now. But I knew better! Still, I couldn't complain. Things had been good but I knew at some point I would have to face a hater. I would have to stand up to him on different terms than in the streets. The weapons I chose to fight them with on the streets only made my problem worst. I played into their hands busting, cussing, and fussing. I had become their entertainment. I couldn't physically fight them. And I didn't know how to walk away. As I got dressed for school each morning I told myself, "Please don't flip out today! Don't ruin it for yourself and your brother"

Not exploding became even more important after I met Lanesha. She was in my Science class. She was the most beautiful girl! She had smooth bronze skin, dark curly brown hair, with brown eyes. The teacher paired us together for a class project. I hadn't told the crew about her because she was a Parker. I planned to tell them at lunch; see what they thought about me talking to a Parker. Well, homeroom was over; time to start the day. I walked pass Lavelle's class on my way to first period. Just like at McKenzie when I would go to his classroom to borrow extra milk money. I stuck my head inside the door.

"Hey, looking for someone?" a voice behind me said.

"Hey Lavelle, I just stopped by to say hi," I answered turning around.

"I was behind you the whole time. I was wondering where you were going. Well, get moving or you'll be late," he warned.

"Okay! Catch you later," I answered, breaking into a jog.

At the end of gym class I told the guys I had to do something and I'd meet them in the cafeteria. I met Lanesha at her locker. It was just around the corner from mine! I wanted to ask her if I could walk her to class after lunch, but I needed to talk with the crew first. Out of respect, I didn't want to talk to her behind their back. My cousin Mae might never speak to me again if she found out from someone else I was talking to a Parker girl. So we talked about our schedules and classes instead. Well, it was lunch time. I needed to break the news to the crew.

"Where have you been," Benny asked as I got in the milk line.

"I was at my locker," I answered.

"I was at my locker too and I didn't see you," he said.

"I was on the other side," I admitted.

"Who's on the other side?" Mae asked.

"I'll tell y'all when we sit down," I smirked.

Benny gave me that "what the hell is going on" look. Our lockers were next to each other, and I wasn't there when I said I was.

"I said I'd tell you when we sit down," I assured him with a smile.

"Yo, yellow cake today!" Booker said.

"No way! I answered

"Yes, way," he confirmed.

"That yellow cake is happening!" Mae affirmed.

We all agreed. She stood behind Booker with her hand on his shoulder. Benny Lee was still giving me the evil eye. He knew I was keeping something from him. We got our milk and yellow cake and sat at our favorite table. I started a conversation about first marking period grades so I could gradually ease into what I wanted to say. Everyone bit but Benny Lee.

"Okay, so what's up Jay Gee?" he asked sarcastically.

"Well, there's something I wanted to talk with y'all about," I said.

"What's wrong, you having those crazy gun visions again?" Booker prodded.

"No Booker, I met a girl…like you have," I said as I looked at Mae sitting next to him.

"Why do you have to talk to us? You never have before when you decide to do all your girly action," Benny Lee called me out with a smirk.

"She's a Parker!" I divulged.

All heads dropped and turned toward me. Their eyes questioned my motives.

"See, there you go again! You're always doing some crazy shit!" Benny fired at me.

"Ah, is this some of your James Bond bullshit? Are you for real?" Booker asked.

"I know I didn't hear you say she's a Parker?" Mae asked with a sister-girl attitude.

"Guys, I wouldn't kid about something like this," I confirmed.

"He's for real!" Booker stated.

"Today was the first time I went to her locker. I was going to tell y'all about her," I explained.

"Sure you were!" Benny said pushing his trash to the center. You know how those dicks feel about their girls. There are only five of us. We can't beat their whole neighborhood!"

"I already beat one, but all of them? Well…if I can catch'em one at a time…" Otis bragged.

"Who says we have to fight them? My brother goes out with Parker girls all the time," I offered in my defense.

"Ah, do I have to remind you your brother is a super star! He can go out with whatever girl he wants and no one will say a word. Those creeps are praying he won't hit on their girl. Now you, on the other hand, ain't no super star. They'll beat your ass!" Booker surmised.

"She better be pretty! It would be a shame to get your butt kicked over some ugly, no good, Parker girl." Mae scowled.

"Why can't you just hang out with our Townie girls? You know how we feel about Parkers!" Elijah moaned.

"Guys, I didn't go after her. It just happened. The teacher paired us together to do a science project in class. I mean she wears perfume and lip gloss. I walked behind her one day, caught a whiff of her shampoo, and I was gone! And yes Mae…she's beautiful!" I drooled.

"Ah man, forget it! He's gone! His nose is so wide open you can drive a truck through it. We gonna have to fight all of them," Booker said.

"Look, I haven't said anything to her about my feelings. I wanted to talk with you guys first," I confessed.

"And what did you think we would say?" Benny asked.

"I don't know. Maybe give me some advice or something. I knew you guys would be pissed. But honestly I didn't go after her. Honestly. But I know she likes me too" I admitted.

"If you are willing to get your butt kicked over her then there's nothing we can say to make you change your mind," Mae said.

"As crazy as this might sound, I say if you really like her, go for it! Just watch your back," Otis warned.

"I want you guys to meet her. She's the nicest girl ever! She's kind, never says mean things. You would never know she's a Parker. She doesn't act like them at all. Come with me to meet her after lunch.

Then you decide. If you think she's a snob I won't tell her how I feel," I pleaded.

"Joseph, we've been through some crazy shit together. But this is the craziest! We all could get our asses kicked daily because of your "Horny Toad" feeling! She better be hot...no, she better be super-hot," Benny demanded.

We disposed of our trash and waited for the bell to ring. Bouncing off bodies, we tracked our way to the lockers. My heart fluttered like a rabbit. Mae, Benny, and I grabbed our books from the lockers. Elijah and Otis were over our shoulders.

"Okay, now where is she?" Benny asked. "I'm telling you, she better be hot. I'm not going to get my ass kicked over a skank from the Parks," Benny reminded.

"Her locker's on the other side. Come on!" I responded leading the way.

We made a right turn at the corner. Another right at the next and there she stood!

"There she is in the peach colored skirt. Come on, hurry!" I instructed.

"Hello Lanesha!" I greeted.

"Hello Joseph. Or should I say, Jay Gee?" she asked with a smile.

"These are my friends I was telling you about. This is my cousin Mae...Booker, Benny Lee, Otis, and Elijah."

"Hi!" They exchanged greetings.

"Hey I know you! You're in my gym class. We were on teams today," she said to Mae.

"Yeah, that's right. We kicked butt too!" Mae bragged.

"Sure did, give me five on that!" she said as she gave Mae a high five.

"And you and I have English class together," she said to Benny Lee.

The meeting couldn't have gone better! Benny nodded and Booker winked.

"Let me get my books and I'll walk with you," Lanesha said.

"She's cool. I like her," Mae whispered.

"Thanks." I exhaled a sigh of relief.

Elijah and Otis gave me a pat on each shoulder and a nod of approval. I turned to each with a smile. I turned back to see if Lanesha was ready. What I saw next made me want to die on the spot. Coming up the hall, 12 lockers away was Cray. His butthead friend from Ray's was with him. Son-of-a-bitch! Suddenly a noose was around my neck, and Cray was holding the other end. The moment I had dreaded for days, months, years, was coming toward me. There was no place to hide; I wouldn't have done it anyway. Daddy said, "Keep your head up." I wanted so bad to blink and disappear.

I took a deep breath and braced myself. I knew if he pulled that noose with a name, I would kick the horse from underneath me, hang myself. Either way, I was dead. To have him disrespect me in from of all these people, including Lanesha and not say anything, I would be a pussy for life. And if I flipped out, I would lose Lanesha and commit social suicide, not to mention ruining Lavelle's reputation. Please hurry Lanesha, I thought.

As he approached, I looked the other way, hoping he would walk past. Not at chance.

"Well...look what we have here! I didn't know they allowed little mulatto mutts in West Side High. This is going to be a fun year having you around!" he announced to the crowd of on lookers.

He and his friend laughed. He stared me down, taunting me, waiting for a response.

Booker gave his books to Mae. He wasn't a fighter, but he had heart. Otis and Benny sat their books next to the lockers. Elijah pulled my upper arm. I stood my ground. Casey said, "Face your fears if you wanted to overcome them." So I stood there, face to face with the devil himself. He had just ripped the scab off my worst wound. I bled profusely. Six cuss words danced to the tip of my tongue. They sat there waiting to burn a hole through that sadistic smile of his. I had three "Your Mama So Fat" jokes that would embarrass him for life! Teachers stood at their doorway, the crowd formed a perimeter. The crew and I snarled, as did Mae.

"Well, aren't you going to say anything, mutt face?" he taunted.

I glanced over at Lanesha. She pulled her books up to her chest. I shifted my focus back to Cray. With my crew on my flank, we readied to jump him. We'd get our asses kicked but get some good shots in. But somehow, losing this fight wasn't good enough for me. I wanted to embarrass him for life in front of all those kids. My mind was drunk with years of anger, my body convulsed, clenching my fist and teeth.

I couldn't let him get away with it. I was doomed either way. I thought, *It would feel mighty good to embarrass this turkey neck, cauliflower ear, breaded dragon face dick for life.* The time had come for me to trash this punk! I opened my mouth….

"Is everything alright Lil Bruh?" a voice behind said.

I didn't have to turn around. It was Lavelle. Milt, Steve, and Louis; friends of his from the football team, went and stood behind Cray and his butthole buddy. I thought, *now you bitches, how do you like these odds?* The crowd looked on. The bell rang. No one moved!

"Alright, get to your classes. You're all late!" a teacher yelled.

No one moved.

"Are you alright Joseph?" Lavelle asked again.

Cray and his loser friend were sweating bullets. I could smell the yellow seeping from his pores. Ah Cray, talk your shit now, I thought. I steadied myself to throw my books in their face and punch that motherfucker in the balls as hard as I could! When he fell to his knee, I'd spit a hawker in his face, and seal it with an Ali right cross!

"Let's kick his ass!" Benny whispered.

I turned to look up over my shoulder at Lavelle.

"I'm good," I said.

"You sure?" he asked as his voice deepened glaring at Cray.

He was ready to make Cray's face a casualty on the 6 o'clock News!

"Yep I'm sure!" I confirmed.

I stepped hard toward Cray. Lavelle's hands dropped from my shoulders. My crew stepped hard too.

"Hi, my name is Joseph. My friends call me Jay Gee," I said as I extended my hand.

Cray paused. He looked at me, then at Lavelle. He shook my hand.

"Cray," he said with a nervous look.

"I know!" I answered as I turned and walked away, Just in time as security came running down the hallway.

There was a big sigh of disappointment. Everyone wanted to see a fight. Lavelle and his friends showing up gave me a chance to breath, to think, and remember what Mr. Thompson told me to try. I was about to ruin it for everyone and lose Lanesha in the process.

Benny and Otis picked up his books as Lanesha walked by.

"See you after school," she said.

"Okay! I answered.

Benny and Lanesha went to English class. Lavelle and his friends walked me to my class. They joked about how they thought the crew and I was going to jump Cray.

"Thanks guys for showing up when you did. I was getting ready to blow it Lavelle. I was getting ready to unload on him so hard they would've arrested me. I was about to cuss him out and talk about his mama so bad, the kids would have laughed at him for life!" I bragged.

"Well, I have a confession to make. My friends and I have tailed you guys since the start of school. I figured this would happen sooner or later. You don't have anything to worry about anymore. You stood up to him, and half the school saw it. Once the word gets around school it shouldn't happen again. So where did you get the introduction thing from?" Lavelle asked.

"Mr. Thompson told me to try it the next time someone called me a name. He told me not to let them define me. He said I should define myself. And I should stop responding to those names. They aren't my name. And to stop letting them manipulate me," I explained.

"Man that was some good advice," Louis said.

"You made that kid look like an ass when you introduced yourself," Steve added.

"You did good Lil Bruh," Lavelle said as we arrived at my class.

"Where are you guys off to?" I asked knocking on the door.

"It's cool. We have lunch," Milt said.

"Alright, catch y'all later. Thanks again," I said walking into class.

The remainder of the school day was a blur. The teachers taught, but nothing resonated. I reflected on how Lavelle and his friends had been looking out for me since day one. How I was able to use what Mr. Thompson taught me. How I didn't embarrass myself or Lavelle. How my friends seemed to like Lanesha. The bell rang! School was over. I agreed to see Lanesha after school. I also wanted to apologize for ignoring her when Cray showed up. I hurried to my locker.

"Jay Gee, that was really cool what you did 5th period," one kid said with a high five.

"Yeah Jay Gee, that kid was a dick for calling you names!" another one said.

"You made him look so stupid when you introduced yourself!" a third one offered.

"Thanks guys. That loser's been calling me names for some time now. I felt it was time he knew my real name," I said, putting my books inside my looker.

"That was so awesome," the first one said. "See you tomorrow."

"Yep, see you tomorrow."

They bid farewell. "See ya."

"So what were you going to do, jump him or cuss him out?" Booker asked as he, Benny Lee, and Mae appeared.

"Cuss him out and talk about his mama!" I answered without hesitation.

"I knew it! Pay up Booker," Benny cheered.

"Pay up?" I asked.

"Yeah, before Lavelle and his friends showed up, these two Yoyos bet on what you were going to do," Mae squealed on them.

"I saw your fist clenched," Booker chuckled." I said to myself, it's going down. I gave my books to Mae. I knew I would've gotten one good shot in before he knocked me out!"

"Nah man, I couldn't let you guys get suspended for fighting. But if I cussed him out and busted on his fat mama, all the punishment would've fallen on me," I revealed.

"Oh, but you wanted us to fight a whole neighborhood over your super-hot girl!" Benny joked.

"Yeah, she's pretty. I like her," Mae admitted.

"Oh no, I have to go! I promised to meet her at her locker. I think

I'm going to ask her for her phone number. Wait for me at the front gate," I said on the run.

I turned the corner, and there she was putting her books away.

"Hey Lanesha, I'm sorry about what happened 5th period. That kid's been bullying me for a long time," I explained.

"I thought you and your friends were going to jump him! You looked so upset. I got scared for a moment. Then your brother showed up. Everyone thought you and your friends were really going to go after him for sure!" she expressed.

"I'm glad my brother showed up or I might have done something real stupid," I said, sheepishly looking down.

"You were great! You made him look like an idiot when you introduced yourself to him. That was the best!" she said as she took my hand.

We walked toward her bus. We small talked on the way. As we drew near, she reached into her purse.

"I've got to go. Here's my number. Call me tonight," she said as she boarded

"Thanks, I will," I said as her bus pulled away.

I unfold the note. It was her phone number with a message; "I think you're pretty neat! Call me tonight." I thought, *Lord, I've died and gone to heaven! I got her number and I didn't have to ask!* I ran back toward the school. I needed to cut through to catch up with Mae and the crew. I looked up to find them standing in the hallway. Those nosey turds! They were watching the whole time.

"Well, did you get it?" Booker asked as I skipped passed them smiling.

They ran to catch up.

"Stop, what did she say?" Benny asked grabbing me by my shoulder.

I stopped, pulled out the note, and gave it to him.

"I knew it! Pay up again Book," Benny said as we walked out the front gate.

He handed the note to Booker. He and Mae read it. I was glowing like a firefly, flying even higher.

"I told you not to take that bet. I knew he would get it. I could see it in her eyes 5ᵗʰ period. You're not going to have any milk money the rest of the week, and you're not borrowing any from me!" Mae scolded Booker.

"This turned out to be one of the best days ever!" I announced.

"Speak for yourself! I'm out 20 cents," Booker complained.

"That'll teach you not to beat against me Book!" I bragged as I grabbed him and gave him nuggies.

"Well Booker, I have a confession to make. I knew he would get it. When she and I were walking to English class, I took a big chance," Benny said.

"Oh no, what did you do Benny?" I asked with anxiety.

"I told her you liked her!" He confessed.

"You did what!" I said with widened eyes.

"Well, I wasn't going to have some beauty queen Parker girl lead my best friend on! So do you want to know what she said?" he asked, toying with me.

"Ah, yes I would," I answered with anticipation.

Silence

"Come on Benny, stop jiving me man! What did she say?" I asked, grabbing him by the shoulder.

"She said, "I know. I like him too"!" He answered giving me nuggies.

"Hey Benny, that's not fair. You knew he would get the number. I shouldn't have to pay up for that bet!" Booker challenged.

"You're right Book. But you still owe me for the first bet!" Benny agreed.

"Why didn't you tell me?" I asked Benny.

"I just did!" He answered with a smile.

"I mean earlier?" I asked.

"How could I? We all came up to the lockers and you broke camp shouting, "I'm going to ask her for her number." And off you went! I was going to tell you on the way home, like I just did!" he finished with a shove to my shoulder.

We laughed.

"Man I can't believe Cray showed up. He tried to make me hang myself after everything was going so well," I exhaled.

"That was crazy! I know you wanted to punch him," Mae said.

"Mae, I thought about punching him in places no man wants to get hit," I confessed.

"I told you he was ready to fight! I was right Benny. I don't owe you anything," Booker argued.

"That was his thought Booker! The bet was, "What was he going to do"!" Benny corrected.

"Everyone in my 5th period class was talking about it," Elijah said.

"Mine too!" Otis added.

"Man, are you kidding? The whole 7th grade class knows what you did! That's all they talked about in my last three classes. How you made a freshman look like a fool. I don't think you'll have any problems from the Parkers over Lanesha either. They were hyped about how you stood up to Cray," Benny said.

"What made you do that, the introduction thing?" Booker asked.

I explained, "The day when they rushed Lijah to the hospital, I went to talk to Mr. Thompson. I mean…I lost it! I told him everything; about Lijah, the Parkers laughing, my haters, my angry visions – everything! He told me to stop letting the bullies manipulate me. He said stop responding to those names; they aren't my name. And to stop letting them define me, that I should define myself. He said to either ignore them or introduce myself to them. That would take the fun out of it for them."

"I'd say!" Benny smirked.

Elijah added, "No doubt! Cray wasn't laughing when you stuck your hand out. And he knew he better shake it or Lavelle would rearrange his face!"

"Man, I'd pay money to see that," Otis said

"Look guys, I promise I'll never cuss, fuss, or bust on anyone again if they call me a name! I've been letting them jerk me around for far too long. Well, no more." I announced.

"What! Say that again," Benny insisted.

"Yeah, I want to hear it again too!" Booker echoed.

"I believe you," Elijah smiled.

"Seriously guys, I will tell them my name or just ignore them," I confirmed.

"Well it's about time!" Otis said.

"I bet you'll tell 'em your name every time! I can't imagine you ignoring them. But telling them your name is 100% better than you flipping out," Benny joked.

We all laughed, Mae too.

The crew took the McKenzie Bridge home. Mae and I continued to my house. I called Lanesha that night. We hit it off well. I got permission to walk her to class. I had never felt that way about a girl before. It was special. I could have laid there and dreamed about her all night.

I was glad I didn't flip out. That would've ruined everything! I stood up to him without responding to his name calling. I did what Mr. Thompson suggested. I didn't let him define me. I also remembered the "Rules of Engagement." I knew I had him beat when Lavelle and his friends showed up. And he knew it too! I didn't have to inflict any unnecessary punishment, although I really wanted to. For once I stuck to the script and it paid off. It also delivered me one of the hottest girls in my class. Mama said, "In one's life some rain will fall. It helps you appreciate your sunny days." Finally, the sun was shining on me. But there would be more rain.

CHAPTER 33

CONVERSATIONS IN THE GTO

Basketball season had arrived. I practiced all fall. The sport had taken the place of the hunts! Well, not all of them but most. I had little time for the crew on the weekends. They understood. I did make time for Benny Lee. We chilled at the creek, played pinball, and sometimes he'd help me practice hoops at the McKenzie Court. I continued to slip in a shoe shine caper with him every now and then at the Farmer's market.

Rumor had it the coach didn't keep a lot of underclassmen on the 7th and 8th grade team. I had practiced all that time and didn't know who the coach of the team was. At dinner, I announced my plans to try out for the team. I asked Lavelle who was the coach for my grade.

'I thought you knew. It's your favorite teacher, Mr. Thompson," he said.

"No, no way!" Not Mr. Thompson?" I asked.

"Yep, it's Mr. Thompson," he confirmed.

I thought *No way was I going out now. He would never pick me. He knew my whole life story! Why would he keep some angry, hurt, pretender, maniac kid who came to him for therapy during his lunch period?*

I called Lanesha. I told her I wasn't trying out and why. She had her own problems. She was trying out for the cheerleading squad. She was nervous as well. Her advice to me, "You won't know if you can make it until you try out!" I didn't sleep well.

My goal all fall was to try out for the team. Lavelle's words were bouncing around in my head as I got dressed for school, "If you really want to do it, don't let nothing stop you!" I told Mae and the crew about my dilemma on the way to school. They all agreed I should try out. After history class I reluctantly approached Mr. Thompson.

"I understand you're the basketball coach?" I asked.

"Yes I am. Are you trying out for the team?" he asked.

My mind said no, but my heart spoke first.

"Yes I am."

"That's good. I saw you play a couple games last year. You're pretty good," he praised.

What, he saw me play! He thinks I'm pretty good! I froze for a second.

"Wow, thanks! I was told you don't keep many 7th graders," I said.

"That's because most aren't very good! Most need another year to improve," he admitted.

My heart sank to the bottom of my Converse! His next class started to come in.

"Well, I got to go. Thanks for the information," I said as I walked toward the door.

"You're welcome. And don't forget tryouts are in two weeks!" he shouted.

"I won't!" I shouted back.

I talked it over with Lanesha, Mae, and the Crew at lunchtime. They didn't know what to make of my conversation with Mr. Thompson. The same was true when I talked with Lavelle. He just reminded me, "If you really want to do it...," I always followed Lavelle's advice when it came to basketball. I went out for the team.

I thought I would die! I never ran so much in all my life! Lavelle told me to be first in everything; first out the locker room to practice, first in the sprints, laps, be first to volunteer if the coach needed help. I wasn't first in everything, but I was in the top five in most. On the last day of tryouts, Mr. Thompson said he would post a list of who made it on the bulletin board in the boys' locker room. No sleep once again.

"Well, how are you feeling?" Benny asked as Mae and I crossed the street.

"I don't know. I guess like last year," I answered.

"You think it's going to be the same results?" Booker asked.

"Man, I sure hope so! I played hard but the 8th graders are very good," I answered.

"I'm sure it's going to be the same result!" Elijah said

"Thanks Lijah." I gave him a pat on the back.

"Well if you don't make it you can always be the manager!" Otis joked.

"I won't be the manager! Not for the Parkers," I fired back.

We all laughed.

"Good luck! Like Lijah said, you'll probably make it," Mae encouraged.

"Thanks Mae. I tried my best. Well, we'll know in a few minutes!" I said.

The crew went with me to read the list. Mae waited outside. As the guys entered the locker room there were five kids in front of us at the board. Two of them turned and walked away.

"Congratulations!" one of them said to me.

"What?" I asked in a high pitched voice.

"You made it," he said.

"I did?" I asked.

"Yep. You're the only underclassman to make it," he said.

I stepped up to the list and there it was, #12 Joseph Graham. The last name on the list! I turned. The crew was right behind me looking over my shoulder. I broke through and ran out the locker room. The guys ran behind me. They all piled on, taking me down to the sidewalk. They gave me nuggies of congratulations, sending my afro in four different directions. Mae expressed her joy with a scream. We stood to our feet.

"I told you you'd make it," Elijah said.

"Yes you did Elijah," I responded.

"Now I have some place to go after school," Benny said.

"Yep, just like at McKenzie," Booker added.

I was the only underclassman Mr. Thompson kept! Lanesha made the cheerleading squad as well. It was the best possible outcome. Our accomplishments gave Lanesha and me a chance to steal a few extra kisses at the away games. I got some grief from my Parker teammates. They were angry because I made it and their friends didn't. I didn't fly off the handle. I could hear Mama saying, "Don't let the devil steal your joy!" Mr. Thompson had told me, "It's time to lay some things to rest!" There comments stung a little but I chose not to participate!

We were the last team to practice in the gym. It was night when we finished. The Parker kids had rides waiting for them. I didn't. I walked the five blocks home. One day, I was last coming out the locker room after practice. Mr. Thompson was locking up.

"Where do you live?" he asked as he turned the key to lock the gym door.

A couple Parkers snickered as they walked to their rides. I didn't say anything. Sensing something was wrong, Mr. Thompson didn't ask again.

"Let's go," he said, loud enough for all to hear.

They stopped in their tracks. Jaws hit the ground as Mr. Thompson and I walked passed them to get to his Candy Apple Red GTO. I thought they'd dropped a load in their pants! We all admired Mr. Thompson's ride, wondering what it felt like to cruise around in it.

Once we got inside he asked, "Now, where do you live?"

"Jefferson Quarters," I answered in shame.

"Where's that?" he asked.

"I'll show you," I answered with my head down.

It was a short and quiet ride. I mostly stared out the window. We got as far as the turn onto the rocky road.

"I'm good from here," I said.

"No, it's dark. I'm going to take you to your front door," he insisted.

I wanted to crawl under the seat. I was so embarrassed. But I couldn't change his mind.

"I live in the first house. The front door is on the other side," I spoke softly.

I was happy for the ride but sorry he had to see where I lived. After history class the next day, he called to me as I was leaving.

"Graham, can you come here a minute?" he asked.

"Yes Mr. Thompson."

"Can you stop by during lunch today?" he requested.

"Sure!"

"Good! See you then."

When I came back to his classroom after eating with the crew, he greeted me with a smile.

"Come in!" How was lunch?" he asked.

"It was good. Loud as usual," I joked.

We laughed.

"Now you know why I eat in here," he said.

"That's why I come down here, for a little peace and quiet," I confessed as I sat down.

Pause.

"I thought you decided not to let anyone define you."

"I did! I told you how I handled the problem with Cray."

"You did and I'm proud of you for that. But why did you let those guys intimidate you last night after practice?" he inquired.

"They make fun of where I live. Most Parkers do," I said, looking away.

"Look, you must accept who and where you are in life! That means the good and the bad. Enjoy the good and let the bad motivate you to be, do, and want better. I thought you told me you were a Townie; proud and true."

"I am!" I perked up.

"Then act like it! Don't ever be afraid to tell someone where you come from. Most successful people didn't start out rich! They had to fight, struggle to get to the top. So where do you live?" he asked.

"Jefferson Quarters."

"Where?" He asked louder.

"Jefferson Quarters!" I answered louder.

"And be proud of it! Graham, in life it's not about where you start. It's about where you finish! So work hard to finish well. In the meantime accept the good and the bad about your life. And work hard to finish well! When people find something they can use to hurt you with they'll use it every time! Remember take the fun out of it for them. They'll stop using it."

"I will. Thanks Mr. Thompson."

"You're welcome. See you at practice."

"I'll be there!"

I don't know how I got through the rest of the day. All I thought of were the words of my basketball coach. I couldn't remember anything from my math class. I wrote down every word Mr. Thompson said. He was the smartest man alive!

There were other rides home in the GTO. His ride was so sweet inside and out. I finally got him to let me out on Franklin Street. I'd run to my backdoor. He'd watch from the tinted windows. I'd waved good-bye when I opened the door. He drove off. We shared several conversations along the way. Some were light hearted, others more meaningful. Sometimes just silence. He made me appreciate my differences.

"Graham, the world would be a boring place if we all were the same; dressed the same, look the same, acted the same! Our differences give us our identity, our uniqueness. They're a big part of who we are. Accept your differences, embrace them," he said during one ride.

Mr. Thompson opened my eyes, my mind. If there was ever a Double-O, it was him. He could have kept any 7th grader but he kept me! He saw something in me. He spoke about it often. Everything he said made sense to me. He also made me stop hiding my academic abilities. He cornered me one day during one of our lunch sessions.

"What do you want to be in life?" he asked.

I pondered the question. When you're in grade school you get that question a lot. You give some kiddy answers like, "Fireman, Police Man, or an Astronaut. I could sense he was looking for more. So I chewed longer, thought deeper.

"I want to be good. I want to be a good basketball player, a good friend, a good person."

"Do you think it's any fun to be good at something and no one knows you're good?"

"Heck no! That's why you work hard. To prove to everyone, to show you're good."

"Do you think you're smart, good at your school work?" he asked.

Boom! Drop the mic! The smartest man alive had stuck again! He caught me in my deception. Our eyes met. We both smirked. His brows did an inverted smirk.

"Yes, I'm good with my school work."

"Then why do you continue to try and hide the fact that you're smart? Your real friends don't care if you're smart. They like you for you. And being smart is as much a part of you as everything else."

The room got quiet. You could hear a rat piss on cotton. My mind flashed back to Lindsey. He told me, "It can't be much fun if you can't be your true self!" I wanted to put my head under the desk. Mr. Thompson began to shuffle papers on his desk. He knew he had me. He was the older kid in the boxing match. He didn't close in. He knew the Rules of Engagement.

"I guess I've been pretty dumb for doing that, huh," I said.

He suggested, "Graham, very few things you do are dumb! Reckless, maybe a little careless, but never dumb. Once again you allowed others to define you! You felt you needed to act a certain way to get them to like you, accept you. I don't know, maybe you did. But I bet it's not that way now! And if it is, you should find some new friends!"

I confronted the crew on the way home with the new intel.

"What if I told you guys I was smart? How would you feel about me?" I asked.

"Why do you ask that? You think we don't know you're smart?" Benny asked.

"Ah Joseph, we check to see who have stars next to their name in each class!" Booker said.

"I also check the honor roll list as well!" Elijah added.

"So why didn't you guys ever say anything?" I asked.

"Because you never made a fuss over it! We all check to see if your name is on the Honor Roll. Makes me feel good to know my blood brother made it," Benny confessed.

"Me too!" Elijah and Booker agreed.

"And you never try to make any of us feel bad when we don't make good grades," Otis stated.

"Never!" Elijah seconded.

"Did you really think we didn't know you were smart?" Benny asked.

"Well…"

I started but Booker jumped in.

"How could we not know you were smart when you use words we have to look up in the dictionary?" Booker joked.

"Or sound like the teacher when you talk sometimes!" Otis chuckled.

"Man, we've always known you were smart!" Elijah confessed.

"But you never threw it in our face! You're smart, you have a car, you live in a house with a phone but you never mentioned it. You never try to make us feel bad," Benny stated.

"Never!" Otis confirmed.

"That's my cousin. He's no loser. He's a true Townie!" Mae praised.

"Thanks Mae! Thanks Guys," I said.

"Townie! Townie!" They chanted.

"Townie! Townie!" I joined in.

Once again, Mr. Thompson had placed another jewel around my neck: "Your real friends are your friends no matter what! They accept you for you." The Crew never judged me because I never judged them!

Like Mama said, "Treat people the way you want to be treated!" Like Benny once told me, "We all pretend!" In other words, you might pretend for other people but you don't have to pretend for your friend. I stopped hiding my academic abilities.

The last jewel Mr. Thompson presented me with, which completed my string of gems, came during a Black History lesson in class. He explained why some blacks were so critical of other blacks. He said it went back to slavery. There were different classes of slaves. There were house slaves, carriage drivers, Blacksmiths, and field slaves. The field slaves became jealous of the house slaves because they were treated better. Many of the house slaves were off-springs of the Master's sexual encounters with the female slaves. Their off springs were light skinned with a thinner, curlier grade of hair. Some could pass for white. They were made house servants. This was why my crew always chose me to knock and ask for mangoes in White Town. They knew my light skin would be favored. The field slaves called the house servants "House Niggers", Half Breeds, and Uncle Toms. In turned the house slaves called the field slaves "Field Niggers" and made fun of their Negro features. They called them, "Big Lipped", "Thick Lipped", "Big Nose", "Blackie", and "Darkies".

Everyone tried to tell me my bullies were jealous. But Mr. Thompson gave me historical proof. It wasn't someone's thoughts or feelings. This was fact! My anger toward the name callers began to dissipate. Now I knew the names they called me were a form of jealousy passed down through generations of anger and resentment toward light skin black people. But we, black people, must stop criticizing each other for the way we look. *If we're going to say, "Black is Beautiful", then show love to "All Shades of Black." Respect the light as well as the coffee shades. Together we fight for all shades of black! "Black is Beautiful" referred to the people and the rainbow of colors within our race.* Thank you Mr. Thompson, I finally stopped bleeding.

I didn't play much that season on the 7th & 8th grades basketball team, only in the 4th quarter. I was learning the game, gaining experience to lead the team next year. But I could never repay Mr. Thompson for all he taught me that school year; on and off the court. Those conversations in the GTO and the lunch sessions were liberating. He made me realize, I was looking for love, acceptance in all the wrong faces. He led me to the mirror and told me to love what I saw. Accept what I saw. Respect, honor, and appreciate what I saw in the mirror. Only then could I move forward in life. You don't know where you're going until you first accept where you've been. What you have endured. He freed me! He helped me break my chains of fear, anger, and feelings of inferiority. He gave me strategies to help me get through one of the toughest times in my life. I would never forget him. I couldn't wait to play for him the next year.

The toughest part of that basketball season came during the District 8, Class 4-A Championship game. Lavelle blew out his knee. He tore his ACL. I cried all night when it happened. They repaired his knee but he lost all his athletic scholarships. Although, after rehab he could still out perform most athletes, no college would take a chance on his knee. Daddy called in a favor from an army recruiter friend. He signed him up. Lavelle passed the physical. Mama wasn't happy about it. But like Daddy constantly told us during his drunken rants, "I'm the captain of this ship! You all are just members of the crew." In other words, his word was law in that house. Lavelle was scheduled to ship out August 10th. When he was in the hospital we had some one on one time.

"Well, now it's up to you Li'l Bruh to get that college degree," he said.

"Don't say that! You can still play," I answered with cracks in my voice.

"No, the doctors say it won't be the same. I won't have the same speed and quickness," he shared.

"What does he know?" I asked on choked words.

"Well, I do know this. You must continue to work hard and get to college. Remember, if you really want to do it…!" He recited.

"I will!" I promised.

Now I had two promises to keep!

The school year was coming to a close. There were two weeks until summer vacation. An all-school assembly was announced for 2:00 pm. That was strange! We usually had assemblies by grade. It was the last day of regular classes for the seniors. Maybe they wanted to do something special for them, I thought. It took forever to get everyone in the gym. Booker and Otis found Mae, Benny Lee, and I, and sat with us. Booker's hand rested on Mae's thigh. I swore if it moved up any higher, I was going to punch him right in the gut!

"Hi there, can I join you guys?" A voice spoke from above.

We turned and looked up.

"Hi Lanesha, sure you can!" I answered as I elbowed Otis in the arm.

He moved over. She sat next to me and took my hand. Mrs. Daily, the Principal, stood at the microphone.

"Good afternoon students. I won't keep you long. I have a letter I must read to you. It's from the School Board. It concerns the court case: Brown vs. The Board of Education," she stated.

Mr. Thompson taught us about that case. It happened way back in 1954, sixteen years ago. What did it have to do with us now? I asked myself. She continued,

"Because of this case all schools in the state must be desegregated. All public schools must be integrated. You are hereby informed that at the end of the 1969-70 school-year, West Side High will be closed!" She announced.

I thought the roof would come off! The older kids yelled, screamed, and cried,

"No! Please No!" they begged.

Lanesha and I managed a disheartened look at each other. No words. Shock!

"Let me finish. Please, let me finish!" she shouted into the microphone.

Moans and groans vibrated from the crowd as the volume lowered.

"All underclassmen will receive a letter in the mail stating your new school assignment. Once you receive your letter you must report to that school to register for classes. There is no more West Side High," she concluded.

And just like that, with the reading of a letter, my life as a Jaguar was over! I had waited all my life to attend West Side High, to start on the varsity basketball team someday. Now, after one year, it was over! Yes, the classes were overcrowded. Yes, the books were old and outdated. But the school was the pride and joy of the community. My favorite teacher, the one who made me realize my potential, I would never see again. He had been ripped away from me by a letter. It was by far the lowest day of my life!

The 7th grade section was fairly quiet as we left the gym. I gave

Lanesha a hug. We both were afraid of losing each other due to the new school assignments. The walk home was solemn. We were angry but didn't know how to express it. We only spent a year at West Side. We didn't have as much invested in the school as the upperclassmen did. Our sentiments were based mainly on our family's tradition. All of our siblings attended West Side High. We expressed their pain and our disappointment as best we could.

By the time I got home, Mama had gotten the word. It was on the 12 o'clock news. In the weeks that followed, there were meetings held all over the neighborhood concerning the school closing. They tried to come up with a plan to fight it but to no avail. During most meetings the vote was 50/50. Several community leaders said the education was better at the white school. They reported the white schools had current books, materials, and supplies to better educate the kids. Besides, it was the law! So it was final, there was no more West Side High School.

After 16 years, desegregation of public schools was being enforced. All public schools had to be integrated. We were going to be bused to the all-white schools, just when life was starting to make sense to me.

CHAPTER 34

WILL I SEE YOU AGAIN

Jeanie got married. She married Arthur Mason, the guy she met at church; the real proper talking guy from Ohio. I knew she was going to marry him the first time I asked her about him. I saw it in her eyes. Her face lit up like neon whenever she talked about him. That left only Lavelle and me at home. And he would be leaving in two months.

Like the previous school year, I didn't hang out much with the crew on the weekends. My adventures had become dives for loose balls, taking charges, and scoring as many baskets as possible. Basketball had become my hunt! I played the sport every chance I got. It was the outlet I needed to release my aggression after I quit boxing. I joined a summer league team at West Side High. The county turned the school over to the city. The city used the facilities for summer recreation programs. I tried to get Benny Lee to sign up for the Summer Football League, but he didn't have the money.

I got him to go with me to a couple of my games. He often left before the game was over. I would find him at Fountain Park playing checkers or ping pong in the Recreation Center. On days I didn't have a game scheduled, I would go to the gym to watch the other teams play. See who the good kids were on the other teams. Benny Lee and I still managed to hang out on the weekends; an occasional movie or a shoe shine run at the Farmer's Market. We even did a mango hunt or two in White Town for some quick cash. We laughed reminiscing about times past.

In the summer of 1970, I attended my first basketball camp. It was the first time I stayed anywhere overnight. The camp was sponsored by the Manopa Wolves, a professional basketball team. On Saturday nights during the winter I listened to a couple Wolves' games on an old car radio. The house radio was broken. We had an old junk car parked on the side of the house. It didn't run but the radio worked. I'd be out in that old black Buick dreaming I was in the pros.

One night, during pre-game, they made an announcement about the Wolves' Summer Basketball Camp. They gave the price and said discounts and scholarships were available. I ran into the house yelling for paper and pen. I ran back with articles in hand to copy the information. I waited until half time to hear the announcement again. I copied all the information. I sent a letter to the team telling them how much I loved the game and requested a scholarship to the camp because my family didn't have much money.

A week later I received a letter from the Wolves with a note, "Fill out the application and enclose $40. You have received a scholarship to camp!" Once again, I ran through the house yelling and screaming. When I showed the letter to Lavelle and Mama they couldn't believe it. Neither could I! Jeanie and Casey help pay the $40 fee. My acceptance and confirmation letter came two weeks later. I told the crew about my good fortune. They thought it was great. I met with Benny under the big tree to talk about it.

"I wish you were going with me," I said.

"Me too! It sounds like a lot of fun. But I'm no good at basketball," he admitted.

"That's why you go to camp, to get better," I encouraged him.

"I'm glad you're getting a chance to go. Maybe I'll see you on TV someday," he joked.

"That would be cool! But I have to get a scholarship to college first."

"You can do it. You're smart enough. What does Lanesha think about you going to camp?"

"I don't know. I told her I wouldn't be able to call her for a week. She didn't sound too happy about that!"

"Did you tell her she had nothing to worry about? That it's a sausage fest, all guys?"

"Yeah I told her. She's upset. She hasn't received her school assignment yet. They may ship her to Sea Garden. To be honest, I'm a little worried about that too."

"Well, it'll work out. Don't worry about it. Go have fun at camp. I'll see you when you get back. And bring me something back!"

"I will. Be good Benny. See you when I get back," I encouraged as I turned to walk away.

"What do you mean? I'm always good!" he yelled back smiling.

The day came for me to leave home and stay overnight at camp. My bags were packed. I wasn't worried. I was excited. Lavelle gave last minute instructions.

"Remember what I told you about tryouts; try to be first in everything?" he reiterated.

"I remember."

"Listen and learn! That's what you're there for, to learn," he encouraged me.

"I will," I assured him.

The camp was being held at a college outside of Sea Garden. Casey took me. I got out, checked in, and was escorted to my room by one of the camp counselors. He was a college player hired as one of the camp counselors. I open the door, "What, a room all to myself? Oh Lord, you are too good to me!" I whispered to myself. The college kid laughed at my mini celebration. I dove onto the bed. I laid there until dinner.

I met two kids from Monopa on my way to the dining hall. They were roommates. Their room was one floor below me. It was like peanut butter and jelly when we met. There's an old saying, "You can take the kid out of the hood but you can't take the hood out of the kid!" We three hood rats hit it off right away. It was as if we'd known each other all our lives. We were friends after dinner.

One night we thought it would be fun to scare the younger campers. We waited until everyone was asleep; met in the stairwell around

Midnight. We brought our bed sheets with us and crept down to the grade-schoolers' floor. The camp rules stated we couldn't lock the doors to our rooms. We burst into the tiny totes room, sheet over our head and face. Two of us stood over their bed bellowing ghostly boos and witches' shrills while the lights flickered off and on; scrambling their senses. Oh my word! They screamed, yelled, cried. It was too hilarious! The next day we heard one kid peed his pants. Another cried all night for him mommy. Funniest thing ever!

The three of us met up the next morning at breakfast. We laughed over our shenanigans from the night before. The camp director stood to make the morning announcement.

"Good morning campers! I hope everyone is in a good running mood. I understand a couple of you went down to the grade-schoolers floor with sheets covering your faces and scared them pretty good!" he announced.

The dining hall roared with laughter. He continued.

"Well, I hope you find this funny as well. All of you will run around the pond until I have the names of the characters that played the Halloween-in-July stunt," he promised.

A huge gasp filled the air. Each morning the camp ran two laps around this huge pond to warm up before going to our skill stations. No one knew we did it. As we walked out to the pond we agreed it wasn't fair for the entire camp to run when they had nothing to do with it. We went up to the director and confessed. *There is some good in the worst hood rat! Sometimes all they need is a chance to do the right thing.*

The camp director made us run so many laps, I lost count. We had to apologize to the camp. We also had to sit out our morning game. And it was over. At least we thought so. The camp counselors thought it was the funniest and bravest thing ever. No one had ever done something so crazy at camp before. The college students treated us like celebrities the rest of the week. They talked to us and high fiving us whenever they saw us.

I did well at camp. My team made it to the championship game in my division. We lost by three. The skill work and the organize game play was invaluable! I learned several new skills I could practice for next season. I had come a long way from reading the one basketball book in the McKenzie Library! I received the camp "Hustle Award". Lavelle told me to work hard. I did. It paid off. I received a super cool looking Manopa Wolves T-shirt for the honor. I saved it to give to Benny Lee. He had asked me to bring him something back.

Camp was over on Friday. Casey was there at 2pm on the dot to pick me up. My lips flapped all the way home. I'm sure he and his wife Marilyn wanted to leave me beside the road. But they couldn't; it was my birthday!

When I got home Mama had baked my favorite cake. Yes, the one with the strawberry jelly for icing. After dinner and cake, I went to find Benny Lee. I took the T-shirt with me. As I crossed Franklin Street I began to look for him. I couldn't wait to tell him about camp and scaring the little kids. That's definitely a 10 on the "I dare you" meter.

Once I got near his door I began calling for him.

"Benny! Yo, Benny Lee!" I called out.

Some of his neighbors looked at me like I was the plague. But they always did. They were probably calling me names in their head as well. At least they were nice enough not to call me any of them out loud. I knocked on Benny Lee's door. I held the T-shirt up to the peep hole.

"Hey Benny, It's me Joseph!" I announced.

The door opens. It was his mom, Mrs. Rivers.

"Oh… hi Mrs. Rivers, is Benny home?" I inquired pulling down the T-shirt.

"You didn't hear?" She asked in a low tone.

"Hear what?" I answered with a smile.

"You better come inside," She said in a serious manner.

My smile left. My heart started a drum roll. Butterflies circled my stomach.

"Sit down."

In my head, I debated if I wanted to hear what she was about to say. I had to pee.

She continued. "Benny Lee got arrested! He's in the Juvenile Detention Center in Rising Tide."

"No, please no!" I cried burying my face in the T-shirt.

Quiet!

Only my sniffling could be heard.

"What happened?" I asked wiping my face with the T-shirt.

"I can't go into the details since it's an open case but that's where he's at."

"When will he get out?" I asked as drops of love, hurt, and anger met under my chin.

She spoke softly. "If he's found guilty, he won't get out for a long time."

I couldn't breathe, couldn't think. I was stunned and confused. I tried to stand. No strength. I rocked back twice to get momentum. I stood and waddled to the door. Mrs. Rivers walked behind me. Her head hung low. I turned back to her with my hand on the door knob.

"I'm sorry," I said opening the door.

She nodded.

I walked home in a daze. My emotions spun like the spin cycle on the washer. I felt faint, dizzy, like I was going to throw up. My stomach was in knots, like I was on a roller coaster that kept traveling down. I opened the backdoor. I spoke to no one. I collapsed on the sofa. I wept openly.

"No, no no! It's all-my-fault!' I cried aloud punching the pillow.

My family ran into the room.

"What's wrong!?" Mama asked.

"It's my fault," I repeated through my tears.

"What's your fault?" she asked as she rolled me over to face her.

I sat up. She gave me a hug as she sat next to me. Lavelle and Daddy looked on with concern. I wrestled with the agony to gain some composure. I cleared my throat.

"Benny got arrested! They put him in Juvie," I moaned.

Silence.

"For what?" Lavelle asked.

"His mom said she couldn't talk about it but said he could go away for a long time," I explained.

Silence. I wiped my face.

"It's all-my-fault. If I didn't go to that stupid basketball camp we would have been together. I wouldn't let him do anything stupid to get put in Juvie!" I sobbed.

"It's not your fault son," Daddy consoled me.

"Sure it is! Why did I go to that dumb camp? Now my best friend is locked up in Juvie. This is the worst birthday of my life!" I complained.

"Whatever he did he decided to do it on his own. You had nothing to do with it. So it's not your fault he got in trouble," Lavelle assured me.

Mama had heard enough. She grabbed me by my shoulders. She looked me square in the face.

"Be thankful you were at camp! You could be sitting in that Juvenile Detention Center with him! You don't know what he did or why he did it. So be glad you weren't there!" She said emphatically.

My crying stopped. I still felt empty inside. I knew what Mama said was right. Benny and I had done so much craziness together it was just a matter of time before one or both of us got busted. She was also right in that whatever he did I probably would've been there with him. But it didn't make me feel any better. It didn't take away the longing I felt for my best friend. I caught up with the crew the next day in front of Betty's.

"Yo, what's up?" I greeted.

"When did you get back?" Booker asked.

"Yesterday!"

"How was it?" Otis asked.

"It was fun! We Played basketball all day every day. We only stopped to eat and sleep!"

"Did you hear about Benny Lee? Otis asked.

"I did. I went by his house yesterday. What happened?"

"He got busted robbing cars in the parking lot at the shopping center," Booker informed.

"I heard they had him on camera and were looking for him. Two ladies pressed charges," Elijah added.

"What! When did he start to do that?" I asked.

"He's been doing it for awhile. He didn't want you to know about it. He knew you'd be pissed if you ever found out," Otis informed.

"They finally caught him! Damn shame. He could go away for a long time". Booker said.

"Keep your head up guys. They haven't found him guilty yet," Elijah encouraged.

I couldn't speak. My mouth got as dry as the desert. Their confessions threw me into a large cactus. It poked holes into my reality. I never thought Benny would do something like that. Well, I never thought he would rob the beauty parlor either. He always told me, "We all pretend. We hid who we really are." I'm sure if I were to ask him why he never told me about robbing cars, he'd say, "You never asked me!" Damn it Benny! I missed him so much.

"Where are you guys going?" I asked.

"To the Heart Beat!" Booker said.

"What's playing?" I asked.

"Beneath the Planet of the Apes," Otis answered.

"Tell me about it later," I said.

"And we know where you're going with that basketball in your hands," Elijah joked.

"Yep, over to McKenzie. I learned some new moves I want to practice," I told them.

"Well, catch you later!" Booker said as they crossed the street.

"Yep, later!" I replied.

The rest of the summer was pretty much like that for me and the crew. I hung out with them only a couple of times after Benny Lee went to Juvie. It wasn't the same without him. He was the main reason I was a member of the FCC. They all knew it. Since he'd been gone half of me didn't function. I yearned for my Blood Brother. I thought of him every day. I stopped going to the Franklin Court Apartments. It was too painful.

I threw all my time and energy into basketball and Lanesha. She and I met on Saturday afternoon at the Fountain Park Pool. My flag rose like the morning sun whenever we touched, kissed. I stayed in the water until my sun went down.

Mr. Thompson occupied a lot of gray matter as well; the smartest man alive. He caught this withering bud just in time. A good gardener, he gave me sunshine and water so I could bloom. He tilled the soil of my heart and mind, freeing me from my weeds of destruction. I hoped to see him again someday. But that's how it was in the jungle. Important people in your life came and went without warning.

CHAPTER 35

DO UNTO OTHERS

The day came for Lavelle to leave for basic training. He finished packing, wasn't allowed to bring much. Mama tried to keep a pleasant face but rivers ran under her make-up. Daddy showed little emotion, his tell was his avoidance of conversation. He was often quiet when he was concern. Jeanie and her husband Art came to take him to the bus station. Lavelle and I had our moment.

"So when will you be back?"

"Ah, I didn't leave yet," he joked.

We smiled. He continued,

"Well, I'll have 6 weeks of basic training; getting in shape and learning how to fight and shoot. Then I can come home for a week,"

"But you already know how to fight."

"Yeah...you gave me a lot of practice.

We laughed.

"Sorry about that."

"For you Li'l Bruh, I'd fight 'em all again.

"Thanks."

"You're welcome. Just promise me you'll stay off the streets while I'm gone.

"I will. I don't hang out there anymore. Especially now that Benny's gone. Anyway, I almost lost my life out there."

"What!"

"Yep, three or four times! Don't tell Mama. That's why I spend my time playing hoops and chilling with Lanesha."

"Good, that's what I want to hear; you playing hoops. You're going to be good one day. Keep practicing. Hey, I almost forgot.

He turned, reached into his dresser draw, and pulled out his #20 varsity basketball jersey. The coach gave the players their jerseys at graduation since the school was closing.

"Here, I want you to have it. Think of me when you wear it and know I'll always be with you, rooting for you.

"I can't Lavelle. It's yours. Besides, I could never be as good as you."

"What am I going to do with it? I'm not a player anymore. I'm an army man. You're the player now. And you're wrong. You're going to do great things in basketball. Here, take it."

I reached for the jersey, my body collapsed into his. I held on tight. We didn't speak; silent tears.

"Hurry back," I whimpered.

He gently pulled my head back and said, "Be yourself. You're Joseph "Jay Gee" Graham and nothing or no one else. That's the name you answer to. Be strong, play tough, and always give your best."

I could only nod yes for fear of crying out loud.

"Come on, walk me to the car."

He put on his hat, grabbed his suitcase, and we walked out together. Everyone was at the car waiting. Mama and Daddy said their good-byes. Jeanie and Art started the car. He looked back at me and said, "If you really want to do it...."

I smiled and nodded as he got into the car and waved good-bye.

That first night in the bedroom alone, every creak filled the darkness. I thought of my friends that had moved on: Adam, Lindsay, April, Sheila, Duke, Benny, and Lavelle. Some had no choice, either way they were gone. I felt alone.

I gazed at the stars through my window, gave each a friend's name. They winked, I winked back. Suddenly a tap on my shoulder, I rolled over. Ghost had entered the room; the bullies, the Parkers, white southern society. They sat on my bed begging for attention. Just behind them were the streets, the rocks, and my feelings of unaccepted. I stared for a minute. Then I rolled over, turned my back, and went to sleep; not giving them a second thought.

By my 13th birthday, I was deeply wounded, scarred. I had seen and experienced things no preteen should encounter. The bullying was the worst. They hurt me, frightened me; scared me into dreams of suicide. I bled. To survive, I pretended the hurt didn't hurt. I'd morphed into James Bond, through whom I could hide in the light. I could walk around and no one knew I was in pain.

Eventually, his mask grew too heavy. I got lost over doing things to show my worth in the streets. I put my life in harm's way to prove I belonged, that I was just like everyone else; the effects of bullying. But in reality, I wasn't like everyone else. I was different and it was time to enjoy being me. The bleeding had stop, my wounds were healing. Thank you, Benny, Lavelle, and Mr. Thompson.

My school assignment finally came in the mail; East Side Junior High. It was just across the railroad tracks. I'd passed it several times on mango hunts. I checked with Mae and the crew. We all were assigned to East Side Junior. Although we didn't hang out much anymore, we still hoped to have some classes together.

I didn't have many fears about attending the white school. I did wish Benny Lee could be with me though. After four years of my best friend being at my side, this would be tough. It pained me to think about him. His hearing before the judge was Friday. I checked with the crew. They had no word on the outcome. His family stayed with relatives in Rising Tide over the weekend. There was still hope.

The few concerns I had about attending the white school centered on being treated fair. Would the teachers grade me fairly? Jeanie said I must work twice as hard as the white students to get any recognition from the teachers. I said to myself, *how does she know? She never went to an integrated school.* But Jeanie was usually right, so I listened. My other concern was would the basketball coach give me a fair chance to make the team? I didn't run the streets any more. Basketball had become my life! And if I made the team, would the white players treat me like their teammate? I remembered an incident that happened in grade school.

There was only one white student in the entire school, a girl. She was in my 5th grade class. She was a nice person, worked hard to get along with everyone. But kids were mean to her, specially the girls. Every time the teacher left the classroom they bullied her.

"How many Saltine Crackers are in this box?" someone would shout.

A chorus of kids would shout back, "One!"

I did not participate. One day, they did it until she began to cry. My anger meter exploded. I stood up.

"Stop it! Just stop it! She's not bothering you. Leave her alone," I yelled.

"Why are you defending her?" One girl asked.

"She better get her butt back across that track!" another one snarled.

"She never bothers you guys. But you're always picking on her. Just leave her alone," I begged as the teacher walked in.

I could be faced with the same situation at East Side Junior. I could be the only black in the class and have someone shout, "How many niggers, coons, monkeys are in this class?" And if so, would a white kid stand up for me?

The night before the integration experiment had arrived. I laid in bed thinking, *what would I talk about with my white classmates?* I didn't know anything about them. I would start with, what did they do this summer? Did their best friend get placed in Juvie? Next, I'd ask, what was their childhood like? Did they hunt for bottles, money, mangoes, or mulberries? Did they shine shoes, car surf, or French kiss girls in grade school? Did any of them swim in a pool with a black kid? Had any of them witnessed a riot one block from their home? Did they witness hundreds of police officers and the National Guardsmen marching down the street to keep order? Did any of them witness a gun fight resulting in a man being shot right before their eyes?

A tidal wave of memories flooded my brain. Did any of them almost drown or narrowly escape the deadly sting of a scorpion? Did any of them see the Prophet heal people? Did any of them live on rocks in a house that looked like a box? Then it occurred to me, I had very little in common with them. Heck, I had only a few things in common with most of the black students!

It didn't matter. Those were my wounds. If they didn't prejudge me, neither would I them. I decided, if the white kids gave me a chance, I would do likewise. Why not? None of them had called me, Space Ghost, Casper, Kimba the White Lion; House Nigga, Mutt, Mutter, Mulatto or Albino, at least, not yet. "Treat people the way you want to be treated."

A year ago, I was petrified at the start of school. Now I looked forward to it. I was probably the only kid on the west side of town that felt that way. My joy stemmed from the fact that I wasn't angry anymore. I had accepted and embraced my differences. Benny Lee once said they were the best part of me. I had decided not to hide or pretend anymore. I would be me. But the #1 reason for my elation was all the name callers would be a mile up the road at East Side Senior High. I was too blessed to stress.

"Ring...Ring!"

Who could that be this late? Probably Lanesha,

"Hello, Graham residence. Joseph speaking,"

"Hello Joseph, It's me...Benny Lee..."

THE END

Printed in the United States
By Bookmasters